TASTE ON MY *Tongue*

BETH BOLDEN

CHAPTER ONE

"I'M SORRY, I HAVE to ask," Landon says, the sarcastic edge to his voice contradicting the deference of his words, "but are you lost?"

Ian, Landon's new but still long-suffering agent, shoots him a reprimanding look which typically means Landon is supposed to behave himself.

Landon doesn't mean to be rude, he really doesn't. It's just that behaving is such a buzzkill and this meeting is already boring enough. Also, he definitely thinks his question was at least a little legit.

"I'm a singer," Landon restates his concern, *nicely* this time. "I don't know what my cooking skills have to do with my career."

"I think what Landon is asking is why that's a relevant question," Ian intervenes as the producers sit stone-faced across the conference table. Ian told Landon this meeting was important, and Landon was at least trying to take it seriously until the lady on the far left—a Max Mara suit aging her by at least ten years—asked him if he knew how to cook.

The dick in the middle—*his* Tom Ford suit wasted—cuts in even smoother than Ian does. Even though his watch and the cut of his suit proclaim him to be an asshat, Landon sits up a little straighter and tries to pay attention.

"You earned, what? Third place on *The Voice*?" Landon doesn't like the sneer in the voice of the man he can't help but mentally think of as Tom Ford, but he's still listening. "Strong debut album. Follow-up . . . not so much."

Unfortunately, Tom Ford is not exaggerating. Landon knows he's gotten bitchy over the last year, but nothing has fallen his way in an industry where success depends on the smallest detail.

He came out of the closet at exactly the wrong time in his post-reality show career, right at the moment when all his young girl fans genuinely believed they might have his babies one day. He doesn't regret the honesty, only the timing, and how it decimated what was looking like a decent career.

His publicist had begged him to wait until his third album—his *serious* album, she'd called it and he'd actually laughed in her face—but now she's the only one laughing. He'd done exactly as he'd wanted and now there might not even *be* a serious album to poke fun at.

Ian is supposed to open new doors for him, except that he's just brought him to a meeting where all the producers want to talk about is the one room he almost never voluntarily enters—the kitchen.

"So, to reiterate the question, can you cook?" Tom Ford continues.

Landon doesn't like Tom's attitude, but beggars can't be choosers, which is what he's learned after *The Voice*. The reality show was supposed to propel him into stardom, but all it did was tease Landon with a tantalizing future that he can't quite reach.

"No. Not at all," Landon says. He's tempted to lie, but it would take about five seconds to expose him and it's not worth the risk.

"We like you as a contestant for a new reality show," Max Mara chimes in. "It's called *Kitchen Wars*. You'd be paired with a chef who would help teach you to cook during the show's run."

"I wouldn't have to know how to cook?" Landon is understandably skeptical.

"Not even how to boil water." Max Mara seems to believe he couldn't. And she would be wrong; he boils water all the time for his French press. It's the one thing he *can* do in the kitchen.

Landon still isn't sold. He's a singer; not a cook. Right now, he and Ian are still shopping his next album to different labels, but all he has to do is catch the edge of Ian's gaze to know right away that his agent really wants this for him.

"Next week we're hosting interviews with the casting director and executive producers," Tom Ford adds. "We'd really like you to come in."

The thing is, he doesn't want to learn how to cook. He's lived twenty-five mostly excellent years without any culinary skills. He's not inclined to change the status quo.

"What about *Dancing with the Stars*?" He makes one last ditch effort to avoid the inevitable. "I'd be great on that."

Tom Ford's look is both pitying and galling. Landon has met too many men just like this one during his time in LA. It's like they grow them in factories, pushing out freshly-suited copies every ten seconds. They both know Landon is not high profile enough for *Dancing with the Stars*.

They both know he would be lucky to be cast on *this* show.

"Landon will be here," Ian inserts in an absolutely certain bid to save the last scraps of Landon's pride.

The meeting ends in a pair of handshakes and Ian barely holds in his explosion until they reach the parking garage.

It's already warm, late July in Los Angeles, and the concrete is steaming in the mid-morning heat. Ian turns on him, exasperation clear on his face and in his voice.

"Do you even know who else is on their list? You *need* this, Landon."

He can probably guess who else is on their list. He's very familiar with the others in his position, scraping by and pulling themselves up the ladder of stardom by the tips of their fingers.

"Yeah, but I'd be better than all of them."

Ian's sigh is the definition of frustration.

"You *know* how good I am on TV," Landon insists. "You know because you watched my season of *The Voice* before you signed me. I wasn't the best singer, but I'm *great* on camera. Don't think that Tom Ford and Max Mara don't know that already."

Ian still looks skeptical. "You need this," he repeats. "You need to appeal to a new demographic."

Neither of them bring up the particularly sore point that Landon pushed away the one he already had.

"I'll do it, okay?" he says.

Ian pokes him hard in the chest. Landon grimaces. "You need to be *picked* first."

Landon rolls his eyes. "They both wanted me. That whole *third place* bullshit was a bad negotiation tactic."

He's seen too many Tom Fords over the last few years. They're easy enough to read if you know what to look for.

Relaxing a fraction, Ian nods. "Agreed."

The biggest problem Landon has with LA is that pride is reserved exclusively for those who win. The rest of the pack have to claw their way up however they can, and for Landon, the next rung of his ladder is now *Kitchen Wars*.

Landon knows he nails the interview—he can be charming if required, and between his own introspection and Ian's quiet desperation, he's decided it's required here. Tom Ford and Max Mara are scarce and it helps too that the casting director is friendly and relaxed, which is practically extinct in Hollywood.

He's not surprised at all when Ian calls and tells him he's been cast. Landon walks into the kitchen of his apartment and shoots the stove the most venomous look in his repertoire. "It's just you and me now," he announces to the collective appliances. "God help us all."

Landon really, really, *really* doesn't want to learn how to cook.

But he still wants to sell millions of records, and hear his songs on the radio, and be recognized when he goes to the beach. So he signs the contract despite all his misgivings that there is pretty much no one on earth that will be able to get him to cook, never mind interest him in legitimately trying.

It turns out he's wrong on both counts.

⁂

Two months later, *Kitchen Wars* finally starts filming.

When Landon walks into the studio for his first day of cooking boot camp and sees his chef, he has to instantly revise every expectation. The man in front of him is all long lines, lean legs, and this sculpted torso that literally nobody that cooks for a living should have, all topped off by a wild curly mane that Landon's fingers itch to touch, wide blue eyes, and a pair of lips that send his mind straight to the gutter.

It turns out there is most definitely a man out there that will interest Landon in learning to cook.

The topper is when Landon saunters over, eyes flicking over those long legs in tight jeans and the little glimpses of tattoos he sees through his mostly transparent white t-shirt, the man actually blushes.

"Landon Patton," Landon says, extending a hand. "Unfortunately, it's gonna be your miserable job to teach me to cook."

The man flushes even pinker as he takes Landon's hand. "Um, Quentin. Quentin Maxwell."

For one rather breathless moment, they stare at each other, Quentin's hand clasping Landon's, his palm warm and soft and slightly damp with nerves, and Landon feels his heart start to beat faster. He feels almost breathless with the possibilities, and it's hard to deny that Quentin looks equally blown away.

Quentin reluctantly releases his hand. "I'm a huge fan," he adds. "Really, you should have won your season. Can't believe you only got third place."

Landon can definitely believe it. Third place was far better than he ever thought he'd end up. But you can say all you want about Landon—and many, *many* people have—he's driven to succeed even when the cards are stacked against him.

So Landon just shrugs and leans back, all carelessly but purposefully arranged curves as he tries to figure out if the way Quentin's fluttering his eyelashes at him means he's actually interested in flirting or if this is just Quentin's natural state of being.

"It was a competitive season," Landon says. He doesn't mention that the third-place finish isn't what has him scrambling to get another record deal—if Quentin is actually a fan, then he definitely knows that Landon is gay.

From the way Quentin is staring at Landon like he's a pastry he'd like to nibble on, Landon decides he doesn't much care. Quentin might not be averse to a bit of flirting, which makes everything much more interesting.

"Are you sure you're a chef and not a model?" Landon asks slyly, still gazing over at Quentin. "You're gorgeous."

Quentin blushes again—baby-blue eyes blazing hot. Landon has to stop himself from doing an actual fist pump at his luck. Not only is Quentin insanely hot, he's also adorable; it's a killer combination.

"Not even close to a model," Quentin replies with a bit of an eye roll. "I'm just a baker."

"A baker?" Landon raises a skeptical eyebrow. He was of the impression that this show was more about cooking versus baking. And if there's anything he knows less about than cooking, it's baking.

"Pastry chef," Quentin corrects hastily. "Classically trained. But at heart, I guess I still think of myself as a baker. I want to open a bakery, anyway."

"That's why you're here, to get the money for your bakery?" Landon asks and Quentin nods.

"So how about you, do you bake?" Quentin asks.

It's Landon's turn to flush red. "Um, ah, not exactly." He was really hoping someone else had already broken the news to poor Quentin that Landon is not precisely knowledgeable in the kitchen.

"No cooking either, yeah?" Quentin asks, and he doesn't even seem slightly fazed by the possibility.

Basically, Quentin Maxwell is a way better man—*chef*, Landon reminds himself, *chef*—than Landon deserves.

Landon shakes his head.

"Well, let's get started then." Quentin shoots him a quick, bright smile. "Got a lot to cover today."

"Lead the way, Quen!" Landon exclaims with more enthusiasm than he ever thought he'd be able to dredge up for kitchen equipment.

The kitchens are massive, giant stainless steel work tables crisscrossing the space, punctuated by a handful of enormous industrial stoves. There's shelf upon shelf of kitchen equipment lining the walls. Landon is game for most things—he wouldn't have taken the reality show route in the first place if he weren't willing to take a chance on himself—but this is overwhelming. He doesn't like to approach anything assuming he'll fail, but well. *The Voice* was different. He knew how to sing and how to work an audience and a camera. His grayish-green eyes and feathery light-brown hair show up great on TV—even better than in person, where he secretly worries they wash him out. He doesn't know how to cook *at all*. He can pour himself a bowl of cereal and work a French press like a boss. That's it.

Sudden panic freezes him in place, but Quentin's behind him, laying a reassuring hand on his back. It's large and warm, and truthfully Landon doesn't ever want him to move it, even as he hates the way it sends tiny frissons of electricity down his spine.

Flirting aside, Landon really doesn't need this distraction right now. He needs to be able to focus so that Quentin can teach him how to cook because he is suddenly very aware that he's out of his element.

But before Landon can even open his mouth, Quentin's in front of Landon, and his hand has moved from his back to his shoulder, pressing in comfortingly. "I know, it all looks super scary," he says, seriously. As if being afraid of a kitchen isn't completely ridiculous.

"Terrifying, actually," Landon says, a lot more quietly than usual. "Is it crazy? To think I could do this?"

Quentin's smile is as soft and warm as the hand on Landon's body. It dawns over his beautiful face and somehow makes him even lovelier—inside and out, Landon realizes. He's not just attractive, he's also kind.

Basically, Landon is fucked.

"No, not crazy at all. And it's not just you. I'm here to help—to teach you, really. We're a team." Quentin sounds confident, but Landon is secretly worried that he's blindly hoping at this point.

"A real dream team," Landon says with only a hint of sarcasm, because even if Quentin *is* blindly hoping Landon isn't utter shit in the kitchen, he's still made Landon believe that they aren't hopeless. And that's something.

Quentin's smile widens, that dimple looking awfully appetizing to Landon. Rather too appetizing. *Focus*, he reminds himself, *focus*.

"So where do we start?" Landon asks. Because let's face it, if he doesn't get them back on track, he and Quentin are going to end up making out in the pantry, and while probably really fun, that's not going to get him another record deal.

Quentin eyes Landon skeptically. "Maybe to start we'd better go over the equipment."

This seems embarrassingly basic, but maybe it's better to do this now, before Landon mortifies himself during filming by having to ask how to turn the stove on.

"Lead away." Landon tries to sound enthusiastic, but it's hard to get enthusiastic about kitchen equipment, even when the man doing the teaching is Quentin Maxwell.

As the morning wears on, they begin to grow more comfortable around each other. Landon discovers that Quentin is also a great teacher. He never makes fun of Landon for asking dumb questions—and Landon is sure he asks plenty of those—and he's unfailingly patient as he not only shows Landon the equipment, he makes absolutely certain that Landon knows how to use it and what each item is for. It's a bit of slow going, with Quentin wanting to make absolutely sure Landon understands.

Landon does a lot of things fast; Quentin's slow and deliberate. Landon wouldn't think that combination would work very well, but instead of oil and water, they're fantastic together.

Quentin is showing Landon how to use the stand mixer—"I use one of these every day," Quentin explains as he carefully changes out the mixing apparatus, a large whisk for a ceramic dough hook—when Landon asks him if he knows any of the other chefs they'll be competing against.

"I went to culinary school with Rory Dargan," Quentin says offhandedly, as if this is totally normal. Which to Quentin, Landon is sure it is. Quentin's never been in reality television before. He doesn't understand how the game works.

Landon grunts in frustration as he tries to maneuver the dough hook into the stainless steel bowl so he can attach it properly. When Quentin did it, it was in a slow but absolutely sure motion, and Landon can't quite figure out how it goes. Probably because he's rushing.

"You've got it," Quentin says encouragingly, even though Landon knows he doesn't at all. He rolls his eyes and goes back for another try.

"So you know him," Landon states.

"Rory? Yeah, we're good friends. I wasn't sure about doing this show, but when I found out Rory had agreed, it was a much easier decision."

Landon barely refrains from rolling his eyes again. He can already tell Quentin is too sweet for reality television; Quen is lucky he has Landon for a partner. No, Landon can't cook to save his life, but he's a reality television veteran. He can steer them away from any potential pitfalls and make sure the producers don't eat them alive in the final edit.

"Anybody else?" Landon asks. He finally gets the stupid hook into the stupid tiny hole and congratulates himself more on not saying anything sexual than actually accomplishing the task. When his hands have moved from the bowl, Quentin reaches over and flips the mixer on.

Apparently, Landon's celebration was premature because the dough hook falls into the stainless bowl with a loud clatter.

"Shit." Landon can't help but curse at how bad he is at this.

"You'll get it. Better now than when we're cooking and I need your help with the mixer and you can't actually figure out how to use it," Quentin says sagely and Landon has never agreed more. He doesn't exactly relish the notion of humiliating himself on television because he can't work a stand mixer. It's humiliating enough now.

It takes him five more minutes, but he finally gets the dough hook in.

"Didn't think you'd have so much trouble getting it in the hole," Quentin says with a smirk and Landon can't help but turn to him in mock outrage.

"Quen!" he cries. "I can't believe you!" And after Landon so scrupulously avoided *any* sexual insinuation.

Quentin blushes, but he doesn't look even the tiniest bit ashamed.

"Next time, I won't take it so easy on you," Landon vows.

"Wouldn't want you to," Quentin says with a laugh and wow, Landon doesn't know how he's going to make it through the next eight weeks if he can't kiss this beautiful man a little bit. Surely that's allowed?

He's going to have to wait until after today's boot camp is over to call Ian and ask though, because even though Landon feels very nearly desperate, he's a bit more desperate to stay with Quentin.

Of course that's when Quentin turns things up a notch.

"I'm hungry, let's make lunch," Quentin says.

Landon loves to eat. He's also pretty intrigued at the concept of Quentin putting things in his mouth. He's only human, okay? And Quentin's mouth is so lovely—all wide and pink and plush. Landon wants to do sinful things to that mouth, only about a quarter of which involve food.

"You mean, you're going to make us lunch?" Landon asks hopefully. He was rather hoping the equipment tour could continue. At least the equipment is mostly non-threatening—all except the food processor. In his completely non-expert opinion, the food processor is a fucking terrifying piece of machinery designed to process fingers not food.

Quentin shakes his head. "*We're* going to make lunch."

Landon can't help the wave of apprehension that spreads through him. "How about," Quentin says with a bright smile, "I'll make you lunch, and you can make me lunch?"

Quentin obviously believes this is a fantastic idea, but Landon thinks it's just not fair. Whatever Quentin makes is bound to be delicious. He's a professional; this is what he does for a living. What Landon can make is probably not edible.

"Are you sure?" Landon asks. He's sure Quentin can hear the dubious tone in his voice, but he doesn't mention it and only nods excitedly in the affirmative.

"Why don't we both do something simple, like grilled cheese?" Quentin asks.

Landon had mentioned to Ian more than once that a grilled cheese sandwich was the *one* meal he feels even vaguely confident preparing besides cold cereal. He thinks Quentin suggesting this isn't a coincidence, but that's fine. Landon doesn't want to poison such a gorgeous man the first day he ever meets him.

"I can do that," Landon says.

"Then let's do it," Quentin says with another one of those dimpled grins that will probably make every single person aged eight to eighty fall in love with him. "Grilled cheese sandwiches. Half an hour?"

"Thirty minutes?" Landon scoffs. "I don't think it's going to take me thirty minutes."

Quentin just shrugs, a knowing smile on his face. "You'd be surprised."

It's never taken Landon that long to make a grilled cheese sandwich in his *life*, but he agrees, mostly because there's nothing wrong with having *too much* time.

They haven't gone over where all the ingredients in the pantry are located, but unlike during the show, when they'll get a measly sixty seconds to shop, there's unlimited time today, so Landon spends quite a bit of time perusing the shelves. Like the kitchen equipment, there are quite a few things he doesn't recognize.

After a good ten minutes, he finally emerges with bread and cheese and butter. Simple enough, but it still took him a long time to choose *which* bread because of course they don't have anything a simple as plain white bread, like the kind Landon buys at the store. The cheese selection is as exotic as the one at Whole Foods. He finally finds one that looks like a basic cheddar and picks it off the shelf.

After that, it's simple enough to slice the bread, though the wickedly sharp teeth on the bread knife scare him almost as much as the dreaded food processor. But he cuts carefully and slowly—maybe a bit too slowly though, because his bread slices end up looking a little like he's already gnawed on the edges.

Landon gazes at them critically and wonders if he should try again, but he really doesn't want to because that knife is almost as terrifying as the food processor. He saw Quentin cut through his bread earlier with confidence and precision, his slices looking as pristine as if they'd just come out of the bag.

Landon remembers seeing something about presentation and appearance counting when they're judged, but this is just Quentin. Besides, Landon reasons, Quentin will make sure their bread doesn't look like it's already chewed when it really matters.

The cheese is really, *really* hard, and Landon struggles even more to slice that into even chunks. He typically buys the pre-sliced cheese in the store. The truth is he's never actually cut cheese into slices before, which is a slightly embarrassing thing to admit, so he doesn't. Landon nods enthusiastically when Quentin glances over, clearly watching him struggle with the knife, and asks him if he's doing okay.

Because, let's face it, if he can't even make a grilled cheese sandwich in this kitchen—the *one* thing he believes he can cook—he's fucked. And not in the good way, either.

Finally, both the bread and cheese are sliced and Landon gets the pan heated and his sandwich is cooking and he can take a relieved breath.

Of course, then he gets distracted by Quentin, who's over at his station, looking like he's adding all these glorious flourishes and garnishes. Whatever he's making must be a masterpiece. When Landon finally tears his eyes away and glances back over at his pan, he realizes the edges of his sandwich are looking well, a lot *darker* than he intended.

But that's okay still. He can scrape those bits off. It's nothing he hasn't done before, Landon tells himself, hating that cooking in this kitchen has made him break into a sweat. He wanted to serve something decent and not burned around the edges but *c'est la vie*.

Quentin is such a good person. At the end of what feels like the longest thirty minutes of Landon's life, he presents his plate rather sheepishly towards Quentin and all Quentin does is smile enthusiastically.

"A true Patton original!" Quentin exclaims with real joy and Landon is rather incredulous. His sandwich looks like a nightmare compared to Quentin's, which is two flawless triangles, balanced one on top of the other, their surfaces a beautifully even color, their edges crisp and not even a tiny bit burned.

When he takes a hesitant bite, almost afraid to mar the perfection that Quentin's created, he moans a little. "This is so good," he can't help but say through a mouthful of deliciousness. The cheese Quentin selected was a white cheddar and he's spread raspberry jam on the bread—not something that Landon *ever* would have thought of, never mind attempted, but it adds a perfect note of sweetness to balance out the sharpness of the cheese.

It's one of the best sandwiches Landon has ever had, and he can't even bring himself to look over at Quentin as he finishes it off embarrassingly quick. He's afraid of what Quentin's face will say when he gets close enough to take in the rough edges of the bread and the burned edges that Landon couldn't quite scrape off.

"That was really delicious," Landon says as he takes his plate over to the sink. He can't face Quentin. If he can't do this, then he really can't do anything, and he just *knows* what Quentin is going to say. That he's going to have to find a different, less culinary-stunted partner.

"Landon," Quentin says, and he's suddenly so close that Landon almost drops his plate into the sink. "It's okay. It tasted absolutely fine. I liked it a lot."

Landon laughs a little bitterly. "Just bread and cheese." And he fucked even that up.

There's that hand again, reassuring and big and so warm, on the small of his back. "You have to know—you're not supposed to be a good cook yet. We can change that. We're *supposed* to change that."

Landon's fingers curl around the edge of the plate and he grips it like a lifeline. "I'm totally hopeless, unfortunately."

"Not even close," Quentin says and it sounds like a vow. "I swear. I wouldn't lie to you. You picked a really nice sourdough and the right cheese to set it off. There were a few . . . execution problems. But most of those were the unfamiliar equipment I think. And you *tried*. Do you think every single one of these celebrities is going to try?"

Landon has wondered that himself. "Probably not."

Quentin's hands fall gently to his waist and it's almost shocking how big they are in comparison. Landon doesn't usually feel tiny—he *knows* he's shorter than average—but Quentin feels huge. Quentin tugs him around and Landon's breath stutters at how close they are.

His eyes are so blue and so near and all Landon would have to do is reach up on his tiptoes a bit and he could press his lips to Quentin's. The knowledge simmers through him and Landon can see the precise moment Quentin has the same thought—his eyes darken just a shade, from the edges of the ocean surf to the sky at the height of summer. And Landon knows without question that Quentin wants him.

When Quentin pulls away a second later, murmuring about washing up and then finishing up with the equipment this afternoon, everything is the same between them, but it's different. They didn't kiss, but Landon knows it's inevitable now. There's heat between them, and he knows self-control has never been his forte.

The afternoon passes much like the morning, with Quentin carefully and completely going over the rest of the equipment. Landon is taken aback by some of the more exotic items, like the anti-griddle and the ice cream machine.

"You don't actually expect me to use these, right?" he asks, crossing his arms across his chest. Quentin doesn't seem particularly dumb, but he's showing Landon the controls of the anti-griddle like Landon might actually have to use the thing. And Landon can't even make a grilled cheese sandwich.

"I have no idea what we're really in for," Quentin admits. "I know we're going to need both of us if we want to have a chance of moving on each week. So yeah, you might have to use it, if I'm busy doing something else."

"You want to be as prepared as possible," Landon says, admiring how shrewd Quentin is, underneath the curls and the sparkly eyes.

"I don't want to have any regrets."

Landon understands all too well about regrets. "Should've kissed me, then," Landon says brazenly, because he might as well bring up the moment that's been on his mind all afternoon.

He knows he'll get another chance and this time, he hopes Quentin won't pull away because Landon can't remember the last time he wanted someone this much. He can practically taste Quentin's lips on his and the anticipation is sweet and hot in his blood.

Quentin blushes. "Am I that obvious?" he asks, as if obvious is *bad*.

"I like it," Landon soothes.

"You're just . . . just . . . so pretty up close," Quentin admits with bright-red cheeks flaming bright.

"Thank you." Landon can't help but preen a little. "The feeling is definitely mutual."

At that, Quentin's grin turns a little knowing. "Best news I've heard all day."

After the anti-griddle and their enlightening conversation, they move on to the deep fryer. Landon finds it only slightly less horrifying than the food processor.

"Why is everything so dangerous?" he asks.

Quentin looks genuinely mystified. "If you're careful, it's not, really."

"It's literally *boiling oil*," Landon points out.

But Quentin just shrugs. "Well, let's hope we don't have to deep fry anything."

At four, they call it quits for the day. Landon has zero qualms about asking for Quentin's number—after he's been flirting rather shamelessly all day—and immediately enters it into his phone.

"I'm gonna put you in as Quentin the Baker," Landon says.

"Not the worst thing I've ever been called," Quentin has to admit.

"What *is* the worst thing?" Landon asks, horribly curious.

"I think an ex-boyfriend called me a dick once. Or maybe that was one of my ex-girlfriends." Quentin shrugs, and Landon thinks he's gotten off pretty easy over the years.

"Girlfriends *and* boyfriends, then," Landon says as casually as he can, which is not casual at all.

"I'm more pansexual than bisexual," Quentin admits.

Landon holds his hands up in mock surrender. "Hardly one to judge here."

"What you did was really brave," Quentin says and that note of hero-worship is back in his voice. Landon thought he'd like it but he really doesn't. At least not because of this. Quentin doesn't know the whole story; *won't* ever know the whole story, if it's up to Landon.

"I guess," Landon says with a shrug. "Or really stupid. Depending on who you talk to."

"Well I think it was brave," Quentin staunchly defends.

"I like you, Quen," Landon says, slinging an arm around him and tugging him close against him for a brief second. Only a brief second because any more and they *are* going to end up making out in the pantry.

"The feeling is most certainly mutual," Quentin retorts with a dimpled smile.

"Burned grilled cheese sandwiches and all."

"It was only a little burned," Quentin is quick to add. "A very tiny bit."

"In my defense," Landon says, shrugging his jacket on, "you're a very distracting person."

"Tomorrow, same time?" Quentin asks, not even acknowledging how insanely distracting he is—which Landon kind of loves and hates that about him.

"Sure." Landon would get up even earlier to hang out more with Quentin Maxwell. Which after one day might be a little pathetic, but he's not complaining. Quentin is extraordinary and Landon feels like he's already in deep and they haven't even kissed yet.

"We'll work on your knife skills," Quentin promises. "It'll be fun."

Knife skills sound even less fun than kitchen equipment, but today was awesome so Landon can't complain. Besides, this is all stuff he'll need to know.

"Maybe if I do well, I can get a reward." Landon knows he's transparent as hell. He doesn't even care.

Quentin smirks. "I don't know, Patton. Maybe we should be practicing patience instead."

"Patience is for losers."

Quentin just shakes his head, but he's laughing so Landon will take that as a win and also as a maybe.

"Tomorrow, then."

Chapter Two

After a restless night of half-lucid, hot dreams that all feature a certain blue-eyed baker, Landon gets up early and spends more time than he even did on his grilled cheese sandwich fussing over his hair in the mirror. *What*—his priorities are *awesome*.

He's not proud of how vain he is, but when Landon has a crush, well, he has a *crush*. And this one on Quentin has hit him hard and fast, and part of that is the fact that he's almost certain it's mutual.

The rest of it might be how gorgeous Quentin is, and how supportive and kind and funny too, with a sly sense of humor that seems to match right up with Landon's own. But mostly Landon thinks his crush is nearly unmanageable already because the air practically vibrates with electricity when the two of them are in the room together.

He'd called Ian on the car ride home, and Ian had texted him back an update on the contract not even an hour later. Maybe Landon slightly exaggerated how charming the world is going to find the two of them together—or maybe not. Only time will tell, but Ian was happy with the news that he likes Quentin. Less pleased that Landon *likes* Quentin, but Ian reports that it's technically not against the contract for Landon to push Quentin against the nearest counter and kiss him until their lips fall off.

It's the best news Landon has heard in a long, long time.

Of course there's a second text that advises Landon to at least *try* to keep it in his pants, but he ignores that one.

He wears his tightest pair of skinny jeans and a t-shirt that he hopes shows off his biceps and his tan. He's pleasantly surprised with the results when Quentin practically trips on air when Landon walks into the room.

The only downside is that Quentin's carrying a whole bunch of knives.

"Landon," Quentin admonishes, but with a twinkle in his blue eyes, "please try not to distract me when I'm transporting sharp objects." He sets the knives down on a huge wooden cutting board, and lets out a quick sigh of relief that he's escaped unscathed.

"Distracting?" Landon wonders out loud, all creamy innocence, as he practically strikes a pose in the doorway. "What on earth could you be referring to?"

Quentin snorts with laughter.

Landon takes a sip of his coffee, trying to regroup and refocus. "So why were you hefting those dangerous objects around the kitchen anyway?"

Quentin levels him a frank stare. "The state of your bread yesterday."

"Oh." Landon really wanted to forget that part.

"*Oh* is right," Quentin says, but it's still kind. Landon doesn't think Quentin could be unkind even if he wanted to be. He's got such nice eyes. "We're going to work on your knife skills today."

Honestly, Landon was expecting *more* from the morning. He was expecting maybe a hug, or some more casual touching, but Quentin's just a touch more stiffly professional today—okay, he wasn't stiffly professional *at all* yesterday, but now he seems to have found some distance and it makes Landon want to whip out his phone and wave around that text from Ian that says there's absolutely nothing in their contracts about becoming involved with their partners.

A year ago, he might have actually done it. But after the last situation where he jumped first and looked later came back to bite him in the ass, he's become more cautious. He's still Landon—overly friendly and excitable, but there's a part inside of him that he's not sure he'd open to anyone else again.

Maybe he read Quentin wrong yesterday. Maybe Quentin is just naturally flirty.

What happens is that Landon tries really hard at first, listening intently to his partner's instructions on how he should be slicing the vegetables that he's set out in front of him. But as the morning drags on and Landon's concentration isn't rewarded with anything other than Quentin's genuine-but-still-polite smile, he definitely starts to slack.

Landon isn't aware that Quentin even notices because his tone of voice and demeanor don't change at all. But then they break for lunch—today, Quentin doesn't even suggest any kind of food competition. He just whips up a big calzone and makes it look dizzyingly easy in the process.

When they're finished eating, Quentin pins Landon with a very firm look. "Why aren't you trying?" he asks.

"It's boring," Landon whines, which is part of the problem. The other part is, of course, that it's definitely boring to work on knife skills if Quentin won't flirt with him anymore. Part of why yesterday was so fun from start to finish was the effervescence in his veins every time Quentin stared, blushed, laughed, or was in general blown away by Landon's presence.

"It's not going to be boring when we're on air and you're trying to chop vegetables and you can't manage," Quentin reminds him, still nicely, but it's definitely one of the harsher things that Quentin's said to him. Landon is pretty tough. He wouldn't have been able to make it through the industry otherwise, but for some reason, this one single comment of Quentin's still gets to him.

Landon grimaces. He's hopeless when he has a crush and he definitely has a crush on Quentin, though three hours into today Landon can't help but wonder if he read the situation all wrong yesterday.

"Here," Quentin sighs, "let's see if we can't get somewhere. We only have an hour or so before everyone else is meeting here to go over some basic rules."

"Everyone is showing up today?" Landon squeaks. He's not even done any research yet. Ian sent over some information packets on the celebrities and their chefs two days ago, but last night Landon was far too busy melting down over Quentin's insane hotness to possibly read them.

Quentin shoots him a strange look. "Don't you ever read your email?"

"Yes," Landon retorts. "All the time."

Quentin's face softens. "Let me guess. Only when it's not boring."

Landon would be offended by how easily Quentin has read him, but it's pretty true so . . .

"Pick up the knife," Quentin continues before Landon can interject and probably get them off on another long tangent that has everything to do with flirting and almost nothing with knife skills.

Landon could argue. But for once, he doesn't. He picks up the knife. It's what Quentin called a "chef's knife," earlier—a medium-ish size with a delicately and wickedly sharp curved blade.

Quentin moves behind him. *Close* behind him. Every molecule of Landon's body perks up in interest.

"You're gripping it way too tightly," Quentin says quietly, air tickling the hairs that brush Landon's neck. "*Relax.*"

Landon wants to tell him that it's a little hard to relax when Quentin's practically humping him against the prep counter. He might have yesterday, in a teasing lilting voice—but today, he keeps quiet and tries to do what Quentin says.

"Now, the carrot," Quentin directs. "One-inch slices. Go as slowly as you need to. Remember the rocking motion."

Landon does remember the rocking motion. They'd practiced it without even chopping anything. But when there's an actual physical vegetable under his blade, the feel is totally different and he can't get it right.

"Slowly, *slowly*," Quentin says firmly but gently. When Landon still doesn't go slowly enough for him, he reaches his arms around Landon, neatly caging him in.

Breath stutters out of Landon's lungs. He's barely composed enough as it is, but Quentin invading his personal bubble like it doesn't even exist is both the best and the worst thing that's ever happened to him.

"Slowly," Quentin repeats, and the words churn sluggishly through Landon's brain. It's on Quentin overload right now. The way he feels all around Landon, his muscular arms and torso boxing him in, making Landon feel a bit smothered, but in all the best ways—protected and worshipped and beloved and *wanted* so damn much. The intoxicating smell of Quentin. Lemons and coconuts and a tiny hint of mint and rosemary. Landon wants to flip their bodies and push him back against the counter and eat him whole.

Quentin causes the strangest reaction in Landon. His heart is beating so quick, it practically flutters like a hummingbird in his chest, but Quentin's also so warm that he relaxes Landon right down. It's the oddest combination, but Landon wouldn't trade it for anything. He never wants Quentin to move.

Quentin's hands skim over Landon's and finally come to rest on them. "Just relax," Quentin murmurs and Landon can feel the heat of Quentin's breath on the shell of his ear and it's suddenly too much. His knees wobble a bit and nearly threaten to give out. His cock has hardened in his jeans and he wants Quentin to kiss him so much he can barely breathe.

They begin to move together in unison, moving the knife as one instead of as two.

Landon has been told countless times that he marches to the beat of his own drum. He knows he's a bit odd and more than a little quirky, but he's always enjoyed that he understands and does things differently than the rest of the world. He's dated lots and lots of boys and even a handful of girls, but he's never met anyone he ever truly gelled with.

But Quentin—Quentin is different. A *different* different than Landon, but somehow instead of pushing them farther apart, their differences just emphasize how good they are together, and it feels natural as breathing to move together.

Landon feels a bit faint when he realizes how good their sex life could be if they're *this* attuned to one another and they've literally known each other for less than two days.

"That's it," Quentin murmurs encouragingly. "Just like that."

Landon has never wanted to drop the knife more and forget all about *Kitchen Wars*. He knows to some extent his future career is riding on how well this gamble pays off. According to Ian, he just needs to stay on the show as long as he can. He doesn't even need to win. But to stay, he's going to need to do things like chop vegetables correctly.

The part of him that wants nothing but Quentin, which is pretty nuts because he's *just* met Quentin, wars with the part of him that wants a real career again. Wants to sing and for people to listen.

Then Quentin's head dips closer and out of nowhere, as their knife slices cleanly and perfectly through a carrot, Quentin's lips brush the nape of Landon's neck. "Perfect," Quentin says so softly that Landon can barely hear the words over the roaring in his ears.

And suddenly it becomes very clear. Landon wants both. He wants both, not yet equally, but enough to *know* that he needs to focus on this right now and pray the rest falls into place.

There's a rhythm in Quentin's movements, Landon realizes quickly as soon as he focuses on the strokes of the knife. They sync up quite nicely with Quentin's breathing, which has somehow become Landon's breathing pattern as well. Big surprise.

It's relatively easy to keep moving the knife to that same rhythm, with the same rolling motion that Quentin so painstakingly tried to ingrain in him hours earlier.

Landon chops carrot after carrot, and then they move on to potatoes, which aren't nearly as fun as carrots, but even though it *is* a little boring, Landon focuses anyway. Landon can see in the slow, warm smile Quentin has on his face that he's relieved that Landon has managed to figure out not only how to chop a carrot, but how to balance this.

Who is he kidding? *Landon* is glad.

When they pack up the knives, preparing the space for the rest of the contestants to stop by, Quentin leans in, those plump pink lips distractingly close to Landon's. "Thank you," Quentin says.

"For what?"

Quentin shrugs. "I know today sucked. But thanks for sticking with it anyway. Just . . ." Quentin hesitates, and Landon can practically see the wheels in his head turning, as he tries to figure out what and how much he should say, "this competition means a lot to me. The potential of my own bakery."

Landon feels guilt wash over him. He forgets sometimes how self-focused the world surrounding him can be, and how he can be just as susceptible as the next thoughtless celebrity.

"I want you to have that," Landon says. "I really do. I know that seems crazy. We just met . . ." He doesn't want to say how strange it is to have a crush on someone you don't even know, but it's the truth.

Fuck it, Landon thinks, *he knows anyway.*

"Honestly, I wasn't expecting to like you this much," Quentin admits in a rush before Landon can even get the words out.

Huh. Well it's good they're on the same page. "Me either," Landon confides and loves how the smile blooms on Quentin's face, his cheeks growing pinker. "I got a bit carried away with it. I'm sorry. But I'm good now."

Quentin's cheeks grow a deeper pink; it's insanely endearing. "I did too," Quentin confesses. "I just hid it better. I don't want to get too distracted by it. But it is rather distracting." His eyes rove up and down Landon's form. "*Very* distracting, if I'm being honest."

"We'll just have to focus better," Landon declares. "Because you need your bakery and well, I need a career."

Quentin looks offended. "You *have* a career! You're Landon Patton!" Quentin is maybe the most loyal human on this planet. Landon didn't think he could be even more endeared; he was wrong.

"Some career advice," Landon pontificates dramatically because this particular part of his confession is a bitter pill to swallow and it's hard to say bluntly, especially to someone like Quentin. "Don't come out of the closet before all the pretty young girls fall out of love with you. It's not good for business."

Landon should have known better. The sympathy—or maybe it's empathy, Landon isn't quite sure, only that it's currently tearing a hole in his heart—in Quentin's eyes is devastating. "I didn't realize," he says slowly.

Landon can only shrug. "It is what it is," he explains. "So basically, I need this too. Probably just as much as you do."

The commiserating smile they share warms Landon up from the inside out. "Then we'll just have to win," Quentin declares, which is reckless, because Landon hasn't even checked out the competition yet.

A loud, obnoxious whistle pierces his ears and he glances up in surprise.

There's a short blond man in the doorway, slender, with a cheeky smile. "Maxwell, what the hell is this?" the man asks in a thick Irish accent. "I leave you alone for *two whole days* and you're charming everyone."

Landon stiffens. Is Quentin like this with *everyone*? Who is this guy?

"Rory!" Quentin exclaims, and Landon realizes that the Irishman is Quentin's friend Rory. The butchering expert, or so Quentin had explained.

"He's so brilliant," Quentin had said with a proud smile.

"I certainly hope he's not *too* brilliant," Landon had muttered, only to have Quentin nudge him with a shoulder.

"Be nice," Quentin had said.

Landon reminds himself of the same thing now. Rory is Quentin's friend and Landon needs all the help he can get to make sure he doesn't end up with nothing—no career *and* no Quentin.

Then Rory looks past Quentin and starts laughing so hard he nearly falls over. Landon doesn't quite understand. Does he have something in his hair? On his face? Oh *god*. Here he was, thinking that the last hour was maybe one of the hottest of his life, all while he's had something disgusting on him that Quentin could barely tolerate. Landon is going to have to move. To Antarctica.

"You're Landon Patton," Rory barely manages to get out between gasps. Landon doesn't understand; his name typically doesn't cause this sort of reaction.

"That's me?"

Quentin is glaring at Rory now, no longer quite so overjoyed to see his friend.

"Oh my god," Rory gasps out between giggles, *you don't know.*"

But Landon never gets to find out what he doesn't know, because suddenly there's a girl at the door behind Rory. She's slim but muscular, with long blond hair and a sweet face. Landon recognizes her but for the life of him, he can't place who she is and where he's seen her.

"And who's this, Rory?" Quentin asks, and Landon thinks maybe he's trying to change the subject, but then the reason why the girl looks so familiar becomes apparent.

"This is *Kimber Holloway*," Rory hisses, like she's not right in front of him.

Oh. *Oh.* Landon has to compete against a world class swimmer who owns handfuls of Olympic gold medals? That's just great. "Big fan," Quentin tells her with a smile and they shake hands and she turns to Landon, a bashful smile spreading over her delicate features.

"Not a little intimidated or anything," she says. "Landon Patton. Wow. You are *so* pretty in person."

Landon blushes. He's spent enough time looking in the mirror and at footage of himself that he knows it's not true, but the compliment still feels sweet.

Quentin speaks up. "He really is, isn't he?"

Before Landon can register Quentin's cheeky smile—there's more people filing in the door, and for a minute or two there's chaos as everyone meets and greets. But more importantly, sizes up their competition.

Landon hangs behind a bit, with Quentin next to him, and wishes he'd spent last night studying the contestant packets instead of daydreaming about Quentin and their future wedding and kids and white picket-fenced home.

Quentin leans over every few moments, murmuring into Landon's ear who each of the chefs are, and what their strengths and weaknesses are.

Landon tries to catalog and observe.

There's Rory, of course. He's a butcher originally from Dublin.

Quentin points out Reed Ryan, from Chicago. He owns the world-famous foodie destination, Garnet. Quentin exclaims, perhaps a bit too enthusiastically into Landon's ear, that Reed is famous for his laser sharp focus when he's cooking. He's paired with Diego Flores, who has become rather famous adapting comic books to movie scripts. He's worked on the last few Marvel movies, and is rumored to be moving over to DC for their new *Suicide Squad* film.

There's a bit of reverence in Quentin's voice as he talks about Blair Paulson, who's apparently the pastry chef for one of the Michelin-starred restaurants in London. She looks scarily serious and like she couldn't crack a smile if her life depended on it. Landon knows her partner, Alice Hitchens, a modern dancer who spent several seasons on *So You Think You Can Dance?* Another reality show veteran, Landon mentally notes.

There's Jeff Austin, who Landon wouldn't really call a *chef*, necessarily, because he hosts an exposé-type program that identifies and ridicules bad restaurants. Landon feels sorry for his partner, Jessa, a rather famous child actress. It's not a surprise she's here; she probably needs the attention as much as Landon does. Unfortunately, being paired with Jeff is pretty shitty luck.

Quentin, who seems to have studied the information packet far more than Landon, hasn't met Ezra Gillingham, a rather prominent mixologist in LA, and Landon hasn't met his partner either, Vanessa Neill, a celebrity makeup artist.

Landon has eaten in Paul Flannery's restaurants tons of times when he was growing up in the Midwest, and finds the food adequate enough, but he knows that Paul is hardly there cooking in every one of them each night. He looks like he's far more comfortable in an office than a kitchen. Landon senses blood in the water and files that bit of info away to use later. His partner, Carson Brooks, is also someone Landon knows—a late-night TV host who Landon has visited more than once—and Landon can't help but feel a little bad that someone he knows and likes is paired with someone who might not get very far in the competition.

Then Landon remembers that he's here for his own career *and* for Quentin's bakery. That means sticking around and being *glad* that he knows Carson can't cook either and that he won't be able to save Paul Flannery's ass.

"Do you know him?" Landon nudges Quentin subtly, towards the giant man standing in the middle of the room with fashion designer Nora Hsu.

Quentin frowns. "I think that's Oliver Glines. He runs a bed and breakfast near Nashville. Like major tourist destination, booked for years in advance type of thing."

"Sounds boring," Landon sniffs. "If I'm going to go on vacation, I want somewhere sunny and warm where I can lie on the beach and tan for hours. With a never-ending parade of frosty drinks."

Landon would have to be blind to miss Quentin's very fond look. He suddenly wonders what everyone thinks of *them*—the semi-washed up, very gay pop star and the baker who doesn't have a bakery. He wonders if everyone is already counting them out.

"I really like those little colorful umbrellas," Quentin confesses in a whisper and Landon can't help but giggle helplessly. Why is Quentin so damn cute?

"Can we help you, Mr. Patton?" a voice in front of the room asks and Landon's head snaps up. It's Alexis Leavy, the *Kitchen Wars* host, and she doesn't look very pleased that Landon was giggling with Quentin instead of paying attention. It's like grade school and he's being reprimanded again for pulling Sally's pigtails.

Whoops. If he cares at all about his career or about getting Quentin a bakery, he's gonna have to lock down his focus and pay better attention.

"Sorry," Landon answers with a lopsided smile. "We're all good."

Alexis gives a sharp, serious nod in acknowledgement and continues her explanation of the rules. Alexis is culinary royalty. Her parents both owned famous restaurants in New York, and she writes very successful cookbooks, as well as hosting shows on *The Food Network*. She also has a way of looking at you that cuts you down to size. Landon makes a mental note to *never* end up on her bad side.

The rules are as follows: there are seven weeks of competition. One pair is eliminated each week. Each week, each pair is to make one dish inspired by the theme of the week.

Landon is thinking to himself this seems kind of ridiculously straightforward when Alexis pauses and suddenly a mischievous smile blooms on her face and a feeling of dread settles deep and low in Landon's gut. He *recognizes* that smile. *He* makes that smile when he's about to seriously fuck someone over and enjoy every second of it.

Alexis explains further that each team will start with $50,000 in cash. There's a few enthusiastic whoops. Landon stays silent because he has a feeling they won't be *keeping* that kind of money. No, the money has some other purpose—probably something nefarious and he almost wants to tell Alexis she can keep it. After all, this show is called *Wars* for a reason.

Landon is right. While there is an overall "challenge" each week, there are also several challenges that teams can bid on to "gift" to other teams. Landon feels faint and also like he could use some clarification. "So like, to sabotage each other," Landon states.

Alexis looks like a cat who's just gotten into the cream. "Exactly."

There's buzzing in the room as the various competitors freak out a little. Landon definitely isn't calm either. His cooking skills are negligible. That alone was going to make winning difficult. Add in more complications and suddenly winning looks impossible.

But someone has to win, right? There *has* to be a winner. Why shouldn't it be him and Quentin?

❧❧❧❧❧❧ ❧❧❧❧❧❧

Filming starts in a few days and two days after their meeting, Landon meets Quentin for a beer at a local bar to go over strategy for their first challenge. They've been texting rather nonstop, but Landon is missing Quentin. The bright clarity of Quentin's blue eyes and the softness of his smile, specifically, but he doesn't need to admit that. Landon decides that going over strategy is a perfectly viable reason to meet up.

Or at least that's what Landon keeps telling himself as he sits in a booth, waiting for Quentin to show up.

Finally, Quentin slides in across from Landon. "This was a good idea," he says with a dimpled grin. "I missed you."

Landon didn't even know he was anxious, but Quentin's words calm him down. Quentin wants to see him just as much as he wants to see Quentin.

Landon slides the beer he ordered for Quentin across the worn wooden surface of the table. "I missed you more," he retorts impudently.

Quentin takes a sip of his pint. "You excited about filming?"

Shrugging, Landon scratches the tabletop with a fingernail. "More terrified than excited, if I'm being honest," he admits.

Quentin's face goes soft. "It'll be fine. I think that we're going to fly right under everyone's radar during the first challenge. The most obvious teams to go after will be the ones that look strong. Probably Blair and Alice. Or Reed and Diego."

Landon has made an entire career out of being the underdog, so he's good with this. Sometimes it's better to not be too aggressive right out of the gate.

"I think Rory and Kimber too. She probably cooks for herself. All those athlete types do. Who do you think the weakest links are?" Landon already has an idea but he wants to see if Quentin's on the same page.

Quentin frowns. "It's okay," Landon tells him with a reassuring smile. "It's inevitable. There's going to be weaker teams. It's just good to know who they are going in."

"Well, I'd probably say Ezra Gillingham and Vanessa Neill," Quentin says slowly. "He *does* cook, obviously, but he's mainly into mixing drinks these last few years. He might not be as sharp behind a stove. And she looks a bit, well, um, flighty?"

Landon's own analysis was a lot more cutthroat than that, but it's okay. Quentin's going to cook well enough to keep them in the game and Landon is going to manipulate the game so they win.

"That was my thought too. He's out of practice in the kitchen. Also, Paul Flannery."

Quentin shakes his head right away. "No, he's definitely going to be tough competition."

Landon raises an eyebrow. "He runs that chain of restaurants. I'm betting he doesn't spend much time in the kitchen."

"He actually teaches at one of the most prestigious cooking schools in California. In Napa," Quentin says. "I had a few classes with him."

Well. Shit.

"And he's good?" Landon thinks he already knows the answer, but when Quentin nods enthusiastically, Landon thinks it's definitely time for them to have this conversation.

"Listen," he says seriously, leaning forward and looking right into those spectacular eyes of Quentin's. "I know you know you're friends with Rory. And you know Paul Flannery and practically hero-worship Blair Paulson. But you've got to forget about all that. This is serious. This is for your bakery."

A crease appears between Quentin's brows. "You don't think I can be tough enough?"

"I think you're plenty tough," Landon corrects gently. "I worry about you being ruthless enough."

The cloud lifts off Quentin's face. "That's what I've got you for, though."

"Yeah, but just like I have to learn how to cook, sometimes I might not be available to be cutthroat," Landon explains softly. "We have to learn from each other. I think that might be the key to winning this."

There's a definite glint of *something* in Quentin's eyes as he gazes over at Landon. "Then we'll be the greatest team ever. The Dream Team."

Landon smiles. "The Dream Team. You *were* paying attention."

Quentin just shoots him a look like he's crazy.

"I mean, I said that on our first day," Landon explains. Maybe Quentin doesn't remember.

"I most definitely remember that," Quentin says. "It's funny though, pretty much that entire day feels like a dream, from the moment you walked in, until we left that night. But I remember everything you said. In explicit detail."

Landon doesn't know whether to be pleased or embarrassed. Maybe both. He definitely is pleased at the *explicit* part. He'll almost definitely have one hand around his cock later as he relives the sly curve of Quentin's lips as he says that particular word.

Quentin leans forward a little. His eyes are gleaming in the dim light of the pub, teasing and just the tiniest bit sly. Landon begins to sweat and simultaneously wonder if his first kiss with Quentin Maxwell is going to take place in this rather dingy dive bar around the corner from his apartment.

His lips are dry and parched. He reaches for his pint, only to discover it's empty.

"Another round?"

Landon lets out an exasperated sigh. "You're a bad influence."

"Only one more round though, or else I'm afraid I'll do some-thing I won't quite regret," Quentin teases as he slides out of the booth.

"Someday, Maxwell," Landon calls as he walks away, "you're gonna have to make good on those threats."

Quentin glances back, and there's pure sexual wickedness in his look. Landon shudders a little, every hair on his body rising.

As they drink their second round, their banter grows further charged, the air thickening between them, and Landon revises his theory that his first kiss might take place inside the bar.

It's totally going to take place outside of this bar—Landon is absolutely sure. Quentin's gaze seems permanently stuck on Lan-don's face. On his lips.

When they head outside into the cool evening air, Lan-don's blood is humming with anticipation. Quentin's on his phone, requesting an Uber and Landon stands there waiting with him—waiting for *far* more than that, if he's being really honest.

"You're working tomorrow?" Landon asks. He's typically a lot smoother than this, but something about Quentin makes him nervous. Like this might be the last time he's ever faced with the possibility of a first kiss. It makes his palms sweat, so he stuffs his hands in his pockets and tries to look chill and relaxed, kind of like how Quentin looks all the time.

"Yep." Quentin is a saint and doesn't even point out that he's *already* said this.

Landon knows their time window is closing quickly, and Quentin's not taken a step towards him yet. Landon shifts his weight from one foot to another. He's normally against making the first move, but maybe desperate times call for desperate measures.

Later, he'll think that everything happened so quickly, but it probably didn't. Landon is just a chicken shit.

The car pulls up, and Quentin takes a step and then another and gathers Landon into his arms, giving him a firm, not-very-quick (especially considering the car is just idling there) hug. While their arms are still intertwined, Quentin leans down and brushes a sweet, soft kiss against the top of Landon's head.

"See you later," Quentin says, and before Landon can react, can snatch his arms—and lips—back, he's sliding into the back of the car and Landon is pathetically and forlornly staring at the departing lights.

He pouts during the entire walk home until he collapses on his sofa and pulls his phone out.

There's a single text from Quentin. **Waiting will make it sweeter, don't you think?**

Landon lets out a grumbled expletive. Quentin's not wrong, but that doesn't mean Landon has suddenly discovered patience.

He leaves Quentin waiting for exactly three minutes. He was going to wait five, but he couldn't quite manage it. Then he texts him back.

You're plenty sweet enough.

CHAPTER THREE

LANDON IS REALLY NERVOUS. Far more nervous than he ever was before he performed on *The Voice*. It probably helped that he was a huge underdog—there's no pressure when you aren't expected to succeed. Probably it also helped that he actually *knows* how to sing, and he has no idea how to cook.

Each team has a tiny green room at the television studio, which is nice. What isn't nice is that Quentin's not even here yet. He's still filming his intro package. And Landon has already looked over the room once, but even though it only took a few moments, he does it again because he's bored and nervous and that's not a good combination for him.

There's a comfortable but rather worn brown leather sofa, but instead of sinking into its comforting depths, Landon is perched on the edge, afraid he might crease his button-up. In the corner is a mini fridge with cold drinks. A fruit basket perches on the top, and just as Landon requested, there's a coffee pot and a really miserly selection of instant coffee that Landon had wrinkled his nose at. A tiny attached bathroom and lighted mirror and counter for makeup rounds out the small room.

Landon grimaces. There's just not enough distractions in here. He's tempted to go dig through his bag and find his phone that he stashed there when he arrived, but what would he even do? Check his email? Text Ian for the millionth time that this was a huge mistake and he and Quentin are going to be the first team eliminated? Redo his hair?

Landon taps his foot agitatedly against the edge of the veneered coffee table. He's going to have to cook in about an hour. Like actual real food that people are going to eat.

Not just people. *Judges.*

Simone Lalit, who's rather notorious in the restaurant world for being harsh.

Jasper McDonnell, who's *more* notorious for being severe.

And Zach Emory, at whose restaurant in LA people wait *months* if not longer to score a reservation. Landon has already purposefully ignored how cute he is. Quentin is already enough of a distraction.

Landon feels the knot of nerves in his stomach wrench a little tighter.

That's when the door opens, and Quentin walks in. He's dressed in tight black jeans and he's got on a crisp white chef's jacket, with his last name embroidered in stark black font on the right-hand side.

Quentin's hair is pulled back with a tight headband, little ringlets dangling along his neck as he nods and laughs, his eyes glowing fierce and blue. Landon swallows hard. Quentin looks like the love child of Mick Jagger and Julia Child, and that's way hotter than he ever imagined it could be.

"You look beautiful," Quentin says softly, his own hand reaching up to gently brush the hair that Landon labored over for an hour this morning. The products he generally uses stand up quite well under the heat of the stage lights, so he's hoping the heat of the kitchen won't be much difference.

He knows it's silly to worry over something like wilted hair, but it's a nice change to worry about something he actually has control over.

"I like it like this," Quentin says. "It shows off your features. And they deserve to be shown off." His fingers brush over Landon's cheekbones. The pads of his fingers are rough with callouses but they glide over his skin like it's the finest thing they've ever felt.

Landon blushes. So much for shifting his crush into a more manageable state. His heart is beating rapidly, and when Quentin's hand brushes lower, his fingers ghosting over where it's thumping in his chest, Landon knows Quentin must realize that he's the cause. It would be embarrassing, but Landon wonders if he put his hands over Quentin's heart, would he feel something very similar?

"Are you ready?" Quentin asks softly.

"No," Landon answers honestly. "Not at all. But we might as well give it a shot."

Quentin reaches down and threads his fingers through Landon's and squeezes them tight. Landon thinks he can feel his erratic heartbeat in them. "Let's do it then."

***

Landon's forgotten how quick things move when they actually get on set.

The Voice always moved through acts fairly rapidly, but there was still a stage to reset between each act. During *Kitchen Wars*, there's no break. From the moment they hit the sound stage, it feels like there's literally not a single moment for Landon to catch his breath.

One minute they're being ushered to their respective stations, awaiting Alexis' appearance to give the introduction, the next, there she is, and she's talking and explaining the rules again.

Landon glances down the line and sees a similar shell-shocked expression on every celebrity's face. The chefs are tougher nuts to crack—most seem fairly relaxed and confident. But it takes zero effort to pick out the people who don't cook for a living.

Alexis moves on from explaining the basic rules to the individual rules for today's contest.

"For this week," she says coyly, like she's unwrapping a gift that she knows she'll particularly enjoy, "the celebrity contestants will be doing all the prep work, and the chef alone will be doing any and all cooking."

Landon blanches. He reaches down without even thinking, beneath the stainless steel counter and finds Quentin's hand, grasping it hard. No matter how much he paid attention in the knife skills lessons Quentin gave him, Landon is just plain *not ready* to have to do all the prep for a dish that will decide if they stay at the competition after this week.

He was really expecting—*hoping*, anyway—that Quentin would get to take the lead this week. Unfortunately, that is not looking to be the case.

Alexis continues. "You'll all start with $50,000, to use for bidding on auction items. Placing in the top three guarantees you a payout so you can bolster up your reserves for the next week.

First place gets $5,000, second place $2,500, and third place $1,000. The team with the lowest judges' score each week will be eliminated. And the last team left standing will get to keep their money."

That's when Alexis stops, her voice ringing through the soundstage and lets the finality of her last phrase sink in. She's got a theatrical streak that Landon might appreciate if it wasn't directed at him.

Landon really doesn't want to be eliminated. He wants to stay in this competition and gain a wider audience for his music. He wants to remind the world that he's not that one gay pop star who came in third place on *The Voice* a few years back. He also wants to spend the time with Quentin, and to build Quentin the bakery he wants so dearly with the money they could win.

It's a lot of things to want without any concrete idea on how to go about getting them.

He grips Quentin's hand harder, and feels it squeeze his own fingers back. It's reassuring until Landon remembers that he's the one doing all the prep work this week. It could be him that lets them down.

"This week's auction is," Alexis says, and then pauses dramatically to whip up a silver turreted lid from the table, "salt and pepper!"

There's a single salt and pepper set sitting on the table. Landon is confused. Someone has to cook with salt and pepper? Aren't they *always* supposed to cook with salt and pepper?

Landon glances over at Quentin, hoping he'll be able to add some illumination onto the problem. But before he can murmur a question under his breath, Alexis starts talking again.

"One of the number one tenets of cooking," Alexis says conversationally, as if they're just hanging out, "is seasoning the food properly. However, whoever wins *this* auction will be the *only* team seasoning their food."

Landon can feel Quentin tense up next to him. In fact, the air on the whole soundstage seems to tighten up. When Landon glances down the line, he can literally see the dread etched on every single chef's face. The celebrities look undeterred, but Landon realizes they're simply unaware of just how terrible a fate this auction item is.

The other issue is that Landon realizes he's been so busy flirting with Quentin that they've barely covered auction planning. They'd discussed it once or twice, but mostly Landon had boasted they could make it through to the finale without spending *any* money on auction items.

Suddenly, Landon is thinking differently. He tries to nudge Quentin, but Quentin gives him a tiny little shake of the head, as if to say, "nope, we've got this."

It feels terrifying, a bit like jumping off a cliff with only the wide open blue sea below, but Landon makes the conscious decision to trust Quentin. If he thinks they can do this without salt and pepper, then they can.

"Who'll start the bidding at $500?" Alexis asks gleefully, clearly enjoying the way each chef is squirming far too much.

The bidding quickly goes wild, with almost every team participating at first. But after the bidding hits $2,000, the only pairs left battling it out are Jeff Austin and Paul Flannery.

Landon feels a moment of fear; Quentin had said that Paul had been one of his professors in culinary school. *Surely* he would know better than just about anyone how vital salt and pepper are. If he's still bidding, maybe it's impossible to cook without them.

But a single glance to his right, taking in Quentin's calm expression, reassures Landon.

Jeff Austin and his partner Jessa win the salt and pepper auction at the rather outrageous price of $4,500.

Alexis looks down the line of pairs, and Landon practically feels skewered by her pointed look. He and Quentin were the only ones to not bid on the salt and pepper auction at all. He's not sure if that was smart or stupid; really, only time will tell.

"One member of your team will get sixty seconds to shop," Alexis says, "for this week's theme. Bar food."

They've already agreed that it will be far better for Quentin to do the shopping, and when Alexis counts off the time, Landon frantically cranes his head, trying to find Quentin in the glassed-in pantry, fighting for ingredients to cook their first dish.

Sixty seconds pass so quickly that it feels like Landon hasn't breathed the whole time. He must not be the only one, because Quentin is panting rather heavily when he makes it back to their station with a full basket of ingredients. He shoots Landon a look after Alexis announces their thirty-minute cooking time starts now.

"Fucking hell," Quentin murmurs under his breath. "I thought Rory was going to fight me in the meat locker."

Landon shrugs as Quentin pokes through their basket. "Did you get what you wanted?"

Quentin frowns. "I *think* so. I wanted to keep it simple, since you're doing the prep. And use ingredients that have a lot of natural flavor, since we can't use salt or pepper."

"That's gonna be tough," Landon says, "I only eat deep fried food in bars. Isn't fried food normally salty?"

Quentin shoots him another, even darker look. "We're not deep frying anything. Bar food doesn't have to be heavy and flavorless. Even without salt."

"Right," Landon says brightly, "what are we making then?"

"A burger. Stuffed with brie, with a mushroom ragout on a brioche bun."

Landon is impressed before he realizes that he's going to be the one prepping all those ingredients. The panic must show on his face, because Quentin takes a break from unpacking their basket and lays a reassuring hand on his forearm.

"It's a fairly easy dish to make. Plus, I'll be next to you the whole time, talking you through it."

Landon takes a deep, unsteady breath and focuses. "Okay. What do I need to do first?"

Quentin leads him through cutting the brie into chunks, then forming the ground beef around the cheese. The ground beef feels gross, and Landon can't bear to look down at his hands. Out his periphery he can see the cameras looming down on them as he makes one disgusted face after another, giggling through the slime sliding between his fingers and the responding fondness in Quentin's eyes as he leans down to get closer to Landon.

Landon hopes the cameras catch how sweet Quentin's smile is as he runs to the sinks to wash his hands the literal second the last burger patty is finished.

When Landon returns to their station, Quentin's waiting there with an expectant expression. "Ready to chop?" he asks with a sly twist to his lips.

Landon makes a face. "I hate chopping."

"Chop, chop, baby," Quentin teases. And Landon is pretty sure at least one of the cameras has been focused almost exclusively on them since the thirty-minute countdown started. He knows they're cute, knows they're flirting with each other, almost unconsciously at this point, and realizes they are making really excellent television.

So it's not like he *plays* up the flirting for extra effect, but well, if he bats his eyelashes a moment longer while he wipes and carefully chops the mushrooms and washes the arugula, then nobody can really blame him. The public isn't actually voting for them, but Landon knows how this all really works. If they become crowd favorites, the producers will make sure they stick around.

Quentin cottons on as he moves to set the burgers carefully onto the stovetop grill. "What are you doing?" he asks quietly, leaning in and letting the sizzling of the cooking meat prevent the cameras from picking up on his words.

Landon leans in further. If the cameras catch any of this, it'll just look like two boys who seem very much into each other—which is *technically* true. "What I can to make sure we win," he says and rises up on his tiptoes and presses a quick, fleeting kiss to Quentin's cheek.

His shocked expression melts into pure pleasure. "Darling," he purrs, "I've gotta grab the bacon."

Quentin had said he doesn't typically put bacon on this particular burger, but with the lack of salt on the meat itself, he'd said that he thought the bacon might help offset the lack of salt. Landon doesn't know anything about cooking, but he loves bacon so he definitely approves.

Leaning against the counter, Landon cocks his hip and tries to emphasize the curves he loathed for so many years but has learned to appreciate. He hopes Quentin can appreciate them too. "We should put bacon on everything," he says, "just for me."

Quentin's smile is like the sun. "On everything?"

Landon can see the camera panning in on them from the corner of his eye. He reaches up and tucks a curl behind Quentin's ear. His hair is so soft, Landon never wants to stop putting his fingers in it. But he has to forcibly restrain himself this time around. It's not the time or the place—*yet*. Besides, he does want Quentin quite a bit, cameras notwithstanding, and the last thing he wants is to give Quentin the wrong idea. They'll have to figure out where and how to draw the line.

Landon carefully butters the brioche buns and Quentin toasts them impeccably, leaving their moist, buttery insides the perfect color Landon wants his skin to be when he's spent a week out on the beach tanning.

While Quentin is manning the mushrooms and the burgers, Landon has quite a bit more time to observe the other teams.

Everyone appears fairly absorbed in cooking their own food, though there do seem to be some team breakdowns already—a few of the celebrities and chefs don't actually appear to be speaking to one another—and Landon is again profoundly glad that he has Quentin on his side.

Landon also observes that most of the other teams are making a lot more than just a burger. Most of them have sides, or salads, or other items. When he mentions this particular point to Quentin, suggesting maybe they should have some kind of additional item other than their burger, Quentin just shakes his head.

"This is plenty," Quentin says, pointing to their burgers. "Plus, typical sides are fries or onion rings or other things that will be really hard to season well without salt or pepper. Anyone that's using potatoes is crazy."

Landon decided the first day they met that he was going to trust Quentin, so he just nods and goes back to watching Quentin carefully construct their burger.

They have a solid five minutes to make sure it's flawless and Quentin does, even walking around the plate and nudging the burger a bit to make sure it's structurally sound.

"It's not going to fall apart," Landon says, even though he isn't the expert here. He's more praying it won't, and it helps to say it out loud.

"The mushrooms are a bit wetter than I normally make them," Quentin says, as he fusses with it. "I put in a lot more beef stock to try to compensate for not using salt."

The mushrooms had tasted delicious when Quentin had given Landon a taste, extending a spoon shyly towards Landon's mouth.

Mushrooms aren't the sexiest food in the world to eat, but Landon had done the best job he could, wrapping his lips around the spoon and sucking the morsels off like they were the best thing he'd ever eaten. And it wasn't even that far from the truth.

Quentin had watched with dark, intense eyes as Landon had finally relinquished the cleaned spoon.

"You're evil," he'd whispered into Landon's ear when he'd leaned down to minutely adjust one of the bun tops on the burgers.

"You love it," Landon had whispered right back.

He'd felt so on top of the world right then, watching the tendon in Quentin's neck flex and his long, deep breaths. Landon had been nearly a hundred percent sure that Quentin was only seconds away from literally dragging Landon away to some dark corner and kissing the hell out of him. It's a little bit of payback for the other night, when Quentin left Landon wanting so much more.

It's selfish but Landon almost hopes the cameras didn't catch that rather sexually charged exchange because it feels like more than just a play for the audiences' affection. It feels like so much more. He *wants* it to be so much more.

But this will all end if they can't make it past the first judging session.

Landon's heart is in his throat as the time ticks to a close and they set their plates on the judging table. The judges file in.

Quentin tenses and Landon hears him squeak under his breath when Zach Emory comes into view. And yeah, he's really cute. Almost certainly straight, but still quite cute. If Landon was going to watch a cooking show, he'd totally watch Zach Emory's.

As they get set up for judging, Landon looks down the line at the different plates of food. There's two fish and chips entries. He sees a few sandwiches, with beautifully burnished crusts, an artistically arranged plate of hot dogs and what looks a bit like coleslaw, and another burger. It's just about everything he loves about bar food, and suddenly he's hungry.

The judges work their way down the line of plates, offering even more casual criticism than Landon was honestly expecting and miserly dishing out tiny tidbits of praise.

Blair Paulson's fish is pronounced a little soggy, and the batter flavorless. The fries also don't have enough flavor, despite being apparently soaked in garlic and parmesan. Quentin looks down-right shocked at this development, like he couldn't even conceive of a world where Blair Paulson might make food that doesn't taste like heaven. Of course, it doesn't help that she attempted a dish that even *Landon* knows needs salt to make truly sing.

"And this," Simone says with a disgusted curl of her lip, pointing to Reed Ryan's coleslaw next to an admittedly sad-looking pair of sausages nestled in buns. "This is literally the most pathetic attempt at flavor I've tasted all day. And that's saying something."

Landon cringes, maybe even more than Reed is wincing right now. Reed has kind brown eyes and the kind of body that would probably reject salt even if it was an option. Landon wants to give Reed a hug, and say that everything will be okay because nobody deserves to be publicly humiliated.

Jasper McDonnell reaches their burger and hums almost appreciatively. Okay, so maybe Landon is just hoping that was an appreciative hum. It might have been a completely neutral hum. He hears Quentin take a rather unsteady breath and Landon realizes he's basically bracing himself for the worst—which is so ridiculous because Quentin should have as much faith in himself as Landon has in him.

"A brie stuffed burger topped with a mushroom ragout, sir," Quentin says very politely. He's such a nice guy; he's definitely the nicest man that Landon has ever tried to date. Not that they've ever actually *tried* to date. Unfortunately, none of what they've done so far could even remotely be called dating.

Maybe if Quentin had kissed him after they met for drinks, that could have been considered half a date.

Focus, Landon yells at himself. He can't lose himself in an internal debate about whether he should properly ask Quentin out to dinner when Simone Lalit and Jasper McDonnell and Zach Emory are about to shred their burger with their Michelin star fingers.

"Plate looks a bit empty without a side," Jasper observes and Landon hates that he'd made the very same observation. He's jinxed them.

"If the flavor holds up, I'd much rather have one really excellent item than two mediocre ones," Zach inserts with a crinkled smile.

Landon *knew* he thought he was cute for a reason. "Let's give this a try."

Landon's heart is in his throat as Simone, Jasper, and Zach all pick up the burger. Zach's falls apart a tiny bit, and he can practically *feel* Quentin chanting in his head, praying that it will continue to stay together. One by one, they put down the burger and Landon can hear the beat of his heart in the interminable silence.

"The flavor is definitely there," Zach says with a reassuring smile. Landon lets out a bit of the breath he was holding.

"Not sure I would have picked brie as the cheese," Jasper observes, but it's a lot more thoughtful than snide. As if he's truly trying to decide if brie was the right route to take.

"Maybe a sharp cheddar might have worked better here," Simone says. "A really sharp white cheddar. Would have bumped up the flavor profile a bit. But it's definitely quite tasty. I love the mushrooms and the arugula. Dressing it with lemon cut through the fat of the meat and the bacon really well."

Landon wants to faint with relief. He also wants to fling his arms around Quentin and kiss him all over. In fact, he smugly decides that he is most certainly going to do the latter during their very next break. He can't wait any longer. He doesn't *want* to wait any longer. He also should ask Quentin to dinner. A dinner *date*. He's got to make sure this *thing* is at least in process before he explodes of sexual frustration.

"I do wish there'd been a side," Jasper adds. "The presentation feels a bit simple. A bit empty."

"And mine didn't stay together very well," Zach says with a tiny apologetic shrug. He's nicer than either Jasper or Simone, but he *does* still mention it.

It wouldn't do for the judges to give them a perfect critique with no flaws, but Landon is still over the moon. Based on some of the other comments that were given, there is almost no way he and Quentin will be eliminated today. He can breathe again.

Except Landon does get a bit jealous when it's Rory and Kimber's turn. All three judges rave over his burger too. Apparently he used some exotic mix in the patty, adding flavor without adding salt.

The worst critique of the hour definitely goes to Ezra and Vanessa, who get an askance look at their rather sad-looking pair of Scotch eggs sitting on a plate, with only a sprig of dill as a garnish. Quentin had said that Ezra has a rather good reputation as a mixologist in town, and he's done a lot more work recently with beverages than food. But, Quentin had also warned, flavor is flavor.

The problem with Ezra's flavor is that it's just not enough to even begin to compensate for a lack of salt and pepper. And Simone bluntly asks him if he bothered to season the eggs at all. Ezra just smirks, and Landon decides he doesn't even feel that sorry for him.

Jeff Austin—the only chef who *could* cook with salt and pepper—goes the utterly safe route and has prepared the second fish and chips dish. The judges give a neutral if not overly enthusiastic evaluation. Which is funny, because Jeff and Jessa spent $4,500 on *salt*. Whatever they prepared should be transcendent.

Oliver prepares what is apparently a very tasty steak sandwich. His bread is glorious, a perfectly burnished golden brown and the judges only ding him for a slight lack of salt. The fact that he'd managed to get even *some* seasoning into the pile of meat on the sandwich is an achievement though. Landon is dying to discuss this with Quentin, but he has to stand quietly and not give a running commentary on the *judges'* commentary, which is a lot harder than he ever anticipated.

Finally, the judges move on to the last dish, a shepherd's pie prepared by Paul Flannery and Carson Brooks. The judges like the flavor, but . . .

"The vegetables are really unevenly cut," Jasper says and the annoyance in his tone is ripe. "Meaning some of them aren't cooked all the way through and others are just mush."

That is totally on Carson, who did all the prep, per the challenge. Landon has never been more grateful at how patient and certain Quentin was that Landon be up to speed in the kitchen before the show even started. He never wants to be the reason they're judged harshly, though he supposes in the end, it's probably inevitable. He isn't a professional chef. But still, it must suck to be Carson, and Landon feels a pang of sympathy for him as his face falls during Jasper's comments.

Alexis steps up then, and she looks like she's enjoying herself just a hair too much. It would bother Landon more, but after listening to all the judges' comments, he still feels certain that he and Quentin are safe.

"The judges will need some time to deliberate on their decision," Alexis announces, and everyone files backstage, looking appropriately nervous—even Rory and Kimber. Landon can barely refrain from rolling his eyes. If anyone scored a home run, it was Rory.

Landon just hopes that however long it takes the judges to come to their decision, it's enough time for him to give Quentin a proper kiss.

He shouldn't have even wondered. The moment the door to their green room closes behind them, Landon opens his mouth to give all the opinions he's barely been able to hold back during the judging, but Quentin pounces too quick and he's throwing his arms around Landon, hugging him tightly.

"Thank you, thank you, *thank you*," he chants into Landon's ear, the words innocent, but the delivery husky and far too dirty for Landon to handle. He groans a little and wiggles closer.

"I didn't do anything," he mumbles into Quentin's curls. "Literally almost nothing."

"You were perfect. And perfectly adorable," Quentin explains softly, pulling back a little. Quentin's lovely eyes are shining so close, and Landon actually thinks to himself that he can't wait any longer to kiss him when Quentin leans in and brushes his mouth over Landon's.

He pulls back before it even becomes a real kiss. It's only a teasing little taste of everything Landon wants, but Quentin only stares at him, a smile flirting around the corners of the lips that Landon is dying to keep kissing. "Is this okay?" Quentin asks, as if Landon hasn't been throwing himself at him practically from the first moment they met. As if he hasn't made his appallingly embarrassing crush so obvious.

"Yes," Landon responds right away. "*Yes.*"

"Good," Quentin says, then he swoops in again, faster this time, his lips pressing onto Landon's and it's perfect. Firm and soft and lovely. Landon wants to swoon. Good thing there's a handy door behind them. He collapses against it, his knees turning to mush as Quentin frames Landon's face with his big, calloused hands, tracing over his cheekbones and his jawline with the most delicate, sensual sweeps.

Quentin holds his head and angles him just so and his tongue is so confident and sure, so *hungry* for a taste of Landon. Quentin's kisses are desperate and so real and Landon is nearly stunned by the depth of Quentin's desire, because while he'd admitted their feelings were mutual, Quentin keeps so much of his buried. He's so much better than Landon at keeping it hidden when it needs to be, and it makes the rawness of this kiss that much hotter. Landon loves the idea that he's the only one who can undo Quentin this way.

With a panting gasp, Quentin wrenches his mouth off Landon's, and slides it down his neck, nibbling and sucking every bit of skin he can reach, and the scrape of Quentin's teeth against Landon's tendon has him moaning with zero thought to how thin the walls are and who might possibly be listening.

"Hot," Quentin breathes onto Landon's skin. "So hot. Today. You. I can't."

Landon giggles and it's high and breathy and he's definitely affected by this. His cock is hard and throbbing in his pants, and he's only a few kisses away from forgetting himself completely and just shamelessly rubbing it against Quentin's own.

"Use your words," he teases in a mumble, tilting his head so he can recapture Quentin's mouth with his own.

They kiss and kiss some more, their lips slick against each other, until the only sound Landon can hear is his heart pounding in his chest.

Quentin lifts his head again. "I get what you were doing today," he slurs out, the sound of his voice deep and wrecked. Landon wants to hear it like this all the time.

"What?" Landon doesn't really want to talk. He just wants to kiss. Forever. And maybe, you know, alleviate some of the pressure in his pants. Minor things.

Quentin pulls back more this time, and Landon can see just how blown his pupils are. His lips are plump and red and wet and Landon has to take an unsteady breath. He wants so much. "I want to talk about it," he says. "But we needed to do that first."

Landon makes an unsuccessful grab for the collar of Quentin's chef jacket, but he's already abandoned Landon at the door and has made his way to the couch. He settles down on it and pats the seat next to him. "Seriously," Quentin says.

"What if I wanted to keep doing that?" Landon whines.

"I want to keep doing it too," Quentin admits.

"Okay then," Landon says, reaching again for Quentin, but he ungracefully dodges Landon's grasp.

"Seriously," Quentin repeats in an adorable huff. "I get what you were doing. And that's okay. That's good. I get it."

Landon can sense the "but" coming from a mile away and he tenses up, waiting for it. "But," Quentin continues, "I don't want to confuse me or confuse you. I like you. I'm pretty sure you like me. I just don't want you to think that it's just flirting for ratings or whatever. I want more with you. I don't want to just fake it for the cameras."

Landon's heart melts like ice cream in July. "Really?"

"I'd love to take you out on a real date, actually," Quentin admits rather shyly—which is very cute because literally not two minutes ago, his tongue was in Landon's mouth and his hands had been wandering in the direction of his ass.

"Are you asking me out?" Landon asks, hope blooming in his chest.

Quentin nods. "Just . . . I've got to work early tomorrow in the bakery. So not tonight. But definitely this week. Maybe I could make you dinner at my place?"

"I'd love that," Landon says, feeling unnaturally shy himself. "Really love that."

Quentin cuddles close into him and Landon leans over, kissing him again because he can't really help himself.

Five minutes later, and they're still kissing. Landon's neck is crimping from the uncomfortable angle and he's just about to say *fuck it*, and climb right onto Quentin's lap when there's a knock on the door.

"Damn it," Landon grumbles. He was *so* close to maybe getting some in their green room. During the first week. He couldn't have envisioned today going better.

"That was quick," Quentin says, and he sounds disappointed. Landon loves it; he is definitely going to try to keep him. He turns to Landon. "You shouldn't be worried. I think we're pretty safe."

It's truly unfortunate, but Landon forces himself off the couch, and saunters over to the mirrors to try to fix his hair. He's going to have to institute a "no touching above the neck rule" when they're on breaks between filming. Just the fact that he might be forced to makes his heart sing and his body feel lighter than air.

"I'm not," Landon admits. "We did good. There's at least two or three teams that I think might go. But not us."

"Might even have a shot at the top three today," Quentin says slowly, as if he's afraid saying it out loud will jinx their chances. Quentin is quirky and cute; he might *actually* think that. Landon is forever endeared.

"No might about it," Landon insists.

Quentin walks up behind him and Landon is a bit distracted—and okay, probably more like *mesmerized*—by the few quick swipes Quentin gives to his hair. The haphazard, carefree way that Quentin treats his looks is kind of inspiring to Landon, who typically spends far more time than is probably healthy obsessing that every hair is in its proper place.

Quentin doesn't care, and lets his hair flop wherever—and of course, it looks perfect.

Landon can't decide if he's endeared or actually jealous as hell.

He spends the next two minutes fixing the damage Quentin wrought on his hair, and even though they're two minutes late, it's worth every glare he gets when they finally arrive back on the soundstage.

After all the teams are assembled, the cameras roll and Alexis steps forward, first listing off the teams that are safe—neither in the bottom or top groups. It's an unsurprising list.

Paul Flannery and Carson Brooks.

Reed Ryan and Diego Flores. Reed looks like he's about to fall to the floor and kiss Alexis' high heels. Which might make for some interesting television.

Jeff Austin and Jessa. Landon thinks with a sniff that if you're going to spend all that money on salt and pepper, you should make sure your dish is good enough to make it in the top three. Unfortunately, there isn't a confessional-style interview on *Kitchen Wars*, which means that the only person he can possibly say such a catty remark to is Quentin, when they're finally alone again.

And when he gets Quentin alone again, the first thing on his mind isn't going to be all the snarky comments he held in during the judging session.

"That leaves five teams—the bottom two and our top three."

Alexis drags it out as long as humanely possible, but Landon's still not nervous. In fact, he was way more nervous that their name might be called in the initial group. But poor Quentin is looking a bit worse for wear.

Landon is a reality television veteran. He knows better. He really, really does. But when he sees Quentin flush and then go white, then green around the edges, Landon doesn't even *think*. He just acts. It doesn't matter if what he does is in full view of cameras—he realizes later that even if he *had* thought about it, it still wouldn't have mattered. He *still* would have comforted Quentin.

He reaches out his hand and tangles Quentin's fingers with his, giving him a comforting squeeze. Landon can feel the tension melt out of Quentin, even from that one small touch, and he doesn't even care that probably four separate cameras caught it. This is still just for them, even if the show manages to record it for the public's viewing pleasure.

"In the bottom two, Blair and Alice," Alexis announces. "And Ezra and Vanessa."

Quentin grips Landon's fingers hard and Landon says *fuck it,* and glances up at Quentin's face. He's beaming with a full complement of dimples. "We did it," Quentin mouths at Landon.

They end up in third, which is not quite as amazing as Landon was secretly hoping for—but is still *far* better than Landon ever expected, considering that he can't cook at all. He nearly jumps into Quentin's arms when Alexis says their names.

Rory and Kimber win first, which considering what he was able to accomplish with no salt and pepper, is well deserved. Oliver Glines and Nora Hsu come in second, and Landon can see the edges of Quentin's smile darkening a bit. Landon wants to smooth away the wrinkles and tell him it's going to all be okay, even if Quentin didn't know anything about Oliver. It's not Quentin's job to scout the competition.

To nobody's surprise, Vanessa and Ezra are eliminated for their unpalatable Scotch eggs and suddenly, the day that Landon has been dreading since he found out about *Kitchen Wars* is over and it's been amazing. Completely the opposite of everything Landon was sure it would be.

It even turns out that he doesn't want to leave, even when they're back in their green room, packing up.

"You wanna come over?" he asks Quentin, before he can think about it and think better of his offer.

Quentin looks genuinely regretful. "I've got an early morning tomorrow and a few days this week at the bakery; I'd better get some sleep."

Landon tells himself that this is *not* a rejection. It almost works. "But," Quentin continues with a sweet, little bit sly smile, "would Wednesday night work for you for dinner?"

Wednesday night is amazing. The only downside of Wednesday night is that it's literally four nights from now. Landon points this out, unable to keep the pout off his face

"Absence makes the heart grow fonder, though," Quentin teases, wrapping his hands around Landon's waist and drawing him closer. "I promise you'll like me even more by Wednesday."

Quentin is probably teasing but is probably not wrong. Landon huffs a little, but most definitely allows Quentin one kiss that turns into about three before they finally break apart.

"Text me then," Landon begs a little when he finally manages to remove his mouth from Quentin's.

"Of course." Quentin looks a bit mystified that this is even a concern which reassures Landon like nothing else. Not that he should really need reassurance when his lips are still wet from Quentin's mouth and there's a big enough bruise on his neck that Landon should be *really* glad they aren't filming again for a week.

"Good." Landon licks his lips and only barely refrains from leaning in again. He needs to find some self-control. Quentin's hot enough that he's evaporated all of what Landon had.

They part reluctantly only when Ian texts Landon for the tenth time, no doubt desperate for an update on how the day's filming went, and if he will need to miraculously dredge up another reality show for his client to appear on.

"Tell him you're wonderful," Quentin says with a parting kiss. "And everyone loves you."

Landon spends the first ten minutes on the phone with Ian in a daze, wondering just *what* Quentin meant by that particular comment.

"Landon," Ian finally grinds out in an annoyed voice, "for the love of god, *please*, pay attention for once."

"Sorry, what?" Landon knows he's distracted. It's not his fault. Quentin is brilliant and perfectly daze-worthy.

"God damn it, Landon," Ian grumbles, but there's a brusque kind of affection running through his words. "I said they're going to leak the *Kitchen Wars* participants tomorrow. So I'm setting up some paparazzi for you at the studio."

Landon makes a face even though he's on the phone and Ian can't see it. "I'm not going to the studio tomorrow."

"You are now," Ian insists. "You're a singer. It's important to remind people you make music."

"Right."

"I'll text you time and address. Look good."

"I'm going to pretend you didn't just say that," Landon grumbles.

"Landon," Ian insists gently.

"You're the one who wanted me to go on this show!" Landon exclaims.

Ian changes the subject, and Landon lets him because he's probably right. And going to the studio will give him something to do tomorrow. He has a few songs he wouldn't mind tweaking with better equipment than he's got in his apartment, anyway.

CHAPTER FOUR

THE LIST OF CELEBRITIES and their chefs on *Kitchen Wars* leaks first thing the next morning.

Landon wakes up to about a thousand texts and emails from people he hasn't heard from in months. He forwards most of them on to Ian and tells himself as he takes a shower and makes his coffee that this is all good. He's good.

Ian texts the address of the studio and time the pap will be waiting for him. Landon fusses over his hair and debates endlessly between a red scoop neck t-shirt that displays his collarbones and a vintage Rolling Stones t-shirt that makes him look like a *real* musician.

Finally he reaches for his phone and opens a text to Quentin.

Which one???????????? I'm getting papped today at the studio.

Quentin's reply is quick. They've texted pretty consistently over the last two weeks, not as much as Landon would have liked because if it was as much as Landon would have liked, they would never stop. But Quentin is always fast to respond with cute, silly comments and a string of bizarre emojis to whatever nonsense Landon sends him.

You'd look blindingly hot in the red. But wear the Rolling Stones shirt. You're trying to make people take you seriously.

Quentin is so right. Landon *does* look hot in the red shirt, but he wants to be taken seriously more.

When Landon doesn't respond right away—he's tugging on his tight black jeans and slipping on a pair of Vans, checking his hair one last time in the mirror—Quentin texts him again.

So which one will I be thinking about later?

Landon giggles. **Naughty. Since you can't behave yourself, you'll just have to wait and see.**

He slips his phone in his pocket and resolutely doesn't look at it until after he's done parading slowly and a little bit pathetically in front of the studio door. It's amazing that anyone actually believes this farce, Landon thinks as he sinks into the comfy leather couch in the studio. Amazing that him walking in front of a place where you could possibly make music is in fact confirmation that he *is* making music, but people apparently will believe anything they're told.

There's been no response from Quentin, and Landon pushes aside his disappointment. He knows Quentin's busy at the bakery this week, probably prepping for the onslaught of new visitors brought about by his new celebrity chef status.

Instead of pouting, Landon decides to keep himself busy. He pulls out his guitar and works for hours on several old songs, tweaking and fiddling with the melodies and lyrics. Ian has talked about leaking some of his studio sessions to try to generate some interest from labels who might potentially sign Landon to a new contract.

Of course, to make this plan work, there has to be good music to leak in the first place, and Landon is determined to hold up his end of the bargain.

Ian calls a few hours into Landon's studio time.

"What?" Landon answers. "I'm busy. You know. Making music. Doing the thing for which I'm actually famous."

Ian ignores Landon. Landon thinks that's pretty unfair; he's supposed to be the client, and technically in charge. "Jessa had an interview with Ryan Seacrest on KISS today. When asked about you, she said you looked pretty close with Quentin."

"Is there a question in that statement?" Landon asks.

Per usual, Ian cuts right to the point. Ian and a sharp knife have a surprising amount of things in common. "Landon, what's going on with Quentin?"

"We have good chemistry. I *did* mention that." Landon doesn't feel like he's ready to tell Ian that he and Quentin have kissed or that their first date is this week. Eventually, he'll need to tell him, but he's just not ready yet. For now, Landon feels like it's perfectly acceptable to focus on how cute they look together on the show.

"You did." Ian sounds quite testy.

"Maybe that's what Jessa meant."

Really, Landon is just a terrible liar.

"Landon," Ian warns, and it all just tumbles out of Landon's mouth.

"I really like him. He's sweet and kind and funny and we kissed and we have a date this week."

"*Landon,*" Ian says and it's practically an exclamation point in verbal form.

"I know, I know. I'm not supposed to date my partner." He doesn't care; he's not giving up Quentin. End of story.

"Actually, that's not necessarily true. But it's risky."

Nobody needs to tell Landon that. Of course, he thought he'd been cured of his annoying tendency to fall too hard, too fast, but Quentin appears to be the exception to all those rules he'd made for himself last time everything fell apart.

"I just want you to be sure you're not making a mistake," Ian says gently.

"Quentin's not a mistake." Landon isn't sure of a lot of things, but that is one thing he is almost certain of.

"Just be sure." Ian pauses. "And try to keep it PG on the show please."

"It's like you don't know me at all," Landon scoffs and he can practically feel Ian's subsequent eye roll.

He hangs up, but five minutes later there's a text from Ian.

Ryan Seacrest. Tomorrow morning. 7 a.m.

Landon groans.

Landon likes Ryan Seacrest, ubiquitous host. They always have a fun conversation when he calls in, and Ryan was supportive when Landon came out of the closet.

That does not mean that Landon likes waking up so early or that Ryan will be easy on him when he's scented some potentially hot gossip.

"Landon, I didn't know you even knew how to cook," Ryan says casually, and Landon doesn't have to be a genius to know where this is going.

Landon stares at the sheet and picks at where a thread is beginning to come loose. The phone is pressed against his ear, damp and sweaty from his nervous palm. He considers dodging. He could do it easily. Ryan would almost certainly recognize it, but he won't call him out on the radio. They're friendly enough that he'll probably let it slide.

But Landon isn't certain he wants to dodge. So he leaves the decision up to Ryan. "Well, that's the point, really," he drawls out, equally as casual. "There's someone who's teaching me."

It sounded way less obvious in Landon's head, but something about the way he talks about Quentin, even when he's not saying Quentin's name, is not subtle whatsoever.

"Quentin Maxwell, right?" Ryan sounds so sly, even though he must realize that Landon practically served him this subject on a silver platter.

"Right." Landon has to practically bite his tongue. He wants to ramble on and on about Quentin for hours. Talk about how his eyes shine like precious stones, how soft and curly and sweet-smelling his hair is, and the way Landon feels when Quentin gazes at him like he's something important.

But he doesn't.

After all, this is Ryan's *job*. He needs to work a little harder for the dirt.

"You know, Jessa was on the other day. And she wouldn't stop talking about how you and this Maxwell were attached at the hip."

"We've only filmed once so far!" Landon protests, but it's pretty weak.

"Moving fast are we, Patton?" Ryan teases.

"Quentin's a great person," Landon says, and he's smiling even though there's nobody who can see. "I think he's going to be the perfect partner for me."

He hopes that's true in more than one way. But he doesn't need to say it; Ryan is quick enough.

"We'll have to keep an eye on you two," Ryan says, and then he's plugging the premiere of *Kitchen Wars* in a few weeks and then they move on to talking about some of Landon's new music. "A new sound," Landon says, "definitely more mature,"—even though he's still trying to figure out what this newer, more mature sound actually sounds like.

Ryan says all the right things, enthused for new tracks, says they're looking forward to hearing more from him.

The interview ends, and almost immediately his phone rings again. Landon doesn't even check it before he picks up. "So how was it?" he demands, sure that Ian will have about a million corrections, even though Landon himself thinks it went pretty damn well. With Ryan's help, he hinted all over the place that he and Quentin are more than friends and hopefully, there will be quite a few people who will tune in just to assuage their curiosity.

"I liked it," Quentin says and Landon is so surprised he almost drops the phone.

"Oh, it's you," he says rather stupidly.

"Did you not know who it was?" Quentin teases.

"I thought it was Ian, actually, ready to complain about the interview." Landon pauses. Makes the decision to be more honest than he normally would. "But I'm glad it's you."

"We listen to KISS every morning in the bakery," Quentin explains. "Was surprised to hear your voice this morning."

"Good or bad surprise?" Landon asks.

"Really, really good surprise. Just a bit taken aback to hear Seacrest interrogating you like that."

Landon can't help the laughter that explodes out of him. "Oh, we go way back. Anything he said—I wanted him to say it."

"You told him ahead of time?" Quentin sounds confused.

Landon isn't sure that he wants to go into how he knows how Ryan thinks. Just like the radio host, Landon likes using flirtatious banter as a weapon, as a shovel to dig deeper, past all the surface crap. There was even a time when Landon might have had a little bit of a crush on Ryan. That's long past, but Landon still understands him.

"Not exactly," Landon hedges.

"I mean, you sounded so ... *Landon* with him," Quentin says, and Landon thinks he might detect a hint of jealousy in his tone.

"He's a good guy," Landon says breezily. "Was really supportive when I came out."

"Right, right," Quentin says with a bit of a nervous chuckle and Landon takes pity on him.

"There's no reason to worry," he says gently. "Trust me. I didn't say anything I didn't want to say. And Seacrest knows that."

There's a long silence. Landon is almost afraid he's said too much.

"I just don't get this the way you do," Quentin says softly. "You understand everything that's going on underneath, all the media stuff. I just bake."

"You're better off baking," Landon says and to his own surprise, he sounds serious and in fact, rather jealous. "This media stuff, as you put it, can be ugly. I don't always like that I understand it. But with my career, I don't have a lot of choice sometimes."

"You'll help me, yeah?" Quentin asks. "When we do interviews?"

There's nothing sweeter than Quentin sounding like there's nothing to be lost in asking for help—in asking for *Landon's* help.

"Of course," Landon says, tucking his knees up under his chin. "Anytime you need it."

"You're the best," Quentin says and Landon can practically hear the smile on his face. "I gotta get back to these croissants, but I can't wait for our date."

Landon smiles back even though Quentin can't see it. "Me either."

⁂

Landon doesn't care that his first date with Quentin is at his place, and that it'll probably be very casual. He still spends a good hour in his closet, trying to decide what to wear.

It's sort of cheating, but when he sees the flare of color out of the corner of his eye, Landon smirks and makes an instant decision.

Quen isn't going to know what hit him.

Half an hour later, the cab pulls up to the building with Quentin's apartment. Landon fluffs his hair and slides out of the cab. He's almost entirely certain the driver's eyes are still on his ass as he walks up to the building, so the jeans he picked must be doing their job.

Really Landon isn't sure if he wants Quentin to open the door, fall to his knees and use that insane mouth for something useful or if he wants Quentin to open the door, make him a delicious and intimate dinner, then propose marriage.

He thinks he's got either option pretty well covered.

As it turns out, Quentin opens the door and neither fantasy comes true.

Okay, his mouth does go a bit slack when he takes in the red shirt of doom—doom being the place any guy goes who sees it and doesn't end up wanting Landon goes—and that is very gratifying. Exactly what Landon was going for.

"Gorgeous," Quentin murmurs. "Really, you're just stunning."

Landon preens a bit. Quentin is a smart boy; Landon practically runs on praise.

And really, Quentin doesn't look too shabby himself. He's wearing a slightly transparent black button-down, the buttons nearly an afterthought, and Landon is salivating at the thought of tracing every single tattoo with his tongue. His hair is down and looks so soft and lovely, Landon is really looking forward to getting his hands in it *finally*, even if they're only making out on the couch.

"It's a good thing I'm not hiding you away tonight," Quentin continues, and *what?*

Landon is confused. He thought he was getting a romantic candlelight dinner, cooked by Quentin Maxwell's own hands. He was mostly expecting them to not even make it through dinner. He'd picked his outfit purely for initial impact and then how good it might look on Quentin's floor.

"We're not staying in?" Landon squeaks.

Quentin smiles. "I've got a surprise for you actually. Wanna wine and dine you; spoil you a little, to be honest."

Landon wavers. He sees his fantasy of a cozy romantic evening, with a couch and a bed and several convenient horizontal—and maybe a few not-so-horizontal surfaces—fading, but at the same time, he really can't argue with what Quentin's suggesting.

"I love surprises," Landon says.

"So do I," Quentin responds with a grin. He reaches over and slides one of those huge hands, warm and definitely big enough to send Landon's heart into a rabbiting mess, over the curve of Landon's hip, just where his red shirt meets his tight black jeans. "I was especially surprised—and *pleased*—to see this make an appearance."

Landon tries really hard, but he can't help his blush. "Didn't want to disappoint."

Quentin leans in, leans *down* really—which is a kink that Landon didn't even think he had, but from the way his heart is pounding, his pulse going absolutely haywire, he most certainly has a size kink when it comes to Quentin—and just nuzzles his nose into Landon's neck, lips just teasing with the sensitive skin along the tendons. Landon takes a shuddering breath. Quentin smells *so* good, like pine forests and soft velvet and butter. "Couldn't even if you tried," Quentin murmurs into Landon's ear and he can't help the shiver that rockets through him.

Landon feels his bones melt into jelly. He wants to sink into Quentin and let them fall back through the doorway into Quentin's apartment and not come out for a good forty-eight hours. He wants Quentin to dismantle him and put him back together.

The problem is that Quentin is a fucking tease and just as Landon is about to sag into him, Quentin pulls back, though he's still keeping a mighty friendly grip on Landon's hips. "We've got to go," Quentin groans a little, sounding positively pained as Landon glances seductively up from underneath his eyelashes. He knows what this particular look does to men, and it *definitely* affects Quentin. There is absolutely no question of that, from the hot piercing look Quentin shoots him. But he's on a mission, apparently, and he lets go of Landon, one hand sliding down to tangle their fingers together.

"Are you going to tell me where we're going?" he asks as they head down the stairs to the street.

"Surprise," Quentin retorts with a dimpled grin. "But you'll like it. *And* it's close."

When they turn a corner, Landon glances over in surprise. They're in front of *Sur Ma Langue*, pretty much *the* French restaurant in LA—a restaurant that even *Landon*, who knows zilch about fine dining, has heard of.

Glancing over at Quentin, Landon is speechless at the stars sparkling out of his blue eyes and the smile playing at the corner of his lips.

"*Here?*" Landon exclaims. "You're taking me to *Sur Ma Langue?*"

Quentin shrugs, and now he's the one blushing. "Don't get too excited, I know a guy."

"Quentin, I've got to be honest." Landon spares his t-shirt and jeans a brief look. "I'm not really dressed for this place."

But Quentin just shrugs. "Trust me. Like I said, I know a guy."

It turns out that Quentin is one hundred percent *not* exaggerating knowing a guy. He does know a guy—the head sous chef, to be exact. It turns out they went to culinary school together, and he owes Quentin what sounds like a whole bunch of favors. Landon shouldn't be surprised, but he still is when they're shown to a table that's in the far back corner room, very private, and there's candlelight everywhere.

There's fat, chunky candles clustered in niches spread through the creamy walls, and wrought iron candelabras warming the corners of the room, and tiny tea lights scattered on the table set for two, their flickering wicks reflecting onto the china and crystal.

It's a statement and Landon can't quite catch his breath.

He can't quite believe that all this is for him.

"Do you like it?" Quentin's voice is low and sweet and Landon can't seem to find his.

Landon's entire life, he's had the rotten luck of always caring more, of always falling harder and faster and deeper. He spent most of high school in love with a good friend he knew wasn't gay. He let his most recent ex-boyfriend, Steve, push and prod and coerce him out of his closet at exactly the wrong time, and then watched as Steve made it clear he'd never really cared about Landon—only about the publicity he could bring to his career.

Landon has known plenty of people who cared about him for what he can do, for the way he sings, for the songs he can write, for the privilege he can bring them with his fame or his money or his name, but he has never, ever believed that someone cared as much as he did.

He'd mostly come to grips with it; made it into a little joke. *"Oh, here's Landon, falling hard again."*

This time Landon feels like he's not the only one launching off a cliff, flailing through the air, arms and legs cartwheeling madly, air rushing by, riding the exhilarating high of falling.

Quentin's right there with him, and it's the sweetest thing he's ever experienced.

"Yes." It doesn't feel like enough, but it's all Landon has the breath for.

Quentin is a perfect gentleman—it's been so long since Landon was on a real date, he's almost forgotten what that means. He pulls Landon's chair out for him, and he's this ridiculous, flawless combination of proper and seductive, letting just the tips of his fingers brush the small of his back as he makes sure the chair is at the right distance from the table.

It's the wildest, sexiest thing Landon has ever experienced, and they still haven't gotten to the food.

There's no menus, first off, and Quentin just smiles, dimple and all, when Landon asks what they're eating. "The chef is preparing something special for us tonight," he explains, and not for the first time, Landon genuinely wants to ask if it's *right* that all this is for him.

It's not that he doesn't think he's worth it. He knows he is. It's just been so long—really, *forever*—since anybody else acted like that was true. It makes Landon want to reach out and grab on to Quentin and never let him go.

So Landon does exactly that, reaching for Quentin's hand and tangling their fingers together, squeezing tight.

Quentin flushes and looks so pleased that Landon can't help but blush too. "You're wonderful," he tells Quentin far more seriously than he usually talks on dates. He's used to pulling out every flirtatious move in his rather extensive book, but with Quentin, it almost feels as if he can slow down and not have to work so hard to impress him.

"I never thought I'd be sitting here, on a date with Landon Patton," Quentin says equally seriously. It seems they're both comfortable enough to break first date etiquette. "And definitely not already knowing you're so much *more* than how you were on TV."

"More awful? More obnoxious? More pudgy? More incapable at culinary masterpieces?" Landon teases.

"All of the above," Quentin teases right back. It's flirting, but it feels like flirting that you'd do twenty years in, when you've long since learned that impressing the other person is not only impossible, but completely unnecessary. Landon has wanted that comfort and slow-burning firework exploding in his heart for so long and had nearly ruled out the possibility because of the kind of men he usually meets. But with Quentin—Landon suddenly sees a world of potential unfolding beautifully in front of his eyes.

"My hips," Landon groans and gently untangles their fingers long enough to grab a hunk of bread, warm and deliciously fragrant from the basket. "But I don't even care."

"You shouldn't," Quentin says, tilting his head and appraising him. "More to hold on to."

Landon nearly chokes on his bread. "Here I think you're being all polite and gooey and romantic, and then you go and do that," he insists. "It's . . . well . . . it's very distracting."

Quentin beams. "I'll have to keep doing it then.

"Besides," he continues offhandedly, "it's nice that I'll be able to cook for you. I want to feed you all the time."

Landon glances up from where he is generously buttering his bread. The butter smells heavenly—so good in fact that Landon is very seriously contemplating eating it without any bread whatsoever.

"And yet here we are," Landon points out.

"There'll be lots of opportunities to feed you," Quentin says very confidently and for once in his life, Landon feels not an ounce of shame for being a sure thing. He's more than happy to be a sure thing if Quentin is involved.

The waiter comes over, and formally presents a little round plate with some sort of brown substance on it. Landon frowns when they've left. "What's this?"

"Pâté?" Quentin asks with an absolutely delicious little French accent that makes Landon melt like the butter smeared on the bread in his hand.

Landon still glances at it dubiously. "What's that?"

"You'll like it. Trust me." Quentin carefully selects a thin slice of bread from the basket and spreads a thick layer of the brown goop on it.

Then Quentin's leaning over the table and *okay*, Landon is willing to try just about anything if Quentin's going to feed it to him.

It's rich and soft and an explosion of flavor in his mouth. Landon can't help but groan a little. Quentin looks very smug.

"Like it?" Quentin asks, as if he doesn't already know how delicious it is. Bastard.

For a split second, Landon seriously considers saying he hates it, but then he won't be able to eat any more. It's not very hard to push his pride out of the way and nod shyly.

"Thought you might," Quentin murmurs conspiratorially, already reaching into the basket for more bread. By the time the waiter is back with wine, they've polished off the entire plate of pâté and Landon is seriously considering casually mentioning to the waiter how stingy of a portion that was. But he trusts that whatever to come will probably be just as delicious.

"So tell me why you decided to become a baker," Landon suggests, sipping at his white wine. It's light and very crisp; the perfect complement to the rich food. He feels very spoiled and he's loving every moment.

"I actually fell into it," Quentin admits. "I needed a job and my local bakery was hiring. But I loved it right away. The early mornings, the feel of the dough underneath my hands, the satisfaction of creating something delicious out of such simple ingredients. There's a magic to baking, I think."

"Just really flour and water, yeah?" Landon asks. He's never baked something a day in his life. But he wants to now, if only to maybe experience a fraction of the passion that's ripe in Quentin's eyes.

He says as much and Quentin just throws his head back and laughs long and hard, leaving the gorgeous column of his neck exposed. Landon wants to leave a deep red love bite right along his jawline.

"You don't have the patience for it," Quentin admits. "Baking definitely isn't for everyone. Besides, if we can get you cooking, I'll consider my job well done."

"If I learn *anything*, it'll be solely because of you," Landon admits.

"Don't sell yourself short, Landon," Quentin retorts. "You're more capable than you give yourself credit for. Besides, nobody expects you to be a wonder in the kitchen. You're a singer and a songwriter."

"A washed-up pop act, more like," Landon inserts wryly and Quentin just frowns.

"What? It's true," Landon can't help but insist. It's not exactly true. But it is a little bit true.

"Why don't you tell me what happened?" Quentin asks gently.

They've broken just about every first date rule Landon has. Normally he'd never discuss anything so non-frivolous and incapable of leading to flirtation, but Quentin actually seems interested. So Landon tells him.

It takes the whole salad course for Landon to explain about how much of a public relations nightmare coming out of the closet is. And how so many artists have way more stringent guidelines built into their contracts, but he found a loophole and used it, despite all the advice he was given to wait. Quentin listens intently and just nods as Landon talks. Landon is so grateful at how kind Quentin is that he doesn't even make a peep of protest at the salad, just is silently and pleasantly surprised that anything comprised entirely of vegetables could be so tasty.

The only thing he leaves out is Steve. If Quentin notices or knows how Steve was involved, he doesn't mention it. Landon hopes that Steve will never come up, but knows better.

"What you're saying," Quentin says slowly and thoughtfully, "is that it wasn't *that* you came out, it was *when* you came out."

Landon nods. "Basically I was still too young and too cute."

"Both of which are still very true, I might add," Quentin says with a little smirk.

"Thank you very much. But yeah, it didn't help. My next album didn't sell, my label dropped me and now Ian and I are shopping my new one—or *will* be shopping my new one, when it's done."

"Ian?" Quentin asks, as the waiter clears their salad plates.

"My new agent," Landon says proudly. "He's good. Very respected in the industry. Got me on *Kitchen Wars* to try to 'diversify my image.'"

Quentin reaches for Landon's hand again and he eagerly lets Quentin wrap his fingers around his. Quentin is a great hand-holder. Very promising for the future. It's been a long time since Landon let himself imagine hand-holding and white picket fences but that train has officially left the station.

Quentin's thumb rubs the sensitive cleft between Landon's pointer finger and thumb. He shivers a little as the rough callouses caress his skin. Squirming a bit in his chair, Landon tries not to imagine those hands on other parts of his body and fails miserably.

"How'd your recording session go?" Quentin asks.

Landon doesn't really want to tell him that he spent about thirty minutes on refining an older song that he isn't convinced is very good and about three hours spouting complete bullshit lyrics about blue eyes and dimples and broad shoulders.

"It's a process," Landon finally admits. "A tough one, sometimes."

"I feel that way with new recipes sometimes. I tweak them for months and months, and nothing ever seems right. You'll get there." Quentin squeezes Landon's hand reassuringly.

Landon realizes then that their passions really aren't all that different. They both create things for public consumption—Landon has his music and Quentin his bread and pastries. Landon feels another bit of himself shift into place, a building block of his heart settling in where it belongs.

Normally he'd be terrified that this isn't going to work out. That he's getting in too deep, too fast. But it all feels so easy and comfortable with Quentin. Like their hearts have known each other forever and their minds are just now catching up.

When the main course comes, a delicious Dijon chicken with little perfect potatoes roasted in the wine and garlic and chicken drippings, they finish off the bottle of wine and start another. Landon feels drunk not necessarily on alcohol, but on wonderful food and even better company.

"I wish I could cook like this," Quentin moans around a mouthful of chicken.

"I thought all chefs could," Landon protests with a teasing smile. "Only reason I was considering keeping you around."

"No. *No.* I wish, really. I'm a baker, like I said. I went to cooking school. I could hold my own at most restaurants, *probably.* But I can't cook like this."

"Damn."

"Don't worry," Quentin says with an adorably lopsided grin, "I'm plenty good at other things."

"Like baking?" Landon asks, trying to ignore the way his heart is racing in his chest and how tight his jeans feel—and not from the food he's been devouring all night.

"Sure, that too," Quentin says, the corners of his lips turning up into a rather slyer smile.

The waiter comes to clear away the plates. "Dessert?" he asks.

Quentin glances over at Landon. Landon hesitates. He definitely wants dessert. He's just not entirely sure which variety of dessert he's more desperate for.

His hesitation is apparently all the confirmation Quentin needs. "To go," he tells the waiter decisively enough that Landon suddenly feels a bit fuzzy. All the blood in his entire body has rushed to his cock and when he stands up, it's going to be obvious that he's hard and ready to go.

It takes them ten minutes to get dessert which should be plenty of time for Landon to get himself together. Unfortunately it doesn't happen.

It's just that it's *very* tough to calm down because even as they're making harmless small talk, chatting easily about the different contestants on *Kitchen Wars*, Landon's mind is literally one constantly looping dirty fantasy—Quentin on his knees in front of him, mouthing at the tip of his dick through his pants, glancing up, his eyes wide and blue and as innocent as they are dirty; Landon in Quentin's lap, cock inside of him, rocking relentlessly against his prostate as he sucks the love bite he's been dying to give Quentin all night right into his chiseled jawline; Quentin fucking Landon's mouth, holding him down, making him take it, wrists bound together behind his back as it slides so big and hard between his lips.

The waiter brings their dessert, boxed up. "Pots de crème, chocolate of course, with a white chocolate ganache," he says, and then disappears, leaving them to the rest of their evening and Landon to his imminent detonation.

Landon is a volcano. One touch, and he's definitely going to explode.

Quentin must notice Landon's panicked expression at the thought of leaving and he smiles. "Don't worry, I'm…uh…plenty excited myself."

Landon's temperature ratchets up another few degrees. He swallows hard, his mouth dry as a bone, and licks his lips. Imagines Quentin's soft, plush mouth on them. "Okay. It's a quick walk, yeah?"

Quentin nods, and he looks just about as eager as Landon feels.

When Quentin gets up, Landon feels zero shame in ogling how hot and ready he looks in his tight jeans. Not that Landon is any less obvious. It's a good thing that while they were eating dinner, dusk has fallen and it's grown dark outside, offering up a bit of protection from prying eyes.

The walk to Quentin's place feels like it's over before it even begins. The blood in Landon's veins goes from a simmer to a full-on boil as they walk up the stairs and Quentin unlocks the door.

Landon doesn't hesitate. He doesn't think. He just acts.

He shoves Quentin back up against the door. He's smaller but it doesn't seem to matter as their mouths meet in a kiss that melts all the nerve endings in Landon's body. It's hot and sweet and *longing*, almost, as if they both spent the entire dinner wishing they could get their mouths back on each other, and now it's finally happened.

Quentin licks determinedly into his mouth and Landon can't help the long, throaty moan he makes. He takes advantage of the momentary break in the madness only to delve right back in, licking and sucking alongside Quentin's criminally chiseled jawline, right to the spot he's been fantasizing about since he spotted it. Quentin's skin is equally salty and sweet, delicious really—the perfect finish to a truly wonderful meal—and it turns out that the spot is even better than Landon could have even imagined because when he finally hits it, Quentin's knees actually buckle.

So, that's handy. It turns out that Quentin loves getting a good love bite as much as Landon loves to give one. Landon wants to fucking eat him alive. He does, wrenching his mouth off and admiring the intense red of the mark he's made before diving back to Quentin's sinful, plush mouth. The kiss goes from passionate to insatiable and Landon barely even registers when Quentin exercises his strength and flips them easily. The back of Landon's head hits the door with a solid thunk but the pain barely registers. He's too awestruck watching Quentin sink to his knees in front of him, an image practically ripped out of his earlier fantasy.

Quentin wastes absolutely no time, hands on the button of Landon's pants, unzipping them and pulling them down like he's waited as long as he can.

Like he'd seen a vision from Landon's mind, Quentin is right there, nuzzling at the hard cock in his pants, sending little bursts of sensation sparking through his body. Landon slurs out a pained plea for *more, god, please,* because Quentin's teasing him and he's desperate for more.

Quentin groans and then suddenly there's no fabric between his hot wet mouth and Landon's dick—only damp air. Landon gasps and strains against the desire to just buck up into Quentin's mouth. Normally he likes a good bit of teasing himself, and in a more restrained mood, he might be the one to taunt Quentin with what he clearly wants so much, but Landon is undone by the evening and by Quentin and just pleads for Quentin to do something, *anything.*

Quentin listens and when he slicks his tongue up the underside, then sinks down, tonguing at the head, wrapping his cock up in the most sinful mouth that Landon has ever been privileged to enjoy, it's pure bliss.

It doesn't take long for Quentin to develop a devastating rhythm, giving Landon everything he didn't even know he wanted. Then his hands creep back to Landon's butt, kneading and caressing his cheeks. There's only the slightest hint of a damp finger nudging at his hole before Landon loses it, suddenly and completely. His life flashes before him in a blinding flash of white light and he dies a little, feeling only a tiny niggling shame for his lack of blowjob etiquette as he shoots come down Quentin's throat.

But Quentin doesn't look even the slightest bit annoyed. He only reluctantly pulls off, licking the last of it from his lips and gives Landon the most scorching, devastating look from his position on his knees.

Landon is dazed and still horny, the aftershocks of his orgasm still pulsing through his veins and he only vaguely registers Quentin moving to his feet and grabbing Landon's hand, leading them through the apartment to the bedroom.

There's a bed. That's literally all Landon registers about it. There's a bed and then he's on it and Quentin is crawling up him like a man who's starving to death and Landon is a banquet feast.

Quentin nuzzles into the damp spot on Landon's neck and even manages to *breathe* sexily into Landon's ear. "Wanna ride you, baby," he moans, rutting against Landon's hip, hard and insistent and even though Landon is still a bit dazed, it seems that's all it takes for arousal to start fizzing through his veins again.

But he's not sixteen still, and Quentin seems to be pretty respectful of that fact so they kiss for a long time, Quentin grinding alongside Landon's hardening cock. He's hard long before they can possibly tear their mouths off each other, panting helplessly as Landon stares into Quentin's eyes.

"Want you," Landon moans as Quentin executes a particularly filthy grind. "Wanna fuck you."

Quentin throws his head back and he looks so exceptionally gorgeous that Landon can't really believe his luck. At some point in this evening, he is going to pinch himself and wake up.

But it seems like that's not even close to happening now. Quentin reluctantly leaves Landon's side for a moment, to gather condoms and lube and shed his clothes as Landon watches hungrily, eyes eating up every bit of skin that he uncovers, littered with tattoos and damp with sweat.

"Gorgeous," Landon breathes out unsteadily. "Fucking gorgeous."

Quentin blushes as he slicks up his fingers and Landon makes a sound of protest. "What, you wanna?" Quentin asks shyly, and Landon nods, eagerly.

Quentin's got a little peach of a butt, small and compact and surprisingly curvaceous for its size. Quentin's finger is already tucked inside and once Landon wets his own fingers, he slides one alongside, gasping a little at how tight and hot Quentin feels, how insanely perfect around him. He can't wait to get his dick in there. Can't wait to make Quentin look even more wrecked than he already does, grinding back on their fingers.

His dick is hard and purple, pre-come bubbling at the tip, and it bobs between them. Landon leans over and licks at the wetness and loves how loud Quentin is when he sucks the head into his mouth.

"Gonna come, gonna come," Quentin pants. "Wanna come around your cock."

Landon wants that too. Wants that more than he wants to take his next breath. He carefully slides another finger in and gives it a few experimental thrusts, making sure that all Quentin feels when he finally gets where he wants to be is pure pleasure.

"Ready," Quentin moans, and Landon pulls his fingers out, reaching for the condom. His fingers shake as he slides on the condom and gives himself an extra layer of slickness. He wants this to be mind-blowing; wants Quentin to feel just as good as he made Landon feel.

Wants to make Quentin feel even *better*.

Quentin sinks down on his dick like he's born to it, his rather ungainly body discovering a new grace as he slowly slides down, works his way slowly but steadily down onto Landon's cock.

He's so tight and so hot, Landon screws his eyes shut so he doesn't come embarrassingly quick. Quentin lets out a long drawn-out moan and Landon tries counting to ten as he bottoms out. The problem isn't just the way Quentin feels around him, but the visuals—his abs contracting as he rises back up and sinks back down again, curls bouncing, eyes completely blissed out. Landon shivers and tries to snatch back his self-control, which pretty much disappeared the moment his lips touched Quentin's for the first time.

Landon's hands move to Quentin's hips and grip him tight, probably tight enough to leave bruises, but Quentin only groans dirtier, filthier, spouting phrases that make Landon's eyes roll back in his head as he takes his cock deep and hard. He angles his hips, trying to catch Quentin's prostate and he knows the moment he hits it, Quentin's mouth opening in a silent scream of pleasure. He hits it once, then twice more and Quentin's gone, ropes of come shooting from his cock, painting them both.

Quentin clenching down is all it takes Landon to lose it again, shuddering helplessly as he grinds deep and fills the condom.

"Fuck." Quentin slumps forward onto Landon's chest, and they're both wet with come and sweat and lube and Landon can't even find it in himself to care. This was one of the most overwhelmingly insane sexual encounters of his life. Maybe even the best sex of his life. And it was literally the very first time.

Twenty minutes later, they're finally cleaned up and cuddling again, this time on the couch with Quentin's arms wrapped tightly around Landon. He's got the dessert container open on his lap and he's spoon-feeding heavenly bites of chocolate mousse into Landon's waiting mouth.

"To die for," Landon moans, lips closing around the spoon, refusing to let it go as he tries to clean every last bit off the plastic.

He finally relinquishes the spoon and Quentin steals a bite, his expression thoughtful as he carefully tastes it. "It's good," he finally admits. "Very good. I can make better though."

That gets Landon's attention. "You are absolutely shitting me. This is a tiny bit of heaven in a cup. There *is* nothing better."

Quentin shrugs rather smugly. "I can think of a few things." He taps the spoon on the very tip of Landon's nose, leaving a speck of mousse behind. He leans in, cleans it off with a quick lap of his tongue. "Well, *one* thing specifically."

Landon blushes. He doesn't know what to say. Then he does. "This was the best date I've ever had," he says. Telling Quentin the truth doesn't feel like an uncomfortable admission, but a secret confession, whispered underneath a nest of blankets. Except there's no blankets, there's only Quentin, and he's keeping him plenty warm.

"Me too." Quentin's grip tightens a little, as if he's got such precious cargo he can't bear to let it slip away. As if Landon would. As if Landon *could.* "Gonna be hard to top this one, to be honest."

Landon giggles. Quentin is smiling. He doesn't exactly look worried.

Landon isn't worried at all. They're just getting started.

CHAPTER FIVE

LANDON'S PHONE RINGS WAY too early the next morning.

"What? Who? When?" Quentin moans, his head buried deep into his pillow. "Just make it stop."

"Sorry, it's Ian," Landon apologizes as he tries to hit the accept button through mostly-closed eyes. He begins to move to get out of bed, but Quentin's arm shoots out and wraps firmly around his middle.

"No, stay," Quentin mumbles into the pillow.

"What?" Landon barks into the phone, trying to resettle back into a comfortable position. If Quentin doesn't want him leaving, then he's sure as hell not going anywhere.

"I've got you a meeting with Epic," Ian says, and Landon doesn't even care how smug his agent sounds, he only cares what he's saying.

"How?" Landon squeaks.

"I sent them that new song," Ian says. "You know, the embarrassing one."

"Oh god." Landon can't breathe. "*That's* why they want to have a meeting?"

"They loved it. Said something about what a surprising Ed Sheeran vibe you have."

"I don't have an Ed Sheeran vibe," Landon says blankly. "I can barely play the guitar."

"It doesn't matter. They loved your voice. How much it's improved. They loved your writing. Loved the romance of it. You're basically in. There's great buzz about *Kitchen Wars*. They want to piggyback on that. Hammer out a contract. Announce it fast."

It's hard to focus on anything Ian is saying. It's all so good, but because Landon is Landon, he can only hear one thing.

Fast.

Things don't tend to happen fast, at least in the music industry—*real* things, anyway. Lots of fake garbage that doesn't pan out, all that happens plenty fast. But not anything lasting.

And after what he went through before, Landon wants lasting more than he wants to breathe, sometimes.

"What's the angle?" Landon asks

Ian sighs. "It's real, I swear. They really love you. Fast is just about the timing with *Kitchen Wars*. You've got to trust me here. I wouldn't steer you wrong."

Landon doesn't believe he would. He also doesn't believe that Ian could be fooled into thinking something is a sure thing when it isn't.

"I guess that means I'm going to the meeting," Landon says. He doesn't really know whether to be nervous or ecstatic.

Ian relays the details of time and place and hangs up.

Landon falls back against the bed, nuzzling into Quentin's curls and not even caring that doing so probably breaks about half the rules that exist when you first start dating someone.

Staying over probably breaks the other half, but he hadn't even hesitated. Frankly, he hadn't wanted to leave, and Quentin had seemed even less enthusiastic about the idea.

"Stay," he'd begged Landon, and Landon had been powerless to resist the pleading look in his eyes, and the way Quentin's hands had drifted over his bare skin as they'd cuddled on the couch.

"When do you have to leave?" Quentin asks now, voice still mostly muffled by the pillow.

"Soon," Landon says. "I've got to get back to my place. Change. Get ready for this meeting. Whatever it brings."

"It's what you wanted though." Quentin carefully rotates until they're facing each other.

Landon sighs. "Yeah, but it's hard to know when something's for real. This doesn't seem like it's for real. It's too fast."

"Then make it real," Quentin says softly.

"It's not that easy."

"I never said it was easy," Quentin insists. "The best things, the things you really want, they almost never are."

"What about this?" Landon asks, stroking a loose strand of hair away from Quentin's face. "This feels so easy."

And it does, lying in Quentin's bed together, skin on skin, wrapped up in each other like they've never been anywhere else.

"This is special," Quentin says so quietly, like he too doesn't want to disturb the cocoon they've created for themselves here. "*Different.*"

Landon wants to tell him that *he's* special, that he already cares so much, surely far more than he should at this stage, but he's already broken so many of those generally accepted, and no doubt wise, rules, so he doesn't. Instead he leans in and brushes a single kiss on the tip of Quentin's cute nose. He hopes it says everything that he doesn't think he can yet.

Ian wasn't kidding when he said the meeting was a mere formality.

The Epic people practically fall over themselves in their eagerness to talk about a contract. Landon doesn't know if Ian has prepped them in advance, but they say all the right things. All the things Landon has secretly wished for years had been part of his old contract—freedom and the ability to make his own choices. There's no unpleasant strings tying him up in knots. Not yet anyway.

Ian promises Landon there will be clauses to prevent the strings from ever tying him up again.

They agree for him to go into the studio with one of their favored producers, who happens to be someone that Landon has worked with before.

By the end of the day, as Landon is relaxing in bed, he feels like he can genuinely text Quentin and tell him that things not only went well at the meeting, they went better than he could have hoped for.

So happy for you, Landon is the text waiting for Landon the next morning on his phone. **Can you meet for lunch? Want to see you before filming.**

They're filming again in two days, and Landon has been so preoccupied with the developing Epic contract that he surprisingly hasn't agonized yet over seeing Quentin. Of course he wants to.

Character development, Landon tells himself.

Late afternoon break? I've got meetings this morning til after lunch.

Quentin responds right away and his eagerness is a balm to Landon's confusion.

Perfect. Meet you at the bakery?

❧❧❧❧❧ ❧❧❧❧❧

The bakery takes up almost a whole block—it's sprawling and very busy, if the constantly revolving door with a steady stream of customers is any indication.

Quentin hasn't talked much about this bakery. They mostly talk about the bakery Quentin wants to own someday. In his fantasy, it's small, tucked away in a suburban corner of LA and moms bring their kids to grab an afternoon pick-me-up and students spend the afternoons camped out in comfortable chairs with endless cups of espresso and the homey, comforting pastries that Quentin wants to bake.

This modern, sprawling behemoth of a building doesn't feel much like it has much in common with Quentin's dream and Landon can't help but swear to himself with renewed resolve that now that his dream is well on its way to repair, they're going to win *Kitchen Wars* to secure Quentin's.

He has no real illusions about what he can bring to a relationship—he can be bitchy and whiny, more than difficult at points—but he can give Quentin what he's dreamed about forever.

With his resolve burning in his veins, Landon shoves his aviator sunglasses onto his head, careful not to disturb his hair, and walks in the front door of the bakery.

It's a hurricane of sight and sound. The scent of freshly baked bread and pastries winding around him like a lover and the burst of colors in the pastry case. A million jeweled shades of *macarons*, and not the heavy, thick coconut cookies, but the perfect, delicate shells filled with delicious concoctions that Landon associates so strongly with the romance of Paris. There's vermilion and emerald and ruby and bright garish orange. He wants to taste all of them.

Tarts filled with strawberries and raspberries and blackberries, scattered carelessly but flawlessly over the sheen of vanilla-flecked pastry cream.

He's so entranced by the outrageous displays, each more fantastic than the next, that he doesn't even see Quentin until he's leaning over the case, elbows resting gently on the glass, a smug smile on his beautiful face.

"Like what you see?" he asks so impudently that Landon wonders how could he have gotten so lucky to find someone so in tune with his own sense of humor.

Landon flutters his eyelashes and stares right at Quentin. He's got his hair pulled back, showcasing his incredible jawline.

"Yeah," he says, not once taking his gaze off Quentin, "I really do."

"Lemme grab us some coffee and a plate," Quentin says. "Why don't you find us a table?"

It's a cavernous room, nothing like the cozy, comfortable vision that Quentin's drawn for Landon. But Landon still manages to find a quiet corner, and is just settling down in the comfortable chair when Quentin shows up with a tray.

"Cappuccino, right?" Quentin asks as he slides a white cup and saucer in front of Landon.

Landon begins to nod but is distracted by the incredible plate of confections Quentin deposits in the middle of the table.

"A little of everything," Quentin explains as he takes a seat across from Landon. "A few *macarons*. These are lime and orange, lemon and thyme. Chocolate cherry."Landon's mouth waters.

"And some tarts, I saw you eyeing those," Quentin continues with a smirk. "Strawberry passionfruit and blackberry orange."

"It looks incredible," Landon says, and it's an understatement. "Did you bake all this?"

Quentin looks surprised. "Of course. I told you I did most of the pastry here."

"I'm just . . . *impressed*," Landon confesses.

"I told you I could bake; that I went to culinary school."

It's true, Quentin did. And Landon has seen Quentin cook during their first week of competition, but watching him assemble that fairly simple burger is nothing like the jewel-like beauty and perfection of what's shining on the plate in front of him now. These are works of art.

Landon is flustered. He doesn't feel inferior; if he was going to feel inferior over kitchen skills, that ship sailed a long time ago, but he'd still felt *somewhat* equal in that he and Quentin have both made a career out of creation.

As it turns out, it's really tough to equate the perfection in front of him to some cheesy pop songs that he's had a hand in writing—even those less-cheesy pop songs that he *longs* to write feel inferior.

"Looking around," Landon can't help but lean over and admit in a hushed tone, "I just don't see why you'd ever want to leave this place. Everything is so freaking beautiful."

Quentin looks amused. "Oh, sure it looks alright, but I don't want to make this sort of thing." Quentin gestures to the plate of jeweled *macarons* and the flawless tarts.

Landon shouldn't gape, but he kind of does. "I mean," Quentin continues, a trifle quicker than before, his voice still as slow as maple syrup on a chilly afternoon, "I want to create beautiful things. But none of this, not a crumb out of place, all cold perfection. I want something you don't want to ruin by eating it. Something you can't wait to sink your teeth into. Something *warm* and sweet."

"Quentin," Landon can't help but admit, "that's the greatest thing you've ever said to me."

Quentin flushes and carelessly picks up an aubergine-colored *macaron*. "I suppose you want to make serious songs, then?" he asks.

The problem is Landon doesn't really know what he wants to create. Maybe what he's really envious of is Quentin's certainty.

"Not serious," Landon says, picking at the napkin lying next to the saucer. "But important, somehow. Even if the importance is just making people happy."

"You'll figure it out." Quentin seems so sure. Landon wishes he had a tenth of Quentin's confidence—but the thought of Quentin realizing that is too awful to contemplate, so Landon does what he does best. He changes the subject.

"We should really be figuring out this week's plan," Landon inserts.

The look in Quentin's eyes tells Landon that he isn't as good as he thinks he is at changing the subject, but Quentin is wonderful and lets it go.

"I wish I could figure out what the theme is. Have some sort of idea going on," Quentin says rather wistfully.

Landon takes a sip of his coffee which is strong and hot. Just the way he likes it. "But watching you in action is so inspiring," Landon teases.

Quentin quirks an eyebrow. "Watching me flounder around with no idea what to cook is inspiring?" "Absolutely. I enjoy every second of it."

"You should really enjoy this week then," Quentin says wryly.

"Please," Landon scoffs. "You're so calm and collected. And here I am, flying off the handle because I've been forced to chop something or actually use the oven."

"Hey, you know how to use the oven now," Quentin drawls out, but his eyes are sparkling, and the air between them is crackling with tension and chemistry and the fact that Landon is pretty much going out of his mind with the need to touch Quentin *right now*. Unfortunately, Landon is dumb enough to have scheduled their date at Quentin's workplace.

"Who do you think is our biggest competition?" Landon asks, pointedly ignoring Quentin's statement about the oven. He supposes he theoretically knows how to work the oven controls, but in the heat of the moment, nothing is certain.

"I think Reed and Diego will make a big comeback this week."

Landon devours half a strawberry passionfruit tart and moans at how good the fresh fruit tastes in combination with the cold, decadent pastry cream. "Reed couldn't bake this. How could he possibly stand a chance?" He gestures with the tart.

Clearly, Quentin is both flattered and amused. He giggles, which Landon has figured out he tends to do when he's uncomfortable with a compliment. Or sexually aroused. Landon shifts in his chair a little.

Quentin is just *really* arousing, okay?

"We probably won't be baking tarts though," Quentin points out very rationally.

"But if we did," Landon retorts with a sly grin, "your tart would own his tart's ass."

Quentin laughs long and loud then, the sound echoing through the open bakery like a rather triumphant bell. Landon tries to find something every day that he's proud of; today, he's most proud of the way he can make Quentin laugh like that. That's an accomplishment that he doesn't think will ever get old.

"You know, my mom never had butter in the house," Quentin confesses when he's finally managed to contain himself. "Maybe I'm compensating for the lack during my childhood."

Landon knows to step very carefully around the subject of parents. It's the first time Quentin has said something about his, and Landon freezes. He wants to ask, wants to know everything he can about Quen, even though he's scared.

"Why not?"

Quentin shrugs. "My mom hated to cook and she was terrible at it. Why bother with real butter if you know it'll taste like garbage?"

"It's hard to imagine you growing up somewhere where food wasn't important." It's phrased as carefully as Landon can, every ounce of tact he can find in use.

"They just didn't care." Quentin's eyes go soft and hard at the same time, and the one thing Landon *does* understand is feeling conflicted over family. He certainly feels conflicted enough over his. "They don't really get why I'm here, doing this. They think it's a waste of my time. Of my future."

Landon plucks a perfect blackberry from a tart. "One thing I can tell you for sure, *for sure*," he vows, as serious as he ever is, "is that you're not wasting your time."

The lines on Quentin's forehead smooth out a little. "I know I'm not, but it would be nice if they knew that too."

"My mom doesn't know what to do with me either," Landon confesses, which is the last thing he expected to come out of his mouth. It's apparently being extra uncooperative today. He can't remember the last time he told someone this; he never even told Steve.

"LA is just a lot different than where I grew up," Landon continues and he can't help the thread of bitterness that sneaks into his voice. "She just doesn't get it. Not before. Not today. Probably not ever."

Quentin confirms his sainthood when he reaches over and tangles his fingers with Landon, squeezing them gently. He doesn't say anything but Landon knows that sometimes words aren't enough.

"Let's get out of here," Quentin says, changing the subject. Landon sees his forehead is getting a little damp. Maybe they're both suffering. "My break's over soon."

"Never going to say no," Landon whispers, but Quentin's already stood up and he probably doesn't hear. Which is just as well because nobody needs to know just how far gone Landon is. Most of all Quentin.

❧ ☙

A few scant minutes later, Quentin's got Landon pressed up against the back wall of the bakery, right next to the deliveries sign. The red bricks dig a little into Landon's skin through his t-shirt, but the roughness contrasted with the honeyed sweet pleasure of Quentin's mouth is exceedingly hot. Landon feels lightheaded, head tilting back to rest against the wall as Quentin's lips coast up his neck.

"Quen," Landon half moans, half pants. "*Public.*"

Because if anyone walks by, they'll see Quentin's big body pinning Landon to the wall, his hands determinedly pushing up his t-shirt, the rough pads of his fingers stroking down his abs and lingering at the waist of his pants, thumbs dipping under the fabric, reverently caressing the sensitive skin over Landon's hip bones.

If anyone walks by, they'll see Landon's fingers buried in Quentin's curls, tugging them hard enough to make Quentin moan into the soft crook of Landon's neck, where he's licking and sucking a bruise that'll be hell for the *Kitchen Wars* makeup artist.

And all because Landon insisted on a goodbye kiss, and Quentin insisted he make it a good one.

Quentin's lips disappear from Landon's skin for a second, and Landon, who'd let his eyes drift shut, vision hazy with heat, refocuses on Quentin.

Sometimes it's hard to look at Quentin directly. He's too much up close—skin smooth and pale, touched with just a hint of a heavier cream, freckles dotting his nose and a jawline so sharp it makes Landon weak in the knees. It's easy to miss how Quentin is more than a sum of his parts when the parts are so extraordinary. Those jewel-like eyes, the pillowy pink lips, his hair like a golden halo around his head. Landon doesn't like to think of himself as particularly stuck on the surface of people, but when the surface looks like this, it's hard to move past it.

It's like Quentin hears him. "Gorgeous," Quentin murmurs as they stare at each other, the air thick and syrupy. Landon's grip on Quentin's curls tightens. "Exactly what I was thinking," Landon says.

Quentin's hands slide up Landon's body, from his hips to his chest to his shoulders. He's never really liked his rather curvy, compact body. Nobody's ever really appreciated it before, but Quentin feels like he's making a study of the curves, tracing their undulating lines with his fingertips. It's like Quentin wants to memorize him, and it's a heady thought, that Quentin might be as deep as Landon is.

"Come to my place tonight," Landon can't help but spit out in a bit of a rush. He's desperate and it feels like Quentin is just as desperate himself.

Landon wants to believe it, even as Quentin shakes his head reluctantly no. "I can't. Long shift today. Long shift tomorrow." He sounds disappointed, but in the end, the result is the same: Landon probably losing his mind from unfulfilled lust, a phenomenon that he thought he'd long outgrown.

"Sometimes I feel like we're back at school," Landon confesses, the words leaving his lips before he can shove them back inside his mouth. "A few little stolen moments here and there when nobody's looking. Jacking off until I'm sick to death of my right hand because there's never enough time."

Quentin cocks his head and gives Landon an intrigued look. "Was that what school was like for you? Hiding things?"

Landon tenses. "You're meant to focus more on the jerking off until I'm sick part," he jokes, but it doesn't come out right.

Quentin's gaze softens and swimming in those warm blue eyes, flecks of gold hypnotizing him, Landon feels like maybe Quentin *is* as deep as Landon. Feels like maybe Quentin does understand what he means, how the impossible longing he feels can't ever be sated by the little moments they snatch for themselves.

It's possible even if Landon gorged himself on Quentin, he'd still never get enough. It's a thought that's exhilarating and terrifying, all at the same time. Landon desperately wants to write it all down, but he can't seem to find the words to properly express it.

So he just kisses Quentin instead, trying to pour everything he feels into a simple meeting of lips. It's slick and hot, but it's slow and tender, and when they finally part, breathless, there's a look he's never seen before in Quentin's eyes.

It looks like maybe everything Landon can't seem to say.

"We'll make more time next week," Quentin insists, and it seems more like a vow than a promise.

"I'm gonna hold you to that."

Quentin's hands drop from Landon's body and hang at his sides. Landon feels the loss of his touch so acutely, he nearly reaches out and drags them back. But he doesn't. He's probably already revealed enough today about his own impossible-to-control feelings. It's really hard to care about falling too hard and too fast when it feels so damn good.

They kiss one last time, Quentin practically wrenching himself away from Landon at the end, as if he can't bear to stop. When he walks away after a whispered goodbye, he doesn't look back, and Landon wants to believe if it's because if he glanced back at Landon, he'd not be able to leave at all.

At least that's the way Landon feels.

He seems to be positively overflowing with feelings, as when he gets home, he digs out his guitar and the ragged notepad he'd been scribbling the lyrics of the embarrassingly sappy song into.

A few hours later, he's developing a few rather painful blisters from the guitar strings, but he's still got what he thinks *could* be a pretty killer song. It's sentimental as hell, of course, but after his conversation with Quentin today, Landon is beginning to wonder if that's such a bad thing.

Unfortunately he can't exactly ask Quentin because the song is basically a big sappy cliché of how hard Landon is falling for him.

Before he can chicken out, he does a quick recording of himself playing through the song and he sends it to Ian. He falls onto his bed fully clothed a few moments later and falls asleep almost instantly.

Chapter Six

When Landon lets himself into their green room the next day, it turns out that even though he's a whole ten minutes early, Quentin is even earlier.

Landon looks up into Quentin's smiling face, the dimple threatening to emerge and his gorgeous eyes glowing, and he wonders if they really, truly have to film today. Can't they just lock themselves away in this room and forget the rest of the world exists? Landon doesn't feel capable of cooking today—not that he truly feels capable of cooking *any* day—but it seems like a truly impossible task when all he truly wants to do is lose himself in Quentin.

"Landon!" Quentin beams at him, practically a human version of sunshine, and Landon prides himself on very staunchly resisting climbing Quentin like a tree. However, that doesn't preclude a very friendly greeting and he's just about to fall into Quentin's arms and not even feel the tiniest bit embarrassed about that when there's a voice behind them, coming from the still-open doorway.

Ian's voice.

Damn it. Landon barely manages not to glare at his agent when he whirls around.

He's just about to launch into an interrogation when a look in Ian's eyes stops him up short. "What?" he demands.

"Your song was really persuasive." If it's even possible, Ian sounds even more satisfied than he looks.

"I thought Epic was already in the bag?" Landon asks just as Quentin pipes up with, "What song?"

Ian thankfully ignores Quentin and addresses Landon. "I sent it over and they were suddenly ready to reconsider a few key points of the contract that I didn't feel were as favorable to you as I'd like. But that's all changed and now we're ready to have you sign." He pauses and suddenly, a huge smile breaks out across his face. "You're *very* persuasive, kid."

This would all be really great news except Quentin asks *again*, "What song?" Because apparently he is nothing if not persistent.

Landon wants to bury his head in his hands. Maybe it would be okay for Quentin to hear the song eventually, but he is *not* prepared to let him listen to it today. Not when in approximately twenty minutes, Alexis Leavy is going to be torturing them with kitchen implements and Landon is probably going to have to figure out how to turn the oven on.

Naturally, ignoring Landon's extremely dirty look, Ian whips out his phone, beaming like a proud papa. "You haven't heard it yet?" he asks. "Just wait. It's really his best work. You're gonna love it."

Landon snatches the phone out of Ian's hand with mere moments to spare before he is completely humiliated. "It's not . . . just, it's not ready for anyone to hear yet," Landon explains lamely, sure he is turning red.

Quentin raises a single eyebrow. "Ian's heard it," he points out calmly but seriously. "Apparently a bunch of bigwigs at Epic have heard it."

Landon doesn't want to fuck anything up. He doesn't want Quentin to hear it yet, but he is also fairly certain that deliberately not sharing is going to look shitty. He feels stuck between a rock and a hard place, with no idea which way to turn.

He looks over at Ian, hoping he'll rescue him, which is only fair since he's the one who got Landon into this mess in the first place. "Maybe after the show, yeah?" Ian suggests kindly but firmly. All agent-y. "You've only got a few minutes to get your game faces on."

Landon tries to ignore the way Quentin's face closes off. He's never seen it do that before. He tells himself that Quen's just disappointed because he wanted to hear the song. Just a little disappointment that'll easily be forgotten in the chaos of the next few hours. Hopefully, the next few weeks, if Landon has any say in the matter.

He's almost convinced until Quentin's slightly forced grin. "And Landon is gonna have to cook his sweet ass off," Quentin responds.

"I know how to turn the oven on!" Landon retorts in a high squeaky voice, which isn't even entirely true. It's so transparent to deflect onto his own shortcomings, but Landon needs to say *something*.

Ian laughs, and Landon wonders if it's one of those moments when someone is laughing more *at* you than *with* you. Before he can get a chance to say so, Ian's gone, and it's just him and Quentin again. Quentin's staring at him with a fond, soft look. Landon can almost forget the forced smile from a moment ago—*almost*. He crosses the few feet between them in a second, wrapping his arms around the other man.

"I missed you," Landon whispers into the soft, elegant curve of Quentin's neck.

"Missed you too." Quentin's voice is equally as fervent, leaving Landon more certain that the awkwardness will blow over.

Landon is silent for a moment, letting himself breathe and relax, using the warmth and solid presence of Quentin's body to center him.

"I still don't know how to turn the oven on," Landon finally admits softly, almost too quietly to be heard.

But Quentin is always paying attention. He catches the quiet confession and just hums with complete unconcern. "We'll be fine. *You'll* be fine," he reassures Landon.

Landon just hugs him tighter.

The five-minute knock comes far before Landon is ready for it, but just before they're about to let go of each other, Quentin leans down and whispers, "I got tomorrow off. My place tonight?"

Landon doesn't really feel exactly confident as they walk down to the soundstage, but guilt is a good distraction. He's hiding his music—music that's *about* Quentin—while Quentin is planning dates.

His respite is short-lived. By the time Alexis Leavy is standing in front of them again, that sly smile seemingly permanently etched on her face, Landon's palms are sweaty and damp and his heart is thumping irregularly in his chest.

As he glances down the row of chefs and their celebrity partners, he sees a reflection of his own terror. It was easier last week, he reflects. Easier because they didn't know what to expect. Landon grips his palms together behind his back and prays that he doesn't have to turn the oven on.

"Welcome back," Alexis says, and while her voice is smooth and creamy, there's that edge to it and a gleam in her eyes that Landon knows means nothing good.

Landon glances over at Quentin and sees him swallow hard, his Adam's apple bobbing briefly but sharply. He's nervous too, and that doesn't help Landon feel any better.

"Today, we're going to visit the Far East, celebrating these fantastic cultures by preparing your favorite Asian cuisine."

He must be numb because Alexis' words just slide right over Landon. Asian food. And Quentin is a pastry chef. A *great* pastry chef, but still a pastry chef. Landon tries not to sweat any harder than he already is; the last thing he wants is to look moist on TV.

"As always, we will have a single challenge, as well as the auction items. For today's challenge," Alexis pauses diabolically, "the celebrity will be doing the shopping."

Landon freezes in place. He is sure that the camera will probably catch a look of sheer, unmitigated panic on his face, but he can't make himself care about that right now. He's going to have to go grocery shopping. *Grocery shopping.*

Landon doesn't think he's been past the wine and the cereal aisles in the grocery store for longer than he can remember. Suddenly, though, he remembers Quentin forcing him to use the pantry to find ingredients for his grilled cheese sandwich and Quentin insisting he understand exactly how the groceries are laid out. He might not have an advantage, but he's probably not at a disadvantage.

"Now for the auction items," Alexis continues. "We have two today. Both, I think, will prove rather counterproductive while creating your Asian-inspired cuisine."

For the first, she whips out a large cardboard container of aluminum foil. Quentin looks a little white around the mouth. Landon resolves to bid on this item even if Quentin won't. Whatever they have to do with the foil, Landon wants no part of it.

"You will be required to make all cooking vessels and utensils out of this lovely foil. Opening the bidding at $500," Alexis declares.

Landon bids for his first item with a thousand bucks, and the bidding continues at a fast pace between Landon and Paul and Oliver. Rory drops out when the bidding reaches $2,000 and Paul finally calls it quits at $3,500, making Landon breathe a sigh of relief. He'd decided to hold himself to $5,000 and he's really happy he didn't even have to go that far this first time.

As for deciding who gets the wretched foil, it's really pretty easy. Landon remembers distinctly what Quentin said in the bakery this week about who he fears the most and that's who he saddles with it, Reed and Diego looking on in horrified shock as Alexis generously gifts them the entire jumbo-sized box.

Landon can't help but smirk as Reed's face goes blank and pale and even Diego, who seems about as clueless in the kitchen as Landon himself, look on with barely concealed panic. It's a good moment, maybe the first of the show when Landon feels like he and Quentin have finally wrestled their fate back from anyone who might try to control them.

Quentin must feel it too, because when Landon glances over, there's definitely a gleam of hard-won success in his eyes and in the curl of his lips as he smiles.

The next auction item turns out to be a microwave. Actually, Alexis explains with way too much delight, it's *only* a microwave.

As in the team saddled with the device will *only* be able to use the microwave as a heat source.

Landon loves his microwave. He would probably starve without it. But he assumes from the look of distress dawning over Quentin's features, a microwave is not the most desired appliance for preparing an Asian-inspired meal.

Landon, spurred on by the worry creasing the delicate skin between Quentin's brows, is a bit reckless and bids on it.

"Five hundred dollars!" he announces, and continues until the bidding reaches $1,000, and when Paul and Carson and Oliver and Nora won't seem to let it go, lets them fight it out. He hopes that whoever buys it will be angry enough at the other team for driving the price up that it'll be a knee-jerk reaction to gift it to them.

It turns out that Carson and Paul are a little more strategic than that. Landon still breathes a sigh of relief as Carson condemns Rory and Kimber to using the microwave for the entirety of the challenge.

It's only when the bidding is over that Landon realizes he's *still* going to have to go grocery shopping. He and Quentin have about thirty seconds for a hurried consult on what he should grab. Quentin whispers to him what feels like a *very* long list of ingredients and Landon only hopes that he's equal to the task.

The sixty seconds in the pantry passes in a flash; there's shoving and pushing and Landon isn't only on the receiving end. He focuses on getting the most important ingredients and when he's sure he's secured those, he just starts stuffing random items into his basket. Still, when he reaches Quentin and sets the basket down on their prep station, out of breath from the short run to the pantry and back, Quentin gives him a huge smile.

"You did so good," he says loud enough for the cameras to pick up. "Dream Team!" Quentin holds his hand up for a high five and Landon glances at it for a moment before tugging him into a tight hug instead. He's fairly certain the camera caught his body pressing hard against Quentin's, and if it doesn't end up in the footage selected to air, he would be shocked.

He already knows the camera loves him, and there's no way it doesn't love Quentin too. *Look at him*, Landon thinks with a lovesick sigh as Quentin sorts through the basket of ingredients with a focused expression, the curve of his neck and jaw exposed with his hair pulled back into a puffy bun that Landon is quite desperate to dig his fingers into. He's just *gorgeous* and Landon is beginning to suspect that Quentin is all his to enjoy.

"So what are we making?" Landon asks.

"A staple. Kung pao chicken."

"I order that all the time from the Chinese restaurant down the street," Landon admits. "I like it spicy, though. Should we make it spicy?"

Quentin holds up a hot pepper and the bottle of sriracha that Landon picked up during the quickest sixty seconds of his life. He doesn't even remember putting them into the basket. "Spicy like you," Quentin giggles, his expression melting into a big puddle of fond.

Landon rolls his eyes. "I'm not spicy!"

Quentin leans over the cutting board and smirks. "Oh, darling, you definitely are. And I love it."

Landon mock sniffs, trying to ignore the way his blood is beginning to simmer a bit from the heat in Quentin's gaze. "Okay, Spicy, what should I be doing?"

"Can you make rice?" Quentin asks.

Landon levels a frank stare at Quentin and he blushes.

"Okay, no rice. Can you cut the chicken up into small pieces, and then chop the peanuts?"

Before Landon can even answer, Quentin's bustling around, setting up a different cutting board on the prep station, and hacking their chicken into rough sections with an enormous cleaver that scares Landon just by looking at it.

So he glances away, taking a moment to look at the rest of the groups. Reed and Diego are in the kitchen next to them, and so Landon gets a front row seat on how their battle with the foil is going.

Landon is somewhat dismayed to discover that for his $3,600, he can watch Diego meticulously assemble somewhat sturdy-looking cooking vessels and utensils out of foil as if his hands were pure sculptural magic.

It's hard, but he barely avoids a massive pout on camera. He isn't pleased that the very first sabotage they've bought doesn't appear to be slowing Reed or Diego down at all. If anything, all it'll prove is that when Diego isn't busy creating the next blockbuster script, he's got a future as the next Martha Stewart.

Landon leans over and nudges Quentin, careful not to disturb his cleaver-wielding. "Hey," he murmurs into Quentin's ear after he bends down, "I think we screwed up." Landon pointedly glances over to where future Martha is carefully twisting and folding a large length of foil into a very credible impersonation of a spoon. Landon wants to cry.

To his credit, Quentin isn't even phased. "It doesn't matter," he says staunchly. "Whatever we make will taste better anyway."

It isn't that Landon doesn't trust Quentin. He does. But there's a level of competency in Diego and Reed's movements that he never saw before and now that he has, he can't seem to un-see it.

Before Landon can go into a full-fledged panic over how Diego and Reed are real competition even though they've been saddled with no actual pots or pans or utensils, only a roll of foil, Quentin beckons him over to the cutting board he's set up with the chicken.

"Small pieces," Quentin instructs him, making sure to demonstrate clearly and carefully with the big knife—though it is far smaller than the cleaver he had been using.

Landon spends the next ten tedious minutes cutting the chicken, being careful and thorough, both happy and unhappy that instead of the camera capturing how horribly boring prep is, it's focused on Quentin. He's moving through their station like a whirlwind, seeming to do about ten thousand things at once.

Even if Quentin was the one assigned to tedious tasks, it makes sense to Landon that the camera would eat him up. He's beautiful and charismatic and charming. He can hardly blame the camera for following him all the time—he does it himself, only forcing himself to pay attention to the task at hand because he knows how important this is.

When Landon finally finishes with the chicken, he looks up to see what whirlwind Quentin has managed to accomplish. There's a pan of rice on the stove, there's an entire garden of vegetables in neat, chopped piles. Quentin's whisking the contents of several foreign-looking bottles into a bowl, his bicep flexing as his hand moves briskly. Landon swallows hard.

"All done?" Quentin asks brightly, as if Landon's task hadn't taken him an eternity.

"All done," Landon confirms.

"Perfect. The wok's all heated up, and there's about ten minutes left, so it's about time to start cooking."

Landon doesn't know where the time went. Ten minutes left? Is that even enough time? They've barely even interacted since the countdown started, both very absorbed in their own tasks, with almost no time for flirting or the sly, witty banter that Landon is already sure will be a very prominent feature of their edit on the show. They need to stick out with personality, not just with their flavors; if they're boring, they'll no doubt be shown the door in the next few weeks and Landon isn't ready to give this up yet. So he goes with his gut, which contrary to popular belief, has steered him wrong plenty of times. All he can hope is that his current run of luck will hold.

"Show me," he demands with a bright, crinkly-eyed smile that he knows gets him most things he wants.

Quentin looks surprised for a moment. This definitely isn't the plan. Landon begs with his eyes to *trust him*, and so Quentin, beautifully trusting Quentin, does. Even beckons Landon over with a saucy grin and a quip about things getting spicy.

Landon really hopes the cameras caught that one because it's suggestive enough, especially considering what they'll surely get up to after filming is over, to bring a blush to his cheeks.

He's asked Quentin to show him; Landon doesn't actually expect Quentin to beckon him over to where the giant wok is smoking on the stove, and stick a long, thin-handled ladle into his hand.

"Come on, let's cook," Quentin says breezily, as if Landon isn't staring with something close to abject terror at the wok in front of him. Before Landon can stop him, Quentin's tossing the chicken into the pan and there's a wall of sound and smell and steam as the raw meat hits the hot metal.

"Come on, stir it," Quentin directs, and Landon hesitantly sticks the tool in, flinching a bit at the sheer heat radiating from the wok.

"No," Quentin corrects after Landon half-heartedly moves the chicken around. He can see it beginning to stick and he's terrified that he's going to fuck up their dish because he was stupid enough to try to create some sort of moment for them. "Like this." Quentin's arm winds around Landon and Quentin's hand grips where Landon is holding the kitchen implement.

Quentin's breath is even hotter on his neck than the smoking pan in front of him. But after a few false starts and stuttered movements, their arms begin to move in sync, and Landon finally begins to understand how to prevent the meat from sticking or burning—you move it very quickly, turning and turning it, so it only has a split second on the sides of the pan.

There's still some chicken remnants stuck to the wok when Quentin scoops it out and gently retrieves the ladle from Landon's hand. His eyes are bright with mischief as he tosses the vegetables in. "See?" Quentin says as he works the vegetables with a much defter hand than Landon had even with Quentin's assistance. "Not that scary."

Landon eyes the leaping flame underneath the wok and how the vegetables sizzle as they barely brush the high sides. "I don't much like the idea of my flesh melting off," Landon says.

"I'd never let that happen." Quentin sounds very certain. Landon sees out of the corner of his eye that the camera has caught this entire exchange and despite the risk, he's almost certain his gamble was worth the potential cost.

Quentin tosses the chicken in to mix with the sauce and vegetables and though Landon is nervously eyeing the clock, which is rapidly ticking down, it's only a few seconds before Quentin is plating their stir fry on a bed of rice and sprinkling it with the peanuts he's already toasted.

"Done," Quentin exclaims with a dramatic wave of his hand.

Landon lets out the breath he didn't realize he was holding. They're about to put a delicious (if the scented steam rising from the plate is any indication) plate in front of the judges with about seven seconds to spare. They got some good camera time in. As long as nothing disastrous happens during judging, they should be safe again this week.

Jasper, Simone and Zach carefully and deliberately work their way down the row of plates. Their faces are annoyingly impassive, and they seem to dole out less criticism, but even less praise, than the week before. Landon doesn't really know where they stand. And even worse they go first.

He knows they enjoy their dish of kung pao chicken, though Zach claims to prefer a more traditional sauce. Landon wonders—but can't ask—if it's his fault; after all, he's the one who did the shopping in the pantry and it's highly likely that he ended up forgetting some vital ingredient. But Zach loves the crunch of the peanuts and Jasper and Simone both remark on the flawlessly cooked vegetables. Simone points out that the chicken itself is a bit ragged in spots, and Landon narrowly avoids blushing.

Rory and Kimber are up next.

"Sushi," Zach says thoughtfully as he neatly captures a piece of sashimi with his chopsticks. "A bit of an easy way out, yes?"

Simone sniffs. She looks like she came out of the womb with that disdainful sniff. Landon wishes he could reproduce it. "Most dcfinitcly."

Turns out a microwave-only cooking method makes unpalatable rice and all the judges are unhappy that Rory and Kimber didn't really attempt to cook *anything* of substance. Rory seems unconcerned though, smiling sunnily through the entire critique as if he could care less.

Landon wishes he could steal a bit of Rory's *laissez-faire* flair. He cares a little too much—not just about the show—and he's afraid it's beginning to show. But the good news is that Rory and Kimber, no matter how unconcerned they appear on the surface, aren't a judge favorite today. Landon takes heart that he and Quentin almost certainly won't finish last.

Jeff and Jessa prepared a fairly simple bento box with rice, teriyaki chicken and some delicious-looking tempura-fried vegetables. They're light and flaky and Zach demolishes his portion, poking around for another portion of zucchini as Simone gives her bite of teriyaki chicken an unimpressed glance.

"Still very simple," she points out. "And this chicken is overcooked."

Landon is beginning to discover that lack of execution is just as harmful as a lack of flavor. He thanks his lucky stars that he and Quentin haven't managed to stumble into either of those issues yet.

The trio of judges move on to Oliver and Nora and their plate of noodles and shrimp.

"This is really good pad Thai," Zach enthuses, as he deftly wraps noodles around his chopsticks.

Simone agrees, and Landon can't help the worry that thrums through him.

"Nora," Oliver insists as he defers to the beautiful brunette. "She lived in Thailand for several years. This was mostly her."

"Delicious," Simone observes. "Kudos to you for working to your team's strengths."

Reed and Diego also apparently worked to their team's strengths, presenting a dish of deep yellow coconut curry. "My favorite recipe," Diego points out as the judges each dig in a spoon to the vivid sauce.

Jasper turns to Diego in astonishment as he licks the spoon clean. "You're a genius," he says, and it's far and away the best praise that any team has gotten today. Up until Nora's pad Thai and Diego's curry, Landon thought he and Quentin might finally have a chance to take first place.

Landon is peeved that all that foil seemed to make no difference. He's annoyed with himself for judging the situation so badly and for wasting their money. Maybe he should have Quentin make all the auction decisions going forward, he's just no good at it. It's hard to stand in front of the cameras and pretend not to care.

Alice and Blair are next up and while Quentin has had nothing but praise for the latter as a pastry chef, it's beginning to be clear that's where her talent really lies.

The judges are unimpressed and downright disgusted at points by their Korean barbecue. They don't like the flavor—"This is unlike any Korean barbecue I've ever had," Simone points out rather bluntly—and they don't like the execution either. "Tough and dry," Jasper remarks. "You cooked it until it was dead twice over."

They don't have a single positive comment to say and Blair looks bereft as the judges move on to Paul and Carson, who have prepared a selection of dumplings.

There's several different flavor pairings, which Landon thinks seems like a lot of work, and it shows because while nothing is terrible, nothing is particularly good either. "Perhaps less is more?" Jasper offers as a parting shot.

It's almost certainly a much less stressful judging session than last week, and Landon feels confident that he and Quentin are sure bets to move on to the next round. So much so that his heart barely races as Alexis announces that the team in last place is unsurprisingly Blair and Alice.

Even more unsurprisingly, first goes to Diego and Reed. Second to Oliver and Nora. And again, Quentin and Landon are announced for third. It's definitely an achievement worth celebrating over, but Landon is still a bit annoyed as they pack up to leave the studio.

"Always the bridesmaid, never the bride," he grumbles as he zips up his jacket.

"It's fine," Quentin soothes. "Really. It's better to be underestimated by the others at this stage anyway. We're competition, but just barely. We're not doing enough to lose, but not really enough to win either."

Landon scrunches his nose. "Don't tell me that's on purpose."

"Not exactly on purpose? But I don't mind flying under the radar. Nobody's given us a sabotage yet, have they?" Quentin's eyes twinkle a bit diabolically.

"Quen!" Landon shrieks. "You've been holding out on me!"

Quentin just chuckles and wraps his arms around Landon, holding him tight. Burying his nose into the warm curve of Quentin's neck, Landon feels the tension of the day finally leave him comple tely."Sorry about earlier," he whispers so quietly that because he's afraid both that Quentin will and won't hear him.

But Quentin must have supernatural hearing, because he pulls back a little and looks seriously straight into Landon's eyes. Landon thinks he must be seeing straight to his slightly tarnished soul and reading all the secrets he tries so hard to hide.

"You were right to do it," Quentin says softly.

"I messed up so much today," Landon can't help but admit. "First buying that sabotage that did *nothing* to hurt Diego and Reed, and then springing that on you about the cooking. I could have really messed up our chances." He doesn't bring up the song he wouldn't let Quentin listen to, because that goes deeper than making a bad logistical decision on the show that didn't end up impacting their placement today. He's also ashamed to admit, even to himself, that he doesn't bring it up because he's hoping Quentin's forgotten about it.

"You're wrong. You saved us. I got so caught up in cooking and doing everything perfectly I forgot about everything else. *You* reminded me. *You* lightened the atmosphere and gave the camera something great to capture. As for Diego and Reed, well, I think they just got lucky."

Quentin must see a shadow of doubt in his eyes, because he just gives a sad, bewildered shake of his head—almost as if he can't believe Landon doesn't see how wonderful he was—and kisses him.

It's heated almost immediately and Landon would hate the fact that Quentin distracted him from feeling sorry for himself, except that Quentin's tongue is in his mouth and his enormous hands are on his ass and he can't even remember why he was upset.

"Let's go home," Quentin says when he finally lifts his mouth off Landon's.

Landon knew it was coming; he'd seen it barreling down the road from about ten miles away, from practically the first moment they met and Quentin, big and strong and handsome, blushed like a schoolboy with a crush.

He's still taken completely by surprise when his heart literally tumbles out of his chest and falls right at Quentin Maxwell's feet.

His voice trembles a little and he knows his hand is shaking as he reaches out to take Quentin's. He's in love. It isn't like he never thought he'd fall in love again. It's more like Landon believed he'd be logical and smart about it and allow it to happen, rather than him blundering into it without rhyme or reason again. But clearly love isn't something that he can control, that much is becoming abundantly clear. Landon is just going to have to trust that this time is different. That *Quentin* is different.

"Okay," he says, like Quentin casually talking about going home together is nothing. Like it hasn't just sent Landon careening right off the cliff of good sense. Like it hasn't made him fall in love. "Let's go home."

145

CHAPTER SEVEN

By the time they reach Quentin's apartment in their separate cars, Landon's heart has finally stopped pounding from his recent revelation, and is now pounding with what must be nerves.

It's not that they haven't had sex before—they have, even though it was only once—it's more that Landon has never had sex with Quentin *while he's been in love with him.*

This is a huge problem because Landon knows what he's like when he's in love. He's sappy and cheesy and likes staring deep into his lover's eyes and talking to him about ten thousand times a day, even if it's just silly emojis sent back and forth, or dozens of snapchats. Sure, Quentin liked Landon a lot when Landon was *himself.* But now he's *in love Landon* and he's afraid *in love Landon* is going to push Quentin away.

Realistically, Landon knows it's stupid; knows he's being silly and that his feelings are likely reciprocated. But logic doesn't help make his heart beat any slower as he climbs the stairs.

Landon taps hesitantly on the door, and Quentin calls out, "It's open!"

Landon walks in and nearly walks right back out. Except that he's actually stuck in place, glued to the floor by the scene in front of him.

The entryway into the living room is dark, the only light a few scattered candles. There's a faint smell of vanilla and lemon in the air and it takes Landon a moment to realize what it reminds him of—it's the scent of Quentin's hair. The earthy perfume of Quentin's bed when he woke up that one wonderful morning next to him.

Landon scrubs a hand over his face. He is so, so fucked. How is he supposed to rein in all the embarrassingly sappy bits of himself when it feels like Quentin is trying to lure them out one candle at a time?

Landon gingerly takes another step inside, hoping against hope that he doesn't spot any rose petals haphazardly sprinkled over the hardwood. Candles he can *maybe* handle; rose petals would turn him into a sappy mess and he won't be able to keep Quentin from seeing all of it.

"I'm in the bedroom," Quentin calls out and Landon rolls his eyes a bit. *Of course* he is. Landon resumes his prayer that there are no rose petals.

Except that there are. Landon pauses at the doorway to the bedroom, the visual laid out in front of him stopping him in his tracks for the second time in the last minute.

At least they aren't on the bed. They're clustered around the bed, vases overflowing with not just roses, but other flowers too. The scent they're throwing off isn't as sickly sweet as Landon might have imagined, not with the sheer amount clustered in the room. Instead, it's delicate and floral and lovely.

"It's too much, isn't it?" Quentin asks, and there's chagrin in his voice and if Landon listens hard enough, he can hear the narrowest, sharpest edge of embarrassment there too. And while Landon might feel scared enough of his own tendency towards romance, there is no universe in which he will ever let *Quentin* feel bad about his.

In a way it's a blessing, because sudden fear that Quentin might regret this beautiful statement and wish he'd never done it powers Landon right over the threshold. He wraps his arms around Quen and holds him as tightly as he can.

"It's lovely," he murmurs, craning his neck up so he can whisper it directly into Quentin's ear. "I love it."

I love you.

He doesn't say it even though he can feel the weight of the words on his tongue. Perhaps they're not begging to be confessed right now, but they're present and Landon couldn't ever forget them. At some point, he fully expects that he won't be able to contain them any longer, and they'll come tumbling out, end over end, probably a bit lumpy and awkward, but real and true all the same.

Hopefully whenever that particular moment comes, Quentin will be in love with Landon too, and he won't care that Landon's words aren't perfect. He'll only care that they exist at all.

The way Quentin holds him back, just as close, just as tight, his arms still careful to be gentle, cradling Landon's back as if he is precious—that alone is enough to relax Landon into the embrace. Enough so that he can tilt his head back and kiss Quentin with everything he doesn't quite have the courage to say yet.

"I'm sorry we didn't win today," Quentin says quietly.

Landon is sorry too, but he's sure as hell not going to let Quentin see that. It's not Quentin's fault. Their lack of first places is down to the whims of the judges, not any fault of Quentin's.

"Don't be," Landon murmurs, brushing his hair back and lifting onto his tiptoes so he can leave a trail of tiny kisses along Quentin's exposed collarbone. "You're wonderful."

Landon is just beginning to deepen one to the vibrant scarlet of a love bite when Quentin pulls away unexpectedly. "Tonight is supposed to be about you," Quentin says with a tiny wrinkle forming between his brows.

"What if I want to leave you this love bite?"

Quentin wavers for a moment, and Landon pounces, hoping to push him over the edge. "Personally, I think it should always be about *both* of us, don't you think?"

He barely waits for Quentin's acquiescing nod before pouncing, reaching up to kiss him.

Quentin only takes a moment to catch up, and he's kissing back with so much passion that Landon feels his heart lighten. Surely someone who can kiss him this way *must* have similar feelings?

Before Landon can go on a long-winded analysis in his mind about Quentin's feelings, the bed hits the back of his knees gently, and he realizes that Quentin's been moving them backwards towards the big fluffy white bed in the center of the room.

The bed is an idea he can get behind.

Landon finally lets the worry go and just revels in the feel of Quentin's lips on his, his tongue snaking in to touch his, the way his hands reverently coast over Landon's curves, sliding his t-shirt over his head.

Landon scoots up on the bed and Quentin looms over him, his eyes a deep, serious blue. "You're so gorgeous," Quentin says softly, as he buries his face in Landon's neck.

Gasping a bit at the love bite Quentin is leaving *him*, lips relentless against the sensitive curve of his neck, Landon gasps as Quentin adds teeth, nibbling with just enough pressure to make his stomach swoop.

By the time Quentin reaches the curve of his jaw, he's more than gasping, he's now panting a little, cock thickening up in his jeans. "Feels good, doesn't it?"

There's absolutely nothing hotter than this—touching and being touched by the person you love. Landon has never liked one-night stands; doesn't like the impersonality of the touches. He enjoys his serial monogamy all the way up until the relationships sour, but even then, nothing has ever felt like this before. It's like Quentin's inside his head, touching him from the inside out, knowing what he likes as if he's experiencing the sensations as Landon does. It's heady and Landon has to force himself to shove away the sudden pang of fear that this too might end someday.

It's really not easy, but Landon does it by turning his focus back on the beautiful man hovering over him. Landon reaches down and pulls up Quentin's t-shirt by the hem, lifting it over his head, and slides his palms everywhere he can, reveling in the way the muscles bunch underneath the smooth skin. His fingers drift lower, toying a bit with the button of his jeans, tucking into the sensitive skin alongside his waist.

While Landon has been teasing, Quentin's moved lower, mouthing insistently at Landon's collarbones. He's gentle yet demanding. Landon can feel the insistent desire under every touch, but that Quentin doesn't give in makes the tenderness Landon receives literally awe-inspiring.

Quentin moves lower, tongue reaching out to caress one nipple, and the heat of Quentin's mouth its own kind of insistence. Landon thinks he might be murmuring a litany of half-formed words into his skin and it's not until he quiets and listens hard that he can finally make out what Quentin's mumbling between kisses and nips and love bites. *"God, lovely, so beautiful, stunning."*

Everywhere Quentin's mouth touches, it feels like his words are being absorbed into Landon's body. Landon feels light and free and loved. He knows he's felt this way about someone before—almost certainly feels this much or *more*—but he's never had someone feel this way about him.

Quentin reaches the tiny pouch of a tummy that Landon has always hated. He still hates it, but maybe not quite as fervently as Quentin nibbles at the skin there, caressing it like it's the sexiest six-pack in the entire universe.

Landon is nearly incoherent with love and a hot, insistent lust by the time Quentin's breath stutters over his straining erection.

"God, Quen, *please*," he begs and Quentin doesn't even tease. He just strips his jeans and pants off and his mouth skates up one thigh, nibbling a bit on the flex of muscle as Landon strains to get his hard cock somewhere near Quentin's miracle of a mouth.

"Gorgeous," Quentin pants just before he slides his lips down Landon's length. Landon barely registers it, he's lost in a wave of sensation as Quentin swirls his tongue insistently around the head.

Quentin's hand clamps around Landon's thigh and he gives him so much hot, wet suction that Landon feels like he must be sucking his brain out his dick. Far too soon, he trembles at the heat building in his belly. "Quentin," he begs, "gonna come."

He pulls off instantly. *Too* instantly for Landon's liking; he pouts a little as Quentin sheds the rest of his clothes, his own cock so hard, the wet head bounces against those glorious abs as he reach-es over to grab lube and a condom from the drawer.

"Want you to come on my cock," Quentin murmurs as he slicks up his fingers and helps prop Landon's hips up. "Gonna make you feel so good, baby."

"Already feels good." Landon knows he sounds a bit delirious, but with that mouth all over his body, how was he supposed to sound any different? And it's probably a good thing he got that out first, because Quentin's beautiful fingers—fingers he's been worshipping in his dreams since the day they met—are circling his hole and he's speechless with how much he just *wants*.

Quentin slides a finger in, big and thick, though nowhere near as thick as the cock he's trying to prep Landon to take. "More," Landon manages to insist when Quentin moves too slow, too careful for his liking. He likes it fast and hard, though the romance of this encounter is probably not the right place for dirty fucking.

"Gonna give you everything you need," Quentin reassures him, and slides a second finger in, the stretch around his rim a bit painfully insistent but still so good already. "Anything you ever want."

"Good," Landon can only pant weakly as Quentin slides in and out, still tender, but determined enough to find his prostate on the fourth try.

Quentin's fingers teasingly circle the little nub, and Landon buries his face in his bicep, mouthing at the skin, trying to distract himself enough that he doesn't scream or *come*.

A third finger teases around his rim, and Landon can't contain his moan of acceptance and pleasure. "Make you feel so good," Quentin says, his voice rough and gravelly. He sounds like he's enjoying giving Landon this about as much as he's enjoying taking it. And that's probably the hottest part of this: *how much they enjoy each other.*

Quentin stretches Landon out careful and slow, but with such determined brushes against his prostate that Landon is desperate within a few minutes. "Give it to me," he slurs, not even caring how demanding he sounds. If Quentin doesn't hurry up, Landon is going to come and ruin all those lovely daydreams about coming on that beautiful cock of his.

He gives Landon one more teasing circle against his prostate and then removes his fingers, making quick work of the condom.

Quentin leans in to kiss Landon's slack mouth as he snags his cock against Landon's rim. "Oh fuck, you're gonna feel so good," he pants into Landon's mouth. "Hot and tight and *gorgeous.*"

"So pretty," Landon agrees mindlessly as he reaches up to stroke Quentin's curls away from his forehead.

The head of Quentin's cock slowly entering him punches the rest of the breath out of Landon's lungs. Quentin is so big and hard and it feels inescapable in the best way as Quentin slowly fucks him into the fluffy white duvet.

When he's fully inside Landon, they both let out a moan, their voices harmonizing together in the still of the room. Landon has never felt so full in his god damn life, and he's never loved anything more. Quentin's cock is already brushing his prostate, a white-hot burning shooting through his veins as the pleasure already threatens to overwhelm him.

"Love me," Landon whispers into Quentin's lips.

Quentin gives a short, tortured nod and fucks him at a pace that might have tortured a previous version of Landon, but tonight, Landon just eats up his long, slow strokes. The pleasure is so hot and thick he can only mouth over the exposed curve of Quentin's throat in wet slurps. Quentin doesn't seem to mind because he's moaning just about as loudly as Landon is now, deep and hard every time he bottoms out.

"Close," Landon groans as Quentin's hips begin to stutter, not quite as controlled as before. Landon thinks he's about to come probably, from the pained expression on his face, to the way his fingers grip Landon's hips even tighter than before, and Landon wants nothing more than to come with him.

Quentin seems pretty gone but he's apparently not far gone enough to slide his hand across Landon's hip bone and grasp his hard cock, stroking it insistently.

It's all Landon needs to fall off the razor-sharp edge that Quentin's been building inside Landon since they met at the bakery. He comes with a shout and his teeth grazing Quentin's throat, vision growing blurry as come splatters up Quentin's chest and he feels his hole clench once, then twice around Quentin's dick.

Quentin follows with a deep groan of his own, his hips slamming home and grinding his cock there for a long, drawn-out moment as he comes into the condom.

Landon can't even complain when Quentin finally collapses on top of him, come and sweat and lube smearing between them.

"Wonderful Quentin," Landon murmurs into his damp skin.

"Wonderful Landon," Quentin mumbles back a few long moments later. "Definitely, wonderful Landon."

⁂

They sleep hard for two-ish hours, Landon finally waking up with his mouth full of Quentin's curls and his skin tacky and gross with various dried patches.

The room is dark, the candles long since sputtered out in their own melted wax.

"Quentin," Landon mumbles, pulling away but groaning when his skin literally sticks to Quentin's. Immediately falling asleep in each other's arms had seemed like such a great idea at the time, but now, it's becoming clear it wasn't.

"Ow," Quentin moans back. He must have also discovered where they're glued together.

"Shower," Landon says as insistently as he can, considering he's half-asleep and his front is literally stuck to Quentin's back.

Quentin nods, and Landon slowly, agonizingly peels them apart. When he's finally free, he collapses back onto the bed, panting a little at how much his skin stings.

Landon hears Quentin rustling on his side of the bed and begins to work up the energy to move again. But before he can, he feels Quentin's arms slide under him and suddenly he's airborne, Quentin lifting him bridal-style.

"Don't you dare drop me!" Landon yelps as Quentin moves towards the bathroom.

Landon can feel Quentin's chest shaking with laughter as he finally deposits him, bare-ass naked on the bathroom counter. Quentin leans over and flips the shower on, steam quickly filling the bathroom.

Quentin mumbles something under his breath as he slips into the shower. Landon slides off the counter and follows him in.

Quentin's hair is wet and he pushes it back, eyes twinkling bright in the dim light of the bathroom. "You're precious cargo," he repeats with an impudent grin. Landon really can't let this stand. He takes a step closer, spray misting over his face.

"Precious?" Landon asks, and he hates how high and anxious his voice sounds. Like he's desperate for Quentin to confess his love. Which he is. Completely. Who is he kidding?

Quentin falling in love with Landon and telling Landon first would make everything about a million times simpler. But of course, all Quentin does is shake his hair like a shaggy dog, finishing what the light mist had started and getting Landon all wet.

"Scrub a dub dub," Quentin sings, his smile giddy and light as he pours shampoo in his hands and scrubs first his head and then Landon's. He's got a nice deft touch with the perfect amount of pressure, big hands massaging Landon's head as well as they've massaged all his other body parts.

"You've got a nice voice," Landon points out after he's rinsed his head. He's soaping up his skin now, trying to not notice how gorgeous Quentin's pale skin is when it's wet like this, shining under the light.

"It's okay." Quentin brushes it aside the way he brushes aside most compliments, though typically they're compliments about his cooking—or his truly ridiculous good looks. Landon spent an entirely non-creepy evening last week watching all the YouTube videos he could find that featured Quentin and couldn't help but notice that he prefers to not take the credit.

Landon wants Quentin to have all the credit in the world, especially when they win *Kitchen Wars* and he can finally open the bakery of his dreams.

They finish rinsing off and dry off—they only get distracted by all the bare, naked skin once, when Landon pushes Quentin up against the tiny counter and kisses him soft and sweet, a nice contrast to the way his thumbs are digging hard into Quentin's hips.

Landon finally lifts his mouth from Quentin's when he hears his stomach grumble insistently. "Hungry?" Quentin asks with an impudent grin.

"Oh shut up." Landon makes a face. "You're the brilliant chef. Dinner, *please*?"

It turns out that even though Quentin *is* a brilliant chef, he has no intention of stretching his culinary muscles tonight.

"Pancakes?" Landon asks with disbelief as he watches Quentin dump in flour and sugar and salt in a bowl. He cracks several eggs terrifyingly quick against the side of a large glass pitcher and whisks the yolks separate from the whites.

He makes it so easy—dividing the eggs that way, and Landon can only stare at him agape from his perch on the counter.

"I thought you weren't gonna go super chef on me."

Quentin raises an eyebrow as he gently folds in his egg whites. "Don't tell me you use a mix."

"I *only* use a mix," Landon admits, though he's only made pancakes a handful of times, even from a mix. "My pancakes taste fine."

Even though Quentin is already turned towards his cast iron pan, heating on the stove, Landon can still see his grimace. Sometimes Landon can't really understand how good they are together. After all, they've only known each other a few weeks. Shouldn't it be much harder to be so in sync? Instead it's been as easy and straightforward as those eggs Quentin just separated.

"Okay, time to practice," Quentin insists, beckoning him over.

"I'll just fuck it up," Landon says apprehensively.

"You won't," Quentin promises. "And even if you do, you won't. It's just flour and eggs and a little bit of vanilla. I've got lots more."

Landon slides off the counter, retrospectively glad that he'd put on a pair of Quentin's sweatpants, and approaches the stove with trepidation.

"See those little bubbles?" Quentin asks, waving the spatula in Landon's face until he forcibly grabs it. He absently nods, focusing far more on slapping Quentin's butt with the plastic utensil instead of actually using it to flip pancakes.

"Landon!" Quentin sounds more amused than mad, but there's daggers in his eyes. "Pay attention. This pancake is going to burn if you don't flip it now. See how the bubbles in the middle have all burst? That means it's done."

"Sorry, your ass is just too distracting," Landon says with a smirk. Quentin flushes, and it's worth the first pancake being a tiny bit burnt after Landon finally flips it.

They slowly make their way through the batter Quentin's whipped up, and as it disappears from the bowl, a pile of beautiful golden-brown pancakes appear on a plate on the other side of the stove.

"See?" Quentin impudently tells Landon as he pours maple syrup over his stack of pancakes. "That wasn't so difficult."

"It's a good thing you were supervising." Landon gestures with his fork. "Otherwise, we might have starved."

"You mean, it's a good thing I supervised, otherwise you'd have ended up on your knees and pancakes wouldn't be what you'd be eating?"

Landon is shocked into silence for a good, long moment. *How does Quentin know him so well?*

"How do you know me so well?" he's finally able to splutter out.

Quentin just shrugs and shovels more pancakes into his mouth. Landon can't really blame him; they're delicious. Way better than the boxed mix that he always used to buy for his sisters, but you won't find him admitting that to Quentin. "You're more famous than you give yourself credit for, Landon."

It hurts, a little, Quentin claiming the reason he knows him is because he watched him on TV a few years ago. Parts of that Landon were real, but the real Landon wants Quentin to love him for who he is *now*.

The hurt feels fair, after the awkwardness with the song earlier, and so Landon hooks a thumb under the waistband of the loose sweatpants Quentin's wearing, nearly pushing them right off his hips. Landon knows just how little Quentin is wearing under those—exactly *nothing*—and he doesn't need much encouragement to drop to his knees and begin mouthing at the fabric covering Quentin's already hardening cock.

A blowjob and an embarrassingly quick hand job later, they're tucked back in bed, Landon collapsed across Quentin's chest, Quentin's hand gently untangling the strands of Landon's hair. They're drifting in that space between wakefulness and sleep, and Landon can't even remember the last time he felt as relaxed as he does right now.

It's the perfect moment for confessions, and Landon has one he desperately wants to make. But the words are thankfully stuck to the roof of his mouth, and he finally drifts off, the litany of them repeating in his head.

His last conscious thought is, *thank god I don't talk in my sleep.*

⁂

Quentin doesn't have to work in the morning, but Landon is supposed to be at the studio by noon. He takes a shower, borrows Quentin's clothes that conspicuously do not fit him, and is at the studio by 12:15. Ian just shakes his head, completely unsurprised, but Landon does see a hint of a smile on his face—and if Ian knew where he spent the last night, he makes no mention of it as they walk into the recording studio.

The next few days pass in a bit of a blur.

This time it's not aimless fooling around with shit new lyrics or re-tooling old songs.

Landon is signed and contracted and working on his new album with Julian, his real live producer.

Julian was brought in by the label based on the ongoing discussions about Landon's new serious singer-songwriter vibe. It's to everyone's surprise that Landon announces he wants something completely different.

"I want to write an album about falling in love," he announces midway through the afternoon on the first day.

"I thought we were going in a new direction," Julian suggests, not unkindly. And Landon *did* say he wanted to do that, but it's hard to write something angsty and profound when he feels lit up from within, like the world's largest neon sign that reads "I've got a huge fat crush on Quentin Maxwell."

Or, you know, something a little shorter that could actually fit on his body.

Julian furrows his brow and Landon shifts uncomfortably from side to side.

"Okay, explain to me how this fits into your vision."

"New vision," Landon says. "I wanna do some retro Madonna-esque pop. Like real eightees shit. A story about falling in love."

"I thought we were gonna go the singer-songwriter route," Julian points out.

It hadn't been a bad idea, really, but the idea had never sat comfortably on Landon. He'd wanted to be taken *seriously*, but he wasn't sure he could pull off that sort of Ed Sheeran gravitas.

"Fuck being serious," Landon says, and finds he actually means it—way more than he ever meant that he wanted to go the singer-songwriter route. Sitting on a stage by himself with a guitar and a plaid shirt just isn't for him. "I wanna make fun music that I can dance to in my kitchen."

"I didn't know you used your kitchen."

"Ian told you," Landon groans.

"Ian told me," Julian confirms with a sly smile. "And that you've got a massive crush on your partner. He said it was embarrassing. And he was right."

"It's not embarrassing," Landon argues. "It's inspirational."

And it turns out to be absolutely inspirational.

On the fourth day, Landon is pacing around the studio, ranting about how Quentin is his new favorite color, and they need to work that into a song. Julian is nodding along, writing notes, actually acting like Landon is onto something big, instead of just being a huge asshole in love.

Landon loves Julian.

Actually, Landon loves *Quentin*. With that thought, his phone buzzes.

It's Quentin. Of course, it's Quentin.

Rory is throwing a cast party next week after filming. You in, superstar?

Landon has been doing so much thinking and writing and singing about Quentin that he really hasn't had an opportunity to miss him. But the text brings it all crashing back. How springy Quentin's hair is, how he purrs when Landon rubs his hands through it, the wistfulness in his clear blue eyes as they'd said goodbye on his front step only a few days ago.

It's a no brainer for Landon to reply: **Of course. When and where?**

He sends the text and then instantly thinks of something else. **Be my date?**

Quentin texts back the location of the restaurant Rory works at and the time. And a second message too: **Thought I already was. I'm a sure thing.**

Quentin might think he's a sure thing, but there's no surer thing than Landon at this point. He's flush with love and is far gone enough to be writing songs about it.

"Just a suggestion," Julian points out, "but you might want to tone down the starry eyes a bit when you see him next."

Landon just isn't sure if he can. He's been constructing daydreams in the sky for the last three days. It's gonna be a bit tough to return to the hard, solid ground.

He practices his most neutral expression and Julian just laughs.

"When are you going to play him these, anyway? Because you are, right?"

Landon's throat gets tight. "When the time is right." He doesn't know when that is, but he knows it exists.

"They're a bit . . . well . . . *obvious*," Julian points out. Again, not unkindly. Julian is a great sounding board because he will absolutely tell you if something is shit.

"I want to work on the color song," Landon says, changing the subject. "I think I was onto something."

Julian rolls his eyes a little, but picks his pad right back up. Landon takes that as a good sign.

By the time they leave the studio at ten that night, the song is mostly done and even Julian looks surprised at how good it turned out. "Honestly," he confesses as they drag their coats on. "I thought the whole idea was terrible. Waited to see if you could make anything coherent out of that ranting, and you did. More than coherent, actually."

Landon flushes with pride. "You really think so?"

Julian pats him on the shoulder reassuringly. "Landon, I'm not kidding. It's a gorgeous song. Any guy would be thrilled to have a song like that written about him." He pauses. "You know, if you feel this strongly about him, maybe you should think about telling him. He probably feels the same, at least if what you've told me is true."

The last thing Landon needs is anyone helping unstick the words. He's very okay with the words being stuck. "I'll think about it."

He means to forget what Julian said as soon as he closes the studio door, but instead that's *all* he can think about. They're filming tomorrow, and Landon is afraid he's coming down with an acute case of word vomit.

Chapter Eight

"I missed you," Quentin says when Landon walks into their green room the next morning. He wraps his arms firmly around Landon's middle and kisses him unabashedly.

Landon gave himself a very stern lecture in the mirror this morning. No untoward confessions today, especially before filming and especially when they get to Rory's party later.

There wasn't anything in the lecture about this. "I missed you too," Landon breathes out unsteadily as they finally break apart. "I'm sorry this week turned out so crazy."

"I lost you to a vortex of music," Quentin says with a nonchalant shrug. "As long as I get you back, that's all I care about."

Landon is still breathless. He's rather taken with the idea of Quentin wanting him back.

"I'm right here," he insists softly. "Good." Quentin pulls him in for an even tighter hug. Maybe that's why Landon can't quite catch his breath; he's had his lungs squished by a giant Quentin. "Ready to kick some ass today?"

"I'm ready to do better than place third," Landon confesses as Quentin releases him and he turns to check his hair in the mirror.

"Oh, baby," Quentin says as he nuzzles into the soft hairs at the base of Landon's neck. Landon shivers. "We're gonna do a hell of a lot better than third."

Landon believes him. There's a cocky restlessness in Quentin's movements today, a certainty that he hasn't ever seen before. Or maybe it's just a week without any sex besides the manual variety. Landon is certainly feeling a bit edgy himself.

He believes him even more when they're standing in front of Alexis Leavy and she announces the theme of the week. "It feels so early this morning, I want you to make the judges . . . *breakfast.*"

Landon's heart jumps in his chest. *Breakfast.* They can totally rock breakfast.

"But first," Alexis continues, the evil edge to her voice returning, "the overall challenge of this episode. The chef will be prepping, the celebrity cooking."

Landon would have panicked for sure if Quentin hadn't just taught him how to cook pancakes. This is going to be *easy.*

He turns his head to meet Quentin's gaze and discovers that Quentin is definitely smirking back at him. It isn't much of a stretch at all to imagine that Quentin is also remembering that wonderful evening they spent together, cooking up orgasms and pancakes.

"First, your sixty-second shop. Then we'll move on to the auction portion of the challenge," Alexis says.

Quentin picks up their basket and he's off and running with the rest of the chefs, battling it out in the pantry. Landon watches, not even slightly anxious, as Quentin throws boxes and bottles and containers into their basket with the air of someone who knows exactly what they're doing.

Usually Landon might worry about being over-confident; however, today he just feels like there's no way they can't knock this out of the park.

Sixty seconds later, Quentin returns to their station with a full basket of ingredients and a rather triumphant smile. "Nailed it," he murmurs into Landon's ear. "Don't bother bidding. We can do this."

Exactly what Landon was thinking. He kind of loves how in sync their thinking has become. It's hard not to imagine that it's evidence of their growing feelings.

The first auction item is wheeled out. "A campfire stove," Alexis announces. "Perfect for cooking when Jasper and his kids go camping."

Landon hates camping. He eyes the jumping flames and the small cooking surface of the stove and prays they aren't given this item. Nobody looks particularly concerned though. Rory even looks excited at the possibility. Landon hopes that nobody wastes their money and gives the stove to him.

The bidding is brisk, with Carson and Jeff battling it out for the right to hand it over to someone.

Carson wins with a relatively small bid of only $2,500, and like Landon expected, he gives the stove to Jeff and Jessa. The danger, Landon reflects, of driving up the price on an auction item, is the winner is far more likely to have short-term memory and just give it to you.

Landon remembers stupidly bidding for that tin foil challenge and how easy Diego and Reed made it look. It's certainly made him a more cautious bidder.

Up until when Alexis has her assistants wheel out a rather diabolical-looking prep station, fashioned as a giant lazy Susan, rotating at a steady clip already.

"One word about this fun experience," Alexis explains. "It never stops. Sometimes it might go slower. Sometimes it might faster. But it won't *ever* completely stop."

Landon knows he blanches and the camera probably catches the fear in his eyes. Even if he doesn't have to personally deal with this, he does *not* want Quentin to.

"One thousand dollars," Rory shouts the instant Alexis opens bidding.

"Fifteen hundred dollars," Nora chimes in, with her rather silent partner, Oliver, nodding along. Nora's gorgeous, but rather deadly-looking. Landon would rather not bid against her.

Apparently Quentin has none of Landon's compunction.

"Seventeen hundred dollars," Quentin says before Nora's voice even fades from the air. Shocked, Landon whips his head around to where Quentin is standing. He gives Landon a little disparaging shrug. And honestly, Landon *can't* blame him. The thing looks evil.

"Two," Rory bids again.

"Two five," Nora says. She sounds perfectly calm and perfectly determined to win this sabotage.

"Three," Rory responds instantly. Quentin doesn't chime in this time. Maybe he's decided to let Rory and Nora battle it out.

"Three three," Nora answers.

"Three seven," Rory cries, his features animated and a little bit desperate. Quentin leans over and whispers to Landon that Rory gets dizzy really, *really* easily. Which definitely explains his desire to win.

Nora demurs and Rory wins the sabotage for $3,700.

Landon almost certainly expects him to saddle Nora and Oliver with the awful contraption. He doesn't really even contemplate the possibility that Rory will gesture wildly at Quentin and declare that he's always wanted to see his good friend run around a table.

Landon feels panic rising in his throat. It must show because Quentin leans over again. "It'll be fine, Landon, promise. We're lucky it's just pancakes. I could whip those up upside-down."

Landon chokes out a laugh. "Don't give Alexis any ideas." He absolutely means it. If they're saddled with anything else, he's not sure they're going to make it out of this week.

"Thirty minutes to make breakfast," Alexis cries out, and suddenly there's a lazy Susan prep station in their section and Quentin is rather effortlessly jogging around it as he pours flour into a bowl.

"Landon," Quentin says like he's not currently running around a circling table, "get a skillet and a small saucepan from the equipment shelves."

Landon is getting dizzy even watching Quentin and it's only been a minute. He's grateful to be able to turn away and go scrounge up the equipment that Quentin's requested.

"The raspberries into a pan with some sugar," Quentin barks out, still fairly pleasant, even though the table has begun to diabolically spin even faster.

"How much sugar?" Landon asks, and his own voice is definitely panicked—even higher and even squeakier than usual.

"Oh, a good shake or two." Quentin glances over as Landon experimentally shakes some sugar from the plastic container into the saucepan. "That's good," he says, and Landon sets it on the stove.

Quentin instructs Landon to turn the heat on high. "We're making blueberry sour cream pancakes with raspberry syrup," he informs Alexis when she drifts over by their station, no doubt interested in seeing how well her evil invention is crippling them.

But Quentin, as far as Landon can tell, is completely unconcerned. He whisks eggs into sour cream, pours in vanilla and even manages to pretty successfully grate the rind of a lemon into his pitcher of wet ingredients.

Every few rotations, he'll glance over to Landon for an update on the raspberries. As far as Landon can tell, they're bubbling away fine.

The first problem happens when the table slows unexpectedly, and Landon gasps out loud as Quentin's elbow catches on the edge of the blueberry carton, sending it flying all over the floor underneath their station.

"Shit," Quentin yells. Rory glances up from where he's bent over his cutting board. His *stationary* cutting board.

"Guess you're making sour cream pancakes *sans* blueberries," Rory cackles. "Tough luck, buddy."

"All your fault," Quentin insists. There's an edge of frustration to his voice, but it's still mostly pleasant.

"Is this going to be okay?" Landon hisses over at Quentin.

Quentin just shrugs. "Doesn't matter. We'll make it work. No point in crying over spilled blueberries." He shoots Landon a quick, reassuring smile and Landon tries to smile back, but he's not feeling it. Something uncertain is roiling at the base of his stomach and he's just not ready for this to be over, okay? Not like this, not over a stupid rotating table and some blueberries.

He looks over to Jeff and Jessa's station, praying that they're worse with the campfire stove than he and Quentin are. At this point, it might come down to whoever makes the most mistakes out of the two of them.

Jessa is bent over the campfire, shaking a skillet with what Landon thinks are potatoes. Jeff is coaching her, and it doesn't seem to be going well. Jessa's face is blotched with red and Jeff looks like he's about to throw the skillet across the room.

It cheers Landon just enough. He turns back to Quentin. "I think we might be okay," he says quietly. "Just have to hold on, okay?"

"I said, we're good," Quentin says but this time there's a distinct edge of frustration in his voice. Landon isn't sure that Quentin's even buying what he's selling. He's begun to lag behind the table just a half a step and he looks exhausted, his own face flushed and sweaty. There's only one circumstance under which Landon wants Quentin to look flushed and sweaty and it's not while cooking pancakes.

"We're really close to finishing up the batter, then you can have a break," Landon pleads with as much encouragement as he can muster. "So close, Quentin!"

It must help, because Quentin makes one last push, pouring the wet ingredients into the dry and folding them as efficiently as he can while actually chasing them around the table.

"Heat the skillet," Quentin instructs. "Lots of butter. But make sure it doesn't burn."

Quentin carefully grabs the bowl full of batter off the table and hands it to Landon, who cradles it like he'd carry one of his baby sisters. With respect and care. This is Quentin's future, in his hands. *His* future, too, he's begun to think.

Quentin walks over to the stove, and examines the raspberries. "Those will need to come off the heat," he says, and Landon reaches over and pulls them off.

"Have to puree them yet, and then strain them," Quentin points out.

Landon glances up from where he's carefully monitoring the melting butter in the skillet. "While you're on the rotating table?" he squeaks.

Quentin shrugs, but even he has finally given up on trying to seem positive about it. "What a crap sabotage," he admits. "I'm gonna kill Rory."

"I'll help you," Landon offers.

Quentin reaches over and squeezes Landon's arm. "Knew you would."

"Twelve minutes," Alexis announces and Landon feels his heart race.

"Should I start?" Landon asks worriedly.

"One scoop of batter, carefully," Quentin says.

Landon has just finished pouring the first pancake, his heart in his throat, when Quentin leans in a bit closer, clearly on the pretext of examining how Landon did. "I think Jessa and Jeff are yelling at each other," Quentin whispers.

Landon surreptitiously glances over two stations, to where the campfire is set up. And there are definitely some raised voices and poisonous looks being exchanged. "We can only hope it's enough to ruin their dish," Landon confesses.

Quentin frowns. "We're fine." He does not sound as certain as he did before, and Landon hates what the uncertain edge in Quentin's voice does to his own stomach.

"Of course we are," Landon soothes.

Quentin glances back at the pan. "God damn it," he barks out, "they're burning."

Landon wants to cry. Instead of watching their pancakes, he was off staring at Jeff and Jessa and hoping they'd mess up. And now *he's* messed up.

"It's okay," Quentin says impatiently. "Let's clean it off and start fresh." Landon repeats the same procedure with the butter and the batter, and considers apologizing and promising to pay closer attention, but the look in Quentin's eyes stops him.

"Time to flip," Quentin says. Landon slides the spatula under the first pancake with one purposeful movement—"Like you mean it, Landon," Quentin coaches—and flips the pancake, uttering one long prayer the whole heart-stopping moment it's in the air.

They stare at the exposed side. Landon flinches.

"Turn the heat down," Quentin says, and Landon can tell he's trying to stay patient but between the horrible sabotage from Rory and that only Landon can cook their food, it's impossible to miss that his frustration is mounting.

"I'm going to finish the raspberry syrup," Quentin says and heads back over to the hell contraption with the food processor in hand. Landon glances up briefly to watch him go, then refocuses on their pancakes. He's screwed up enough today; they can't afford more lapses of concentration.

Landon, without Quentin to distract him, focuses solely on the pancakes, making sure to flip them accurately and when all the bubbles have burst in the middle. He works for the last few minutes and nearing the end of their time limit, has a full plate to deliver to Quentin.

Thankfully, Quentin has managed to use the food processor without any accidents, and as the assistants take away the diabolical prep station, he finishes straining the sauce.

Quentin has just enough time to plate the pancakes and to artistically drizzle on the syrup, then to dust the top with powdered sugar.

When the timer buzzes indicating the thirty minutes is up, Landon doesn't think or even hesitate. He feels like he's been close to throwing up for the full time, and all he feels is relief that it's over. He flings his arms around Quentin and squeezes hard. He doesn't care that they're covered in sweat and unidentified food gunk or that they spent the last half of that challenge being the team that gets pissed at each other. All he feels is bliss that they've made it through with a full, delicious-looking plate of food to show for it.

It isn't until Landon pulls away that he remembers there's a camera on them. And that hug was pretty obvious. It's impossible to know if their impromptu embrace will make the final cut, but Landon has a feeling it will.

His stomach winds into tighter and tighter knots as the judging trio makes their way down the line of plates. This week they're near the end, and Landon doesn't think he can take the pressure.

He doesn't even care if the camera records it. Shamelessly, he reaches out and grabs Quentin's hand, using the reassuring weight of it to ground him.

Simone, Jasper and Zach start with Reed and Diego. Landon is still bitter over what happened last week and has zero compunction about half-sneering as the judges take small, speculative bites of the English breakfast they've prepared.

"I'll confess, first, I love beans, but I don't get them for breakfast," Zach says and Landon can't help but agree.

"Beans in an English breakfast is rather *de rigueur*," McDonnell explains and Zach just laughs. "I know," he says. "But so weird to me. They're delicious regardless."

Landon goes from a half-sneer to a full sneer. He's totally allowed to be competitive, okay?

"The eggs are a bit overcooked," Simone points out. "And I would've liked a bit more of a crisp on the bacon and sausage. But overall, well done."

Landon glares as the judges move on and he sees Diego and Reed turn to each other with success and happiness. He would give *anything* for him and Quentin to be able to do that after the judges taste their pancakes.

The next group up is Oliver and Nora. Nora spent all that money on the campfire, and it's no surprise that with their only sabotage being that Nora had to cook their food, there's nothing seriously wrong with their French toast.

"One side of this looks a bit overcooked and the other a bit undercooked," Zach says apologetically. "But the flavor is delicious. I especially like the hint of nutmeg, and what else is that?"

"Rum," Oliver confirms. "I like to think of this as my eggnog French toast. Perfect for the holidays."

"Delicious," Zach comments, and Landon can't help it, he's growing even more nervous.

Good for him, Jeff and Jessa are up next and their tiny skillet of potatoes and eggs looks really depressing. If Landon isn't mistaken, he can even see a bit of a char on their food. Things are not looking good for them.

"This is burned," Simone says pretty matter-of-factly.

"I'd really like to have more food here," Jasper explains. "When I make breakfast for my kids, they'd eat about ten of these tiny little skillets."

Really, that's all that needs said. Landon just prays that their pancakes are just *slightly* better than Jeff and Jessa's skillets. His attitude feels so far from how they began, but at this point, he only wants to stay in the competition. He doesn't want to get kicked off like this, after barely speaking to Quentin through the round.

The trio of judges stop in front of Landon and Quentin's station. Landon's heartbeat is careening wildly in his chest.

"Pancakes," Quentin says politely. "With raspberry syrup."

"The color is so beautiful," Zach observes as he digs into his portion.

"Pancakes are a bit dry and a bit eggy," Simone says. Landon's heart feels like it skips a bit.

"Overall, pretty good," Jasper finishes up and suddenly they're moving on and nothing horrible and awful happened. Nobody even made a face.

Landon feels some relief, and from the way Quentin's hand squeezes his, he knows he does too, but he won't feel completely safe until it's announced they haven't been eliminated.

It doesn't help that the judges go wild over the next pair. "What a gorgeous omelet," McDonnell raves. "A perfect example of a classic French omelet." Landon has no idea how Carson was able to pull out a perfect omelet out of his ass, but it doesn't seem fair. Even though he *does* like Carson.

Rory and Kimber are up next.

"Steak and eggs," Rory explains.

"My steak is pretty well done," Zach says, picking at his. "I usually like a more rare portion."

"Mine's alright, I suppose," Simone comments. "But a more consistent preparation is probably something you should work on."

"A lot of wonderful food today," Alexis says. "As is popularly said, breakfast is the most important meal of the day." She pauses and the tension in the room seems to grow. "Today, in third place, we have Rory Dargan and Kimber Holloway. Second, Oliver Glines and Nora Hsu. First, Paul Flannery and Carson Brooks."

Landon feels very little surprise at the announcement. He knew they were a huge longshot for a placement this week. That doesn't mean it doesn't hurt. Especially considering how much they both wanted to win this week.

"That leaves three pairs that are available for elimination. Landon and Quentin, Jeff and Jessa, and Reed and Diego."

Landon feels Quentin take a deep breath next to him. As hard as this is for Landon, he can't even imagine how hard this must be for Quentin. This is his dream of his own bakery. Landon's career is already well on its way to being fixed. Quentin still needs all the help he can get.

"Landon and Quentin—the judges thought your pancakes were a little dry and overcooked. Jeff and Jessa—your skillets were small and the contents were burned. Reed and Diego—inconsistent cooking of the eggs and meat on your offering."

Alexis pauses again and Landon wants to scream.

"Safe are Diego and Reed."

Landon's pulse rabbits. That means it came down to them and Jeff and Jessa. He can only pray that burned is worse than dry.

"And eliminated today, Jeff and Jessa. Sorry, guys."

It takes a long moment for Landon to realize that it's not their name that Alexis called. It's not their names and by some sort of miracle, even though they pushed their chances to the very edge, they're *safe*. They're not leaving. Quentin's dream is still intact.

Landon's knees sag in relief and he's about to turn to Quentin when a big, strong pair of arms wraps him up and lifts him off the floor. It's instinct but he just wraps his legs around Quentin's waist and lets Quentin cart him around the kitchen like they've just won, not that they barely didn't get eliminated.

And if he whispers into Quentin's shoulder that he loves him, it doesn't matter because nobody can hear him.

CHAPTER NINE

Of course, Quentin apologizes the moment they're alone in their green room.

"God, Landon, I'm so sorry," he murmurs into the curve of Landon's neck as they embrace again. Landon doesn't think his heart has really slowed down yet, and it's all he can do to hang on to Quentin as he holds him close and tight.

"It's not your fault," Landon insists, even as his heart continues to race. He can't believe they came so close to losing it all over something as silly as a lazy Susan prep table and pancakes.

"It just was *so hard* to stand there and just watch, when it was *my* bakery on the line."

Landon nods his head in commiseration but he can't help but think there's an unspoken *and you can't cook,* at the end of that sentence.

It's the plain and bitter truth, but it still hurts.

Not only does Landon desperately want Quentin to win so he can launch his own bakery, he knows that he and Quentin have yet to really talk about what's going on between them. He doesn't think Quentin would disappear out of his life if they were no longer dependent on *Kitchen Wars* to keep them together, but Landon worries anyway.

Landon will often wake up to a text from Quentin. A picture of whatever he's baking or a cute emoji or even a simple "good morning"—and every single morning it's enough to put a smile on Landon's face as he drags his lazy butt to the kitchen for coffee.

They'll text throughout the day and Landon has taken to sending him tiny little snippets of songs—though he's *always* careful to make sure none of the lyrics are obviously about Quentin, even though so far the majority of the album seems Quentin-inspired. Landon regularly ignores Julian's knowing smirk at all the blue eyes that have appeared in the lyrics he's written over the last few weeks.

They've gone on less than ten dates yet somehow Quentin has claimed an undeniably permanent part of Landon's life. So logically, Landon *knows* Quen isn't going anywhere, but his heart still stutters at even the tiniest fraction of a possibility that he might. Especially if it was Landon's fault they were eliminated.

"You're not mad?" Landon asks when they finally pull away from each other. Landon can't seem to unglue his gaze from Quentin's face. He hopes if Quentin notices, he'll chalk it up to the near miss they just experienced.

"Of course I'm not mad!" Quentin exclaims. "The pancakes were *dry*. That's not even on you, that's on *me*. You have nothing to feel bad about. I'm the one who should be sorry."

Quentin leans in and rests his head back on Landon's shoulder. He's got inches on Landon, but he can also make himself small. Like he needs Landon's comfort and nobody has *ever* needed him for that before.

"I'm going to go grab a quick shower," Landon says after a long moment. His heart has finally stopped racing, and now he just feels vaguely sick. All that adrenaline curdling in his stomach.

As Landon showers, he's surprised at how much he wishes they could just go back to his place and cuddle on the couch. He's never felt less like going to a party.

He's fixing his hair in the mirror when Quentin walks out, towel wrapped around his narrow waist. Quentin drops the towel nonchalantly, and suddenly cuddling isn't all Landon can think about. He stares in the mirror, his eyes glued to Quentin's cock, hard and red, brushing up against his belly. It makes his mouth water and his insides melt into mush and *how are they going to make it through the next five hours.*

Landon glances up, and his eyes catch Quentin's in the mirror. Quentin's watching Landon as Landon watches him. His insides go from mush to lava and his hand is trembling as he reaches up to smooth down his bangs.

"We . . .uh . . . I . . . uh . . ." Landon stumbles. He doesn't have enough blood in his head right now to sound remotely coherent.

"I'll wait outside," he finally gets out and he escapes the room, tugging at the tight collar of his shirt because *god*, how did it get so warm so quick?

He'd think it was only him, but when Quentin emerges, his cheeks are flushed and his lips are bitten raw. Landon straightens his shoulders and tells himself that if they can make it through the party without fucking in the bathroom, they deserve an award.

They take a cab to the restaurant where Rory works, which has been closed for the night. Quentin sidles up tight against Landon and when his big hand settles high and hard on Landon's thigh, Landon clears his throat and tries to imagine that it hasn't just turned into the Sahara desert.

"You okay?" Quentin asks softly. There's so much care in his voice and it amazes Landon because he's never had the kind of moment with someone like he had with Quentin in the green room *and* had them care about him, too. It's raw sexuality tempered with what Landon hopes might be love.

He's surprised, but he's actually not lying when he snuggles closer to Quentin and looks up at him with stars in his eyes. "I'm good," he says. "*Great*, in fact."

⁂

Rory's restaurant is a great barn of a place, all exposed rafters and brick and rustic furniture. Quentin shrugs at Landon's questioning look when they walk in. "It's supposed to be 'barnlike.' Don't ask. I try not to."

There's a DJ set up in the corner, playing music softly, and several groups of people clustered through the big open room. They head to the bar where Rory is unsurprisingly holding court. "Quen!" Rory exclaims, moving so fast to embrace Quentin and then Landon that he's really surprised that beer doesn't slosh over the rim of his glass. "Let's get you drinks."

"This place is something else," Landon says to Rory as Quentin deals with the bartender.

"It's a little much," Rory shrugs, "but I can still grill you a steak that'll make you weep."

Quentin places a glass in Landon's hand and he glances down to find, to his surprise, a vodka soda, his usual drink of choice. There's even a sliver of lime balanced on the rim of the glass, *exactly* the way he likes it. He takes an experimental sip and even the brand of vodka is right.

He shoots Quentin a thankful glance, but he doesn't really understand. He's nearly certain they've never talked about Landon's cocktail of choice before.

"Maybe we'll have to come to dinner here sometime," Landon says. He wants to imagine a future with Quentin where they have the time and opportunity to go on dinner dates like any normal couple would.

"I heard Quentin already took you to *Sur Ma Langue.*" Rory makes an expressive face and Landon can't help but laugh out loud.

He's funny, this friend of Quentin's. Even if he's just tried to oust them from the competition. "Very posh of you, Quen."

Quentin just shrugs. "I like to make a good first impression."

Rory throws back his head and downright *cackles*. Landon doesn't understand what's so hilarious. He takes another sip of his drink and prides himself on absolutely *not* choking on it when Quentin's hand settles firm and warm against his back. Like they're here together. Like they're *dating*. Which, Landon is pretty sure they are, but they haven't actually discussed it so he doesn't want to assume.

"Oh, I bet you do." Rory turns to Landon. "You wouldn't believe how ridiculous Quentin was for you when you were on *The Voice*. Never missed an episode. Followed your Twitter. Even had to talk him out of going to try to catch you like all the other fan girls a few times."

Landon doesn't know what's more surprising: Rory's story or the way Quentin's hand tightens on his back as Rory tells it.

"Oh, that's . . ." Landon is legitimately floundering for words. He had no idea Quentin felt that way about him back then. It's reassuring somehow, and nice, and also not at all what he was expecting to hear.

"It's most definitely weird," Quentin inserts, and he doesn't sound happy at all. "Thank you, Rory, for making me sound like a creep."

"Oh, Quen, it's cute. Honestly. I bet Landon thinks it's endearing. Right, Landon?"

Landon turns to Quentin. There's apprehension in his eyes, but they fade as Landon gives him the warmest smile he can. "It's fucking adorable," Landon says softly and the rest of the fear disappears from Quentin's face.

"You two are absurd," Rory chuckles. "Gonna go make the rounds. Have fun and don't do anything I wouldn't."

"What wouldn't he do?" Landon asks as they wander over to an appetizer station. He picks up a beef skewer and nibbles at it.

Quentin laughs. "Not much, honestly."

He hands his drink to Landon and he holds their glasses while Quen fills their plates. Landon doesn't even have to explain what food he wants, because Quentin is already two steps ahead of him. They head towards one of the tall tables scattered with candles.

"I had a feeling," Landon confides across the table, enjoying Quentin's conspiratorial smile in the candlelight.

"Hey, isn't that Rory's partner? Kimber, I think her name is?" Quentin subtly nods towards a tall, slender girl with blond hair that's on her own, awkwardly standing at a similar table. "Maybe we should go talk to her."

Landon ignores the pulse of disappointment that it won't be just the two of them because she looks so very alone. He scans the crowd, but doesn't see Rory. The decision is an easy one. He picks up his drink and Quen trails behind.

"Hey, you mind if we crash?" Quen asks softly and the girl's gaze jerks up from where she's been minutely examining the tablecloth.

"Um, no, of course not, but *why?*" Kimber stutters out.

Landon loves Quentin for so many reasons, but the big, reassuring smile he gives her is high up on the list. "There's lots, but we'll start with, *I'm a huge fan*," he says. "Saw you swim in the Olympics in Rio a few years ago."

Her own smile is swift and brightens her whole face. "You mean, you read the story about me and my mom," she teases, suddenly looking nothing like the tablecloth-gazing wallflower.

"That too," Landon inserts apologetically, because now that she's brought it up, he can't believe he forgot about it. Of course, that was the summer he was going out of his mind in Wisconsin, desperate to get out and do *something* with his life. He remembers reading about Kimber Holloway and her mother—the battle that had raged in the headlines, mother versus daughter, and the arguments over who should really be making Kimber's decisions. At the time he'd been stupidly envious. A mother who *wanted* something for her child, while Landon's mom didn't seem to have the slightest interest or understanding in anything he did. "You went to school, then?" Quentin asks, even as Landon is trying to yank himself back to the present, as far away from Wisconsin as he could get.

"I did." She nods. "I went to Stanford. Graduated last year."

"And now you're doing *Kitchen Wars*," Quen says.

"It seemed like a better idea than training for an Olympics I didn't want to swim in," she admits with a wry smile that doesn't quite reach her eyes. She has kind eyes, soft and brown. Landon wants to like her, even if he doesn't understand her. Even if they're radically different.

"I have to tell you," Quentin says, and Landon is a little confused how and when this conversation grew so serious. "But you inspired me to leave home and go to culinary school even though my parents couldn't understand why I'd waste my time baking for a living."

"I didn't do anything special, but thank you," she says graciously.

If Landon is being very honest with himself, he's still envious of Kimber Holloway. Quentin might have mentioned his less-than-supportive parents, but he's never told Landon this particular story. Of course, when would they have had the time? Their lives are crazy busy, they barely have time to take a breath, never mind for long, drawn-out confessions.

Landon isn't proud of it, but he changes the subject. "You have a boyfriend? Girlfriend?"

Kimber shakes her head no, but Landon absolutely does not miss the way her gaze flits over the crowd and settles on a blond head that's carrying two beers back from the bar. Rory is headed this way.

Well, Landon thinks, *I'm not the only one with a big fat crush on their partner.*

"Kimber!" Rory exclaims as he sets the second beer down in front of her. "Look who I found you with." He's flushed and Landon makes a mental reminder to definitely pick Quentin's brain later about this matchmaking opportunity.

"Let's dance," Quentin murmurs to Landon. Landon can't help but beam up at him. There's a bunch of couples already on the floor, the room has filled up quickly while they were talking to Kimber. It's easy to get lost in the crowd as Quen leads him.

It's a slower jam and Quentin's hands settle inexorably on Landon's hips, warm and big and practically spanning his waist. Landon moves his hips a little experimentally and he can feel Quentin's fingers dig into his jeans. It's a heady feeling, knowing without a single doubt that as worked up as Landon is by Quentin, Quentin is just as worked up by Landon and at the end of the night, they're going to go home and unleash all this pent-up energy in the bedroom.

If they make it home first, Landon corrects himself.

Quentin doesn't have great rhythm but Landon more than makes up for it and it only takes a few moments for them to move together like they've never been apart. Landon throws his head back and groans a bit. He can feel Quentin's breath hot on his neck, and when he brushes his lips across the nape, they're even hotter.

The slower song segues into something faster and more intense and Landon twists in Quentin's hands, facing him and running his own palms up Quentin's shirt, feeling the insistent fluttering of Quentin's heart. His eyes are intent, staring at Landon like he desperately wants to memorize every molecule of Landon's mind and his body.

"You're beautiful," Landon murmurs, reaching up to catch just the corner of Quentin's lips with his own. Quentin pulls back, startled and eyes growing wild.

"Not yet," he mouths over the loud music. Landon thinks he understands. If they kiss now, there's no way they'll make it home. As it is, there's about a ten percent chance it'll happen, and Landon wants it all, wants way more than just a quick fuck in the bathroom.

Landon crowds right into Quentin's space, can practically count the palest freckles on his nose. It still doesn't feel close enough, but it's going to have to do too. Landon tangles his fingers into the curls at the back of Quentin's neck and smirks at the low groan he makes.

They take a break after another few songs to quench their thirst, and Rory shows up briefly at the bar to egg them into doing shots. Neither of them put up much of a fight, and then they melt back into the crowd.

They're both definitely a bit tipsy and any compunction either of them seemed to have before about being too handsy has disappeared completely. Landon dimly realizes that he's grinding against Quentin's firm thigh and it feels so amazing he really can't find it in himself to care. Quentin's hands have crept lower and lower on his backside, until they're hovering right over the curve of his butt. Landon wants it so much he doesn't even care if anyone sees. He rises up and whispers right into Quentin's ear. Pleads, practically. "Do it," he purrs, and Quentin's fingers bite down hard and unrelenting and Landon groans at how good it is.

"Good boy," Landon says and settles back to watch Quentin's reaction. It's immediate and electric. His eyes blink once, then twice, and then there's only one hand on his ass and the other is wrapped around Landon's wrist and tugging him insistently to the edge of the dance floor and then heading towards a corridor.

Landon stops in his tracks, despite the grip that Quentin has on his wrist, when he sees the sign that indicates this is the direction of the bathrooms. Yes, his cock is hard and it's been hard for way too long, but he isn't so far gone that he's willing to settle for a quickie when he could have a nice long fuck in a bed.

"Wait," Landon whines. And yes he does absolutely whine. "Not the bathroom."

Quentin gives him a sweet, lopsided smile. "Not the bathrooms," he confirms. "Rory's office."

There's a moment of hesitation. It's kind of not cool for Quentin to use his friend's office for a hookup. But then, Rory *did* sabotage them today. Did nearly oust them from the competition. Landon decides the payback is *just* enough.

The ferocity of Quentin's lust combined with that adorable smile is just about the last of what Landon thinks he can take. He's appallingly grateful when Quentin types some numbers into a keypad next to an unmarked door and ushers them into a dark room. There's the dark shadows of furniture and Landon has a split second to think it *might* be an office, before Quentin's on him, hands reaching for his cheeks, holding him still and steady and at the perfect angle to kiss him deep and dirty.

Landon whimpers into Quentin's mouth. He can't help himself. Kissing Quentin always feels like a sensory overload, but after the last few hours, his nerves are already strung so tight. Quentin's lips short-circuit them completely, leaving Landon limp and mindless, touching Quentin wherever he can, fingers coasting over smooth muscled planes of his back, tangling in his hair, moaning without a single care for anyone who can hear as Quentin rips his mouth away from Landon's and instantly attaches it to his neck.

Their desperation feels a bit reminiscent of the first time they slept together, when Landon thought he might explode if he wasn't able to touch Quentin, but now that he knows just how miraculous they are together, his need only feels greater.

Landon hopes that Quentin might feel the same way. The way his mouth coasts up his neck, nibbling on the tendon, tasting him, and his hands roam over every inch of him, Quentin certainly seems to want him just as much.

Quentin lifts his head and his voice is so rough, Landon's knees actually wobble a little. "Turn around," he says, and it's not a request. With anybody else, Landon might protest that he's not some little twink to be manhandled around, *thank you very much*, but with Quentin, it just feels natural. Like he's somehow unlocked something inside Landon that he never thought he even wanted.

So he turns around, pressing his hands on the flat wooden surface of what must be a desk. Quentin practically growls and Landon nearly growls back as he feels Quentin's hands go up to bracket his hips and he feels Quentin's mouth bite his butt through his jeans.

If Landon can stay upright, it's going to be a miracle.

"Beg," Quentin says. It's not so much of a demand as before, there's a tiny bit of wiggle room there, in his voice, and Landon knows that if he wanted to, he could take it. Or he could give in and beg the way he wants to and Quentin wants him to.

In the end, it's one of the easiest choices Landon has ever made. He begs.

"God, please, Quentin," he whines, "make me feel good. Make me come."

Quentin's hands reach around, unbutton and unzip his jeans, and slide them down to his ankles. Landon whimpers. He thinks he knows what's coming and it feels like both a nightmare but also a fantasy.

"This okay?" Quentin asks, his voice so low, Landon can barely hear it. That might also have something to do with the fact that Quentin's pulled down his pants and he's kissing and licking and nibbling the curve of Landon's butt. *Worshipping* it, really.

"Yes," is all Landon can get out.

"Your ass . . ." Quentin groans against his skin.

Landon's hands clench the desk edge so he won't just slide down onto the floor, a puddle of mush.

And then Quentin uses those big warm hands to spread his cheeks and Landon feels the first tentative lick of his tongue and thinking isn't an option anymore, Landon can only feel.

There's the gentle roughness of his tongue as Quentin slides it across the wet clench of his hole, the dizziness when he screws it in, opening him up. Landon thinks he must black out a little when Quentin slides a wet finger through his crack and teases mercilessly against where his tongue is buried. It's too much and Landon sobs a little, overwhelmed and in love and not even sure he's speaking words anymore. There's just tiny whimpers and moans and sounds that might have been English at some point, but he's long lost the thread. He only needs Quentin. Quentin's what makes sense of this world. Quentin's lips and his tongue and his fingers.

Quentin bumps him and his cock, beyond painfully hard, hits against the edge of the desk and Landon nearly screams. It hurts and it feels good, feels amazing, even. If only because he got some friction finally.

The finger delves deeper into him, hitting his spot and Quentin chuckles at Landon's moan. "Yeah, baby," Quentin murmurs, "gonna make you feel so good."

"More," Landon manages to get out between sobs. "Yeah, more."

"Gonna come from my fingers and my tongue," Quentin croons, more of a statement than a question. Landon remembers the pleasurable sting of his cock hitting the edge of the desk and just nods, even though there's no possibility Quentin could see him. Quentin will know. Quentin *always* knows.

Another finger, insistent on his rim, tracing where he's already split open. Quentin soothes its entrance with spit and laves of his tongue. "Yeah, you like that," Quentin announces, so smug when Landon cries out at how good it is.

He's never told Quentin, he couldn't possibly know, but rimming always overwhelms him so completely and so easily, and he can come so easily from having his ass played with. Somehow Quentin *must* know this because he just expects Landon to come and so Landon does, the pleasure hot and insistent as it hits him hard. He spurts into his pants and clenches down tight around Quentin's fingers.

"So good," Quentin says with a rewarding little pat on his cheek. "Always good for me."

Landon's knees would give out then but Quentin must know because he's right there, bracing him from behind. With a start, Landon realizes that Quentin's pants are down too and his cock is out, hot and heavy and pushing up against Landon's bare ass.

"Gonna let me come all over you, won't you, baby," Quentin murmurs and again it's not even a question and Landon doesn't even care. Just feels blissed out from his orgasm and wants Quentin to feel as good as he does right now.

Quentin's cock slides so easily into his crack, wet with saliva and pre-come and all it takes is a few thrusts and Quentin's coming all over his shirt, the splatters hot and gooey on his bare skin.

"Fuck," Quentin swears, his voice low and trembling. He holds Landon there for a moment, come everywhere and then gently pushes him forward, making sure Landon's hands are grasping the edge of the desk. "Hold on and I'll clean us up."

He must know where the tissues are because he's back in a moment with handfuls of them and efficiently and quickly cleans them up.

Quentin's hands reach out and carefully unhook Landon's from the edge they've been gripping. "You're all good," he says, and his voice is lighter. Happier. Like whatever they've done has made Quentin as relaxed as it's made Landon.

Landon pitches forward a little and buries his face in Quentin's neck. He can't believe they just did what they did in Rory's office and he didn't protest even once. He can't even comprehend of how much Quentin just makes him forget everything he's ever cared about. His world narrows so completely whenever they're together, it's almost frightening.

"I know, I know," Quentin soothes, stroking his back with long, calming motions.

"I've never," Landon says, regaining a bit of his strength and pulling back so he can look into Quentin's eyes, "I've never done that before. Something like that."

Quentin's expression is solemn and careful. "Did you like it?"

Landon's smile is wry, he knows it is. "I think it was obvious I did."

Quentin reaches up to stroke Landon's cheek. "Landon, all I care about is if you *know* you liked it."

"I did," Landon confesses, and it doesn't feel nearly as hard as he thought it might be.

"I get a bit out of control with you, I think," Quentin says softly.

There's love burning in the back of Landon's mouth. "I do with you too."

Landon thinks he might say it, thinks he is nearly to the point of opening his mouth, as foolish as it might be, when Quentin pulls him close, wraps his arms around him and the spell is suddenly broken. Landon doesn't feel so compelled to confess his love if Quentin's eyes aren't trying to tempt it out of him.

CHAPTER TEN

LANDON AND QUENTIN ARE puttering around Landon's apartment the next afternoon, the day lazy and slow, consisting of them eating cereal in bed, taking a long, hot shower together, and then promptly returning back to bed to snuggle, when Landon's phone rings. He doesn't really want to answer it but it's Ian's special ring—he programmed it when Landon kept ignoring his calls. Landon doesn't want to tell him that "Call Me Maybe" doesn't really convince him any more to answer it, but the shrill blast certainly makes Ian tougher to ignore.

Ian forgoes a greeting and steamrolls right into the business at hand.

"You and Quentin are doing a big interview this week," Ian says. "One of the biggest morning shows in LA."

"Great." Landon doesn't even bother sounding enthused. He isn't the biggest fan of interviews in general, and morning show interviews are typically awful—full of fluff and nothing of substance.

It hits him then; not only is he not going to have to falsify something exciting, he's not going to have to *lie* about how good his love life suddenly is. He perks up right as Ian lets out a frustrated groan.

"No. You're the *only* pair that was selected to do this interview," Ian enunciates. Slowly. Like Landon hasn't been doing this for years.

Landon is a bit stunned. He knew they were doing well in the competition, despite not having a win under their belt, and he knows they're probably pretty fun to watch, but *the only pair*.

Quentin's gazing over at him like he doesn't understand anything. Landon switches his phone on speaker. "Tell Quentin what this means," Landon demands.

"It means you're gonna get a really good edit," Ian explains.

Quentin still looks confused. "It means that we're going to do *really* well," Landon murmurs to Quentin, bumping their shoulders together and not even trying to hold back his brilliant smile.

"Really well," Ian repeats.

Landon manages to tear his eyes away from Quentin's. They're gorgeous in this half-light, glowing and ethereal and so fucking happy, Landon never wants to look away. He re-focuses on the phone call because he very clearly understands now why Ian was so excited about this. "So this interview . . ."

He doesn't even get partway through his sentence before Ian is barking out requests. "Don't confirm, don't deny, play it super coy. You know how, Landon. And all they really need to do is catch the way Quentin looks at you, and it'll all be crystal."

Landon looks over at Quentin and he's blushed bright red. "Also try to get something in about your new music," Ian instructs. "The articles about your signing should hit Monday-ish, so it'll be a great time to talk about it. Mention a few of the songs." There's a meaningful pause and Landon understands exactly what Ian means. He's supposed to hint at the truth—that he's essentially writing an album full of love songs about Quentin. It's Landon's turn to blush, because *he's writing an album full of love songs about Quentin.* It won't be difficult not to reveal too much, because Quentin still can't know.

"Landon, your stylist is going to send over an outfit. I want you to *wear it*, okay? And Quentin, she'll send something over for you too."

Quentin opens his mouth, and Landon is sure he's about to protest. "Yes and yes," Landon inserts quickly before Quentin can. Quentin frowns.

Ian gives a few more sets of instructions, and tells Landon he'll email over the details.

After the call, Landon doesn't feel like he can stay in bed. His blood is fizzing with excitement and he feels light as a feather.

But Quentin's definitely still on earth, in fact, he doesn't look nearly as excited as Landon feels. Not even close.

Landon burrows into Quentin's neck. "What's wrong?" he asks softly, wrapping his arms about Quentin's waist and sending them on a controlled fall backwards into the nest of pillows Landon had gathered for them.

Quentin is quiet for a long moment. Fear begins to grow deep in Landon; Quentin has never, ever shut him out before. With how well everything's been going between them, he really doesn't want them to start moving backwards just when Landon was really beginning to hope that Quentin loved him too.

"I hate interviews," Quentin admits lowly. He laughs, but it doesn't sound like he finds anything actually funny. "I know, it's stupid. This is a great thing. But I don't want to fuck it up for you."

"For us," Landon insists, squeezing Quentin tighter. "And you couldn't possibly. If I haven't managed to fuck up any of our dishes yet, I can't imagine you messing up an interview. Maybe pretend like it's just us talking together."

"Just us talking," Quentin repeats.

"Just us talking," Landon reassures him.

❦

"I feel ridiculous," Quentin complains, as he stares in the mirror at the brightly colored shirt he's wearing. "Like a parrot."

"A gorgeous parrot," Landon insists loyally, coming up behind him to give him a quick hug, giving no shits about wrinkling the Gucci silk shirt.

"It feels nice, though," Quentin admits.

Landon reaches over and tweaks another button undone. Some of Quentin's tattoos are now exposed and he looks a bit surprised. "What?" Landon asks with a smug smirk. "You look *hot*."

Quentin looks back at himself in the mirror. "I don't know, I've never worn anything like this before. I stick to t-shirts mainly. No need and no budget for anything fancier, really." And he doesn't have to add, he doesn't like to draw this much attention to himself. Landon has spent the last few weeks discovering that as much as Landon loves the spotlight, Quentin shies away from it.

"Mainly I would agree with you," Landon says. "The stylist is pretty useless most of the time. I ignore about ninety percent of what she sends over. *But* she did good with you."

"It *is* soft," Quentin says so quietly, his eyes intent on his image in the mirror. "And it's got such beautiful colors."

"Beautiful colors for a beautiful person," Landon can't help but say. He might care about what sort of feelings his words give away, but not right now, not when Quentin is staring in the mirror, trying to decide if he feels confident enough to give a television interview wearing this shirt.

Quentin turns back to Landon, a brilliant smile breaking over his features. "You look gorgeous too, you know," he says.

Landon glances down at the Givenchy t-shirt his stylist sent and his favorite pair of black jeans. He figures wearing half of what she sent was keeping to the promise he made to Ian.

"I'll do." He shrugs.

Quentin reaches back and slides a big palm into the back pocket of Landon's tight-fitting jeans. He squeezes a bit possessively and Landon's mouth instantly goes dry.

Of course that's when there's a brisk knock on the door. Quentin barely gets his hand out before the door opens. Ian walks in and rolls his eyes. "I leave you alone for *five* minutes," he complains, but there's that particularly bright look in his eyes today—the one Landon always associates with pride at one of Landon's accomplishments.

That doesn't stop Quentin from flushing.

"You two ready to go?" Ian asks. Landon can't help but notice that Ian's eyes are almost primarily resting on Quentin. After all, he's the rookie here; Landon could probably do this kind of interview in his sleep.

"All good," Landon answers for both of them.

They move quickly through makeup and getting miked up. They meet Allison, their interviewer, who has kind eyes and a warm smile. Quentin relaxes a bit when he sees Allison, and even more when they start chatting about their favorite places to eat in LA.

By the time they take their seats and the camera starts rolling, Landon is positive they're going to ace this.

"Tell me about *Kitchen Wars*," Allison asks and Landon has to give her major props, she sounds like she *actually* wants to know.

"It's an instrument of torture," Landon explains, all straight face and deadpan voice.

Quentin lets out a huge belly laugh, literally just throws his head back and cackles, like Landon is the funniest person on earth. It's a pretty good feeling, if Landon is being honest.

"Landon Patton, I heard you were a tease," Allison says back with a sparkling smile.

Landon opens his mouth to say something clever and witty, but before he can speak, Quentin jumps in. "You have no idea," he says, and Landon can *feel* his knowing smirk.

Well. Ian *did* say to play it coy and not exactly deny it.

Allison raises an eyebrow. "So you both enjoy being tortured?" she asks.

"Personally," Quentin jumps in again, and Landon is so proud, he's sure he's beaming all over this damn uncomfortable couch, "I signed up because I would love to own my own bakery. Getting Landon as a partner is the real prize though."

"And you, Landon?"

"Oh, you know me, I was just sitting around and thought *hey*, why not do a competitive cooking show? Because I love to cook and all."

"Don't you?"

Landon makes a face and shakes his head. "I'm the worst," he confides, leaning forward a bit. He can work a camera blindfolded. "I feel sorry for poor Quentin here, saddled with someone who can't cook to save their life."

"Is this true, Quentin? Landon can't cook?"

Quentin frowns. "That's actually the best part about *Kitchen Wars*, it helps teach the celebrity to cook. Without Landon picking up some culinary skills over the last few weeks, we'd have been sunk. Could he cook when he started? Not really. But he's learned and caught on really well."

Allison's smile is cat-got-the-cream personified. "Sounds like you're a big fan of his, Quentin."

"Ever since he was on *The Voice*, if I'm being honest." Quentin sounded a bit ashamed of this fact at Rory's party, but today, he just owns it, pride bursting from his voice. Landon can't help it; he blushes. He can almost *feel* Ian's wildly-vacillating rage and excitement as this interview continues.

"So you feel like you're working well together, Landon?"

"We're awesome together," Landon says, and it's the complete truth. He's never been part of such a tight team before. They truly are the Dream Team. He believed they might be back when he first met Quentin, but nothing could have really prepared him for the certainty he feels now.

"Absolutely bananas," Quentin echoes.

Landon giggles. *Why is Quentin so damn cute?*

"Landon, I hear you're back in the studio," Allison says, shifting directions.

"Yeah, I am. With Epic Records. Very excited to be with them. And I've already started recording my new album."

"Anything you can tell us?"

Landon hesitates for a split second. Ian *did* say to hint and to play it coy, and he absolutely doesn't want for Quentin to find out about the album before he's ready to tell him. However, Landon feels like he just can't help himself anymore. He's been holding all this in and some of it was bound to come out at some point.

"It's about falling in love," Landon says, and he knows he's got that sweet Quentin smile on his face. "Falling in love with someone special."

"I can't wait to hear it. It *sounds* special." Allison's knowing grin tells Landon that she understands exactly what—or *who*—he's talking about.

Allison wraps up the interview and it's over. Done. And probably the most appallingly obvious thing Landon has ever participated in.

He doesn't know whether to be excited or ashamed.

Allison shakes their hands and thanks them for such a great interview. "I'll be rooting for you two to win," she says with a twinkle in her eye. "You're a very cute couple. Positively sickening, honestly."

Landon freezes a bit, which is massively ironic, because on the couch, during the actual filming he was as relaxed as he's ever been on camera. But now, he's confronted with someone who thinks they know what's going on and he has no idea what to say. Deny it because he and Quentin have never actually discussed whether they're "together"? Or should he admit it? Landon doesn't know and before he can figure it out, she's already moving on, leaving him standing there, fish mouthed and brainless.

Quentin is quiet when they get back to the dressing room, carefully unbuttoning and hanging up the Gucci shirt, shrugging on his own t-shirt and jacket and getting his things together to leave.

Landon frets, postponing actually leaving by fooling around with his own bag far longer than is truly necessary. He's both dreading and hoping that Quentin will just say something and put him out of his misery.

"Why did you freeze back there?" Quentin asks, and his voice is more wary than accusatory.

Landon still doesn't know what to say any more now than he did ten minutes ago. So he shrugs. Nice and non-committal.

"Did you not like her assuming we were together?" Again, Quentin seems more confused than upset, but Landon isn't taking any chances.

"I think most people will get that impression after watching that interview," Landon says.

"But her specifically," Quentin presses. Landon looks down, he can't actually meet Quentin's eyes when he's demanding answers and Landon has nothing to give him. "She was asking."

"I didn't really think so," Landon says, even though he's just flat-out lying by this point.

"I thought so." Landon glances up and there's a deep frown line between Quentin's brows.

"Did it bother you, her assuming we were together?" Quentin continues, clearly not going to leave it alone.

"Of course not," Landon admits. That much is certainly safe.

Quentin lets out a rather shaky sigh of what might be relief. "Well, then why didn't you just say we were, silly?"

Landon glances up in surprise. "Because we haven't talked about it?"

"I didn't think it was even really necessary to have a conversation," Quentin confesses, all shy voice and flushed cheeks. "I thought it was pretty obvious we were together."

Landon feels answering relief flood through him. "Oh thank god," he gets out.

Quentin flings his arms around him and holds him close. "You are so silly," he whispers in his ear. "I'm crazy about you, *boyfriend*."

I'm crazy about you isn't exactly the three words Landon was hoping for, but it's a really, really good start. He's not complaining.

Also, as they're leaving, he makes the time to quickly text his stylist and make sure that Quentin can keep the Gucci shirt. If he's going to be lucky enough to be Quentin's boyfriend, he's going to be the *best* boyfriend.

Landon waits until they're filming to present it to him. There's no way for Quentin to wear it while they're cooking, but he has an idea that maybe the shirt can be sort of a good luck charm—something they most certainly need. The competition is narrowing; every single pair left is stiff competition, and Landon is still not ready to lose.

Not now, not when they are so much closer to getting everything they both want.

Quentin's eyes when he opens the box are worth every bit of the argument Landon had to have with the stylist when she said she couldn't make it happen.

"This is too much," Quentin says immediately, even though his hands are already reaching out to stroke the soft silk.

"You're wrong," Landon insists. "It's honestly not enough, but I suppose it'll have to do."

Quentin's answering smile is bright enough to power a small city and his kiss is passionate enough that Landon is really disappointed when a knock on the door of their green room tells them it's time to film.

Quentin seems really relaxed even when Alexis walks out and the cameras start rolling.

"Last week," Alexis says thoughtfully, as if she's truly considering this, "we had breakfast. So it seems only fair that this week we should make dinner." She pauses, and Landon can't help but admire her dramatic effect. Kicks off her heels. Smiles and pulls the sharp-looking chopsticks out of her bun. Shakes her hair out. "A typical weeknight dinner. Whatever you'd normally throw together after a long day at work when you're hungry and don't feel like ordering in again."

Landon never gets tired of ordering in, but he can see from the thoughtful expression on Quentin's face that he understands exactly what Alexis is referring to.

"Today," Alexis continues, "we'll be doing our shop before any of our auction items. Sixty seconds, per usual. Off you go!"

Quentin grabs their grocery basket and heads off to the pantry at his usual quick clip. Landon watches with interest as he loads up their basket with what looks like a large amount of ingredients. When the minute is up, he heads back to their station, and Landon peers into the basket, not surprised to see a lean piece of meat, lots of fresh herbs, vegetables, potatoes, even rice. Quentin has prepared and then prepared again if they lose their ingredients or are otherwise sabotaged.

Except then Alexis opens her trap again and sends Landon's stomach to the floor. "Looks like great baskets. Too bad you're not going to keep them." She laughs a bit maniacally and Landon feels legitimately sick. "You're going to have to switch your basket with another team's basket. Everyone except for Reed and Diego that is, a perk of currently having the most money in the bank."

"Oh *please*," Quentin exhales under his breath. Landon feels similarly annoyed. He thought he was over the foil utensil debacle but he's really not.

Alexis calls out the pairs, and Quentin exchanges their awesome basket of ingredients with Carson and Paul. Quentin instantly goes digging through their new basket and Landon thinks from his thoughtful look as he peruses their new set of ingredients they're not so bad off. His sick feeling relents a little, but then Alexis calls for the first auction item.

Oh *yeah*, that fantastic experience wasn't even a real auction item. They *still* have those to go. Joy.

The show assistants wheel out a contraption that has Landon thinking of the lazy Susan prep table and hoping with every fiber of his being that they *do not* end up with it. It's a prep table attached to a diabolical invention—the stair stepper. Landon is proud of how muscular his legs and thighs are and even he doesn't want to put himself through that torture.

The bidding starts briskly and it's clearly between Nora and Carson right away. Landon can't say he's all that surprised. Neither Carson nor Paul are in the best of shape and he's sure that both of them dread ending up with that disaster of a prep station.

Carson wins the stair stepper with a bid of $6,200, the highest-priced auction item to be bought thus far, and as Landon looks down the line, everyone is a bit shell-shocked by the money that's suddenly being thrown around.

Unsurprisingly, Carson and Paul give the stair stepper to Nora and Oliver. No doubt their payment for driving the price up so high.

It comes as no additional surprise that the next auction item, a rounded dome of a pan with only the tiniest flat cooking surface, on which *everything* has to be cooked, goes for another high amount to Nora and Oliver, and they graciously bestow the pain right back to Carson and Paul.

Landon breathes out his own shaky sigh of relief. He and Quentin have new ingredients but they have no sabotages. No devilish prep tables or pans or anything else that will prevent them from getting eliminated. As long as they don't stab themselves in the back, they should be okay.

Alexis calls out the start of the cooking period, and Landon and Quentin start to unload their basket.

"How different is it from the things you got?" Landon asks, looking at similar ingredients to the ones he originally spotted in their basket.

"Very much the same, honestly," Quentin says. "Luckily I was going to go simple—meat, starch, veg."

"So what's the plan?" Landon asks, leaning over on the counter. Belatedly he realizes he's displaying his butt for all onlookers and he didn't even mean to. Quentin shoots him a hot look across the cutting board.

"Flank steak. Roasted potatoes and sautéed zucchini. I think I might do a blackberry sauce with these berries," says Quentin.

"I love blackberries," Landon admits.

"Then *definitely* the blackberry sauce," Quentin adds with a tiny smirk.

Quentin sets Landon to chopping up potatoes, while Quentin starts seasoning the steak, his arms whirling through the jars of herbs and spices, his movements resembling a mad magician. Landon is doing more boring chopping, but it also means he gets a front seat to the struggle that Carson and Paul are having over their horrible pan.

"I can't cook on this," Paul rages. Landon has never seen him rage before, but it's certainly an interesting look. It's also possibly a repeat of last week of Jeff and Jessa with the camp stove. Landon isn't exactly disappointed by this development. He really wants to be safe from elimination and he *really, really* wants to win.

Landon glances over the other way, and giggles inwardly at Nora panting not very attractively as she battles the stair stepper. It looks intense and he is more relieved than ever that he and Quentin didn't end up with that particular nightmare.

He finishes chopping the potatoes and Quentin seasons them quickly and throws them into the oven, roasting them with garlic, salt and pepper. Quentin then hands him a whole bunch of fresh parsley. Landon makes a face. "Am I just here for slave labor then?" he asks imperiously.

Quentin shoots him a smug look. "For your menial kitchen skills, darling, and for your glorious body."

Landon puts down the knife long enough to blow Quentin a very dramatic kiss. He sees the camera catch the whole exchange and can't help but think of the interview they gave this week and the edit they're almost certainly going to get.

He can't even say he's the slightest bit surprised or disappointed. He and Quentin have spectacular chemistry together and it would be a horrible waste for the producers not to take advantage.

After the parsley is reduced to a heap on their cutting board, Landon sidles up to where Quentin is heating up a grill pan on the stove. He shoots Diego and Reed a quick look, and returns his attention to Quentin. "Do you see what they're doing?" he asks, under his breath.

"I'm trying to ignore them," Quen says, and there's that annoyed edge to his voice again. Landon doesn't think Quentin is annoyed with *him*, but it's impossible to say for sure. "Can you open that bottle of red wine?"

Something Landon can do. He has the bottle of wine open in a minute, and Quentin pours it in with the blackberries, drizzling in honey and balsamic vinegar.

"Better if it could simmer for an hour," he huffs at the pan as he swirls it around.

They don't have an hour and Landon doesn't feel he needs to contribute this fact to the conversation. "What else can I do?" Landon asks because he hates feeling useless and because they don't have a weekly challenge that forces him to participate, it feels like Quentin is cooking the entire dish.

"Chop the zucchini?" Quentin suggests.

Being the sous chef sucks, but Landon will do it to win. As he carefully chops, he takes the opportunity to glance around the other kitchens.

Reed and Diego are making tacos. Rory and Kimber, some sort of soup. Oliver is stirring sauce on the stove while Nora sweats and forms meatballs. Carson and Paul have clearly stopped speaking to each other as Paul tries to cook a chicken breast on the smallest pan known to man. It'll be impossible to know where he and Quentin will fall until the judging begins, but his faith that Quentin is brilliant helps reassure him. They *can* do this. He feels even more certain when Quentin is done plating.

The meat fans out, succulent and juicy, drizzled with the bright red sauce. The vegetable sides piled carelessly but artistically. It's a gorgeous plate, and Landon feels the most confident so far as they head into judging.

The judges start with Oliver and Nora. They look even worse for wear than he or Quentin do, and Landon is not surprised because while Nora normally never looks anything less than flawless, she's spent the last thirty minutes climbing the stair stepper of death.

They've prepared spaghetti and meatballs. "Really tasty sauce," Zach says and goes in for another bite. Landon can't help but tense up. "You got a lot of layers of flavor in a short amount of time."

"Really beautiful plate of food," Jasper observes, "but I would have liked something green besides the parsley garnish."

Simone is silent, which Landon can't decide if that's better or worse.

The judges move on to Carson and Paul, and this time, Simone is the first to speak at the very small portion of chicken she was given and the odd way it's been prepared. "It's dry," Simone says skeptically, "and yet feels a trifle undercooked. I've never had overcooked and undercooked chicken at the same time."

Landon has to hide his smug smile. Nora doesn't hide hers at all.

It's clear that Paul and Carson were forced into preparing their dish this way because of the very tiny flat cooking surface of the pan they were sabotaged with.

Zach tries to give a compliment to the Dijon sauce on the side, but it's clear that unless anyone else's dish is worse, chances are not looking good for Paul and Carson.

Kimber and Rory are up next. Landon reaches out and grabs Quentin's hand. He knows the wonders Rory can create with meat. As it turns out, he didn't cook meat. And then Landon remembers that he didn't use his own ingredients. He was stuck with someone else's and he made. . . soup?

Simone frowns. "When you're tired and hungry from a long day, you take an *eternity* to make butternut squash soup? To build flavor layers at a time, then blend, then strain?" She looks absolutely skeptical, but Rory just shrugs.

The flavors are good, but not as developed as either Jasper or Zach would like. "You only had thirty minutes, man," Zach reprimands kindly. "Pick something to cook that's doable in that time limit."

Diego and Reed prepared pork tacos seasoned with spices and citrus. However, Jasper pokes around the plate and says, "I wish there were more sides to go with this dish. It feels a bit unfinished."

Simone nods. "A slaw or rice and beans. Something else besides the tacos."

Quentin and Landon's turn is last, and Landon's insides are curdling as Quentin tells the judges about their dish. "Rosemary flank steak with blackberry sauce," he says, "accompanied by roasted potatoes and zucchini."

Their dish looks more elegant than any other, and from the moment Zach cuts into the meat and doesn't even need the knife he's been provided with, Landon feels incredibly proud.

"This sauce is delicious," Zach exclaims, and takes another bite, and then another. "I'd love the recipe."

Simone nods. "Rosemary and blackberry aren't flavors I'd normally combine but it works perfectly here," she says. "Absolutely delicious."

Jasper doesn't comment, but considering he's eaten half his plate by the time they step away, Landon can't help but give a triumphant smile in Quentin's direction. They've done it; they've *finally* won.

All that's left to do is for Alexis to confirm what he already *knows* is true.

But first, there's the expected announcement that Carson and Paul have been eliminated. Carson looks disappointed but not really surprised to hear their name called out as the pair that will be leaving next.

"A valiant effort," Alexis says kindly, shaking their hands, and Landon thinks she's probably more right than truly kind. They did the best they could with what they had. He isn't sure he or Quentin could have gotten around the challenge of that pan.

"As for our winners, well, it's rather obvious, I think," Alexis says, shooting them an astonishingly fond look. "Quentin Maxwell and Landon Patton. Second place to Oliver and Nora. Third, Diego and Reed."

Landon always wondered what it would feel like to actually *win*. He feels like he's spent his whole life coming second or third. As it turns out, he's waited to win until the best possible time, because *nothing* could possibly feel better than winning with Quentin by his side. They feel like a team in the best sense of the word, and when Landon wraps his arms tightly around him, he tells him he loves him for the second time in two weeks, but this time he feels okay saying it a little louder.

Not loud enough that Quentin might hear, mind you, but a *little* louder. And some day, hopefully someday soon, Landon will feel comfortable saying it loud enough for Quentin to hear it all.

Chapter Eleven

THE INTERVIEW WITH QUENTIN and Landon airs Monday morning, and by Monday night, when Quentin comes over to Landon's apartment for dinner and some snuggling, Landon has personally gained about 10,000 new Twitter followers and Quentin's follower count has tripled. Landon knows from the frustrated emoji Quentin sent that he's not all that happy about it.

Landon is on the couch, attempting to sift through the massive pile of mentions he's gotten after a day at the studio, when Quentin walks in, carrying a bag of groceries. "Hey!" Landon exclaims as Quentin sets the bag down on the kitchen counter and comes back into the living room to give Landon a kiss. "I *do* have food, you know."

Quentin rolls his eyes, fondness radiating from every pore. "Snacks and cereal. I can't make dinner out of pretzels and Cheerios, Landon."

Landon lifts his face and accepts the kiss Quentin drops on his lips. "Hello to you, darling. Did you see that we're famous now?"

"You were already famous," Quentin calls out as he heads back to the kitchen.

Landon mumbles something to himself about YouTube culinary demonstrations and a few recorded karaoke videos he's dredged out of the abyss of the internet, but he doesn't say it loud enough for Quentin to hear. Even though Quen's his boyfriend now, he doesn't *ever* have to know the depths Landon sunk to during the height of his desperation for new Quentin Maxwell material.

He hears Quentin unloading bags in the kitchen, opening and closing the fridge, and then a startled gasp. "Landon! *Have you ever even turned this oven on?*"

Landon has to think for a long moment. He's a bit embarrassed at the answer. "No?" he calls out hesitantly.

"It's okay, it's gonna get a bit of a workout today," Quentin answers back. Landon can hear the smile in his voice and a tiny sigh of relief escapes him.

He's been thinking all day of what he wants to say in response to the attention he knew they'd get, but the amount is staggering and intense. It occurs to him suddenly as he's scrolling and he doesn't hesitate as he types out the tweet.

Love the excitement! he writes, **I'm pumped to tackle @KitchenWars with the greatest partner ever, @Quentin-Maxwell. #DreamTeam4Ever.**

By the time the pizzas are out of the oven and Landon is scrolling through Netflix looking for something good to watch as the food cools to a level that won't scorch their mouths, Quentin has time to glance at his phone.

"Landon," he says very seriously as Landon mentally debates *The Avengers* over the first episode of *Daredevil*—Quentin hasn't seen either, and Landon feels it's his civic duty to educate him—"Dream Team is trending on Twitter."

Landon drops the remote and picks up his phone, frantically scrolling to the Twitter app. "It is?"

"Worldwide," Quentin says and he's clearly in shock, because he must not be reading it right. Landon opens his app and is greeted by the exact same revelation. They have gone *global*.

It turns out, after some digging and Quentin reheating their pizza twice, what's actually happened is that Buzzfeed got ahold of the interview, a two-minute preview of *Kitchen Wars* in which apparently Landon and Quentin feature prominently and then the tweets they've made to and from each other. They gathered it all together into one article titled, "The Cutest Reality Show Couple Ever." Right now, it's the most popular article on their site and has started to be picked up by many, many media outlets.

Then Landon tweeted—and apparently, from what Landon can figure out from the tidal wave of info he's trying to wade through, to many people, Landon's tweet was a confirmation of all the speculation that Buzzfeed spent the day generating.

Quentin's head falls back on the couch. "I don't understand," he says. Unlike when they agreed to be together, he doesn't sound thrilled. He sounds terrified.

Landon's phone rings out shrilly. It's Ian. Of course, it's Ian. Landon debates quickly the pros and cons of putting his manager off while he and Quentin try to salvage what's left of their quiet night in.

Quentin's face is resigned as he glances over at the buzzing device on the coffee table. "You know he won't stop calling if you don't answer," he points out.

"I know, I know," Landon grumbles. But still his finger hesitates over the answer button. It's exciting to become this popular this quickly and it will certainly help both of their public profiles and it will absolutely contribute to the success of *Kitchen Wars*, but it's almost too much too fast.

The first thing Ian says when Landon picks up is, "Quentin needs a manager," and the conversation goes downhill from there.

Thirty minutes and another pizza reheating later, Landon and Quentin are finally off of the call with Ian and are debating whether it's a good idea for Quentin to also become Ian's client.

"I think there are a lot of positives," Quentin says between big bites of pizza. "Like he can work together on our PR. I can't imagine there would be much I'd want to really do separately, PR-wise, from you. Other than the bakery, of course."

Landon just shakes his head. Quentin's so smart, and a wonderful cook, but he's so naïve. "You're amazing," he says softly, "you can't even imagine how many people are going to come knocking on your door. And most of it won't have anything to do with me."

"I just want to open my bakery," Quentin keeps insisting. Landon cracks open a beer and chugs down half before calling Ian back.

"Quentin works tomorrow afternoon," Landon explains to Ian. "Come to my place and we'll talk contracts before he goes. Bring bagels."

Ian makes a grunt of assent.

"I want to state for the record that I wanted him to seriously consider different representation. At least *looking* at different options," Landon says, shooting Quentin an arch look. Quentin just smiles, because he really doesn't know what is going to happen shortly, but Landon does. Landon knows what it feels like when suddenly everyone wants you. He also knows what it feels like when everyone forgets you. The trick is trying to keep your balance somewhere in the middle.

Even after four years in the entertainment industry, Landon is still trying to figure out that technique

"I think that you'll be more than paranoid enough for both of us," Ian says with a chuckle. "He'll be fine. I promise. I'll take good care of him."

They make the final arrangements for tomorrow, and Landon hangs up, grabbing another piece of pizza to avoid looking at Quentin. He's never done that before. Not once since he's met him. Usually he can't look away.

"Landon," Quentin says softly, scooting closer on the couch until their thighs are touching and Quentin is cuddling into his side, "Ian will take good care of me. You trust him to take care of you, right?"

Landon doesn't know exactly how to say this—or if he should even say it at all—but it's one thing to make sure he has a manager who takes care of *him*. But Quentin? Quentin deserves more than that. Quentin deserves the very best. End of story.

"I do," Landon confirms after he chews and swallows. If the bite has trouble doing down, only he has to know about it. "Of course I do. He cares more than anyone else has before. But if we're both his clients, he might . . ." Landon clears his throat. The lump won't go away. It's definitely not pizza. "I'm worried he might try to use our relationship as PR."

"Would he do that?" Quentin asks. "I guess it's better than using a fake relationship for PR."

"It is," Landon says. He can't seem to shake the worry in his bones. Maybe it's the two years of fake relationships he had to endure before he came out—stupid stunts that were fake replicas of a real relationship. Maybe it wouldn't be so bad if their relationship, which is one hundred percent real, had a little light shown on it.

Landon thinks for a long moment, then continues. "What if we made sure to write boundaries into your contract? It wouldn't be in mine, but it would be in yours, and as long as we were together, nobody could force us to do anything."

Quentin nods slowly. "It'll be okay," Landon promises. "Ian *is* a good guy, as managers go. I was lucky to get him, honestly, and you'll be lucky too."

Quentin looks so trusting as he stares back at Landon. Landon also wants to believe his expression could also qualify as loving—and as a hypothesis, it's not so crazy, actually. "Would you mind if we wrote out a few things I want to make sure are priorities when we discuss the contract?" Quentin asks.

"Of course!"

Landon finds a copy of his contract on his laptop and they go over it until late, all thoughts of Netflix forgotten, writing down ideas of clauses that Quentin feels are important to him.

It becomes very clear that Quentin, while not being particularly creative in his search for a manager, is not going to be the type of client who simply lets things happen to him. The final list of requirements is not lengthy, but it is firm. Quentin is going to open his bakery. He wants to prioritize his PR commitments around the bakery and its opening in the near future. Everything has to come back to his business. He is not in this for personal glory. There is a point about relationships. Quentin wants to see all the offers that Ian gets. He wants to make his own choices, with advice from Ian. He is willing to let Ian manage him, but not *control* him. The distinction is so important and Landon is relieved that Quentin never had to learn the hard way how horrible it can be when someone else has complete control over your life.

By the time they fall in bed, Landon's concern is almost entirely dissipated and as they cuddle together under the covers, he thinks he's never been happier.

He always thought it was bullshit when well-meaning people insisted that going through tough times gave you perspective for the good ones, but he's surprised to find that the cliché is actually rather accurate.

They wake up to ringing phones. Landon ignores his (it's Ian) in favor of listening as Quentin answers his. It's the bakery, they are apparently inundated with crowds this morning, all clamoring for Quentin.

Quentin hangs up, still trying to process as he wipes the sleep from his eyes. "I guess I missed the part where the Buzzfeed article listed my place of work," he gripes. "They want me to come in and just make an appearance I guess, stroll behind the counter and look important while they sell out of every pastry in the case." He doesn't sound happy. This is the sort of personal glory that Landon is beginning to realize Quentin just doesn't revel in. But at the same time Landon isn't surprised at the request. It's what he would do if he happened to employ a baker of whom everyone suddenly wanted a piece of.

He *is* surprised a second later to hear banging on the door. Throwing on a t-shirt and sweatpants, he pads to the door to find Ian there, looking rather wild-eyed.

"My god, Landon," Ian spits out when he's finally let in. "You need to answer your fucking phone."

Landon looks at him dumbfounded. "It's two hours before you were supposed to be here," he points out.

"There is a mob of paps around your complex," Ian explains in a huff. "And I already got a call from the bakery. I guess it's a madhouse down there."

"Quentin just talked to them," Landon explains slowly as Ian takes his laptop out of his bag and sets up on the kitchen counter. "They want him to come in, I guess and pimp their pastries."

"He's not going anywhere," Ian said with an edge of pure satisfaction in his voice. "In fact, I think it's safe to say he's not going there again."

"What?" Landon squawks. "What did you do?""I acted in his best interests," Ian says patiently. "He doesn't need to be working for other people right now, he needs to be working for himself."

"That *is* the plan," Quentin says, walking into the kitchen. He's wearing sweatpants too, but he's not wearing a shirt and Landon wants to plaster himself to his front, even with Ian here. "Eventually."

Landon crosses his arms over his chest. "This isn't eventually," he points out.

"What's going on?" Quentin asks, glancing from Landon's aggressive pose to Ian, who looks like he's trying to keep a lid on his own temper.

"I spoke to the bakery this morning," Ian says carefully. "I broached the idea that it's not in your best business interests to bake every day for them right now. Appearances, maybe, but you have a lot of important things to get lined up to start your own bakery and working there isn't going to help you achieve that."

Quentin looks like he's trying to process this. Frankly, it's a fucking shit ton to process, and Landon is impressed that Quentin's doing as well as he is.

"So, you want me to quit."

Landon wants to applaud because at Quentin's words, a look of pure disgruntlement passes over Ian's face, like he just came to the realization that Quentin will be just as much of a pain in the ass as Landon is. Landon's look says, *did you really think I'd fall for him otherwise?*

"Not quit," Ian coaxes. "I don't want you to do the grunt work. Maybe make some appearances. Sign some autographs. Sell some pastries. Give some interviews that boost your old bakery's sales as well as help promote the new bakery. *Your* bakery."

Landon is impressed despite himself. Occasionally he'll have these blinding realizations of just how smart and manipulative Ian is, and honestly, those moments only make him love his manager more.

There's a furrow in Quentin's brow and he seems to be considering what Ian is proposing very seriously. As he should. These first few steps almost always seem to set a precedent for everything to come. Quentin needs to think about himself, first and foremost, while not alienating anyone who's helped him get where he is today. It's yet another balancing act, and it's one that Landon has struggled with.

"If I agree to this," Quentin points out, "I absolutely want to make certain that I do make those appearances and use this sudden popularity to help *them* as well as me. I won't shit on them. They gave me a job right out of culinary school and I wouldn't be on *Kitchen Wars* if I wasn't allowed to creatively express myself in the kitchen there."

"Of course, of course," Ian promises rapidly. "We'll arrange them today, if you want."

"What about today?" Quentin asks. "They called me. They want me to come in early."

"Today, unfortunately, isn't going to work. I've got some investors that I want you to meet with."

The furrow deepens. "I don't want to answer to anyone," he says stubbornly. "I want this bakery to be mine."

"And it will be yours," Ian reassures. "I just want you to meet with them. You could use some startup capital that isn't tied to the show, and they all have an excellent business track record. I think you could use their advice, at the very least."

Quentin leans back against the counter. His face has relaxed and so have his limbs. This feels more like the comfortable negotiation that Landon was expecting when he woke up this morning.

"LA's not cheap, particularly the spaces I have my eye on," Quentin hedges. "The startup capital wouldn't be unwelcome."

"Even better." Ian turns his laptop screen towards Quentin. "I've drawn up a sample contract..."

"No need," Quentin interrupts before he can even finish. He sets the paper they drew up last night together on the counter and slides it over. "I already know the kind of conditions I want."

Ian's glance at Landon is approving. His look and the last ten minutes have gone a long way to reassuring Landon that Quentin is making an informed and intelligent decision. He isn't going to let Ian walk all over him, but he will take advantage of Ian's years in the business.

Ian and Landon have been a dynamite combination. Landon is beginning to see that Ian and Quentin could create the same kind of magic.

Quentin and Ian talk over the list, but it's all essentially done. Ian doesn't want things that clients don't need to give and that's one of the main reasons Landon was so relieved when they agreed to work together. He'd had too many years of managers demanding and then just *taking*.

Landon eats a bowl of cereal and takes a shower and when he's done, the contract is printing and Ian looks up at Landon next.

Quentin goes to take a shower and Landon and his manager are left alone in the kitchen.

"I want you to go outside," Ian says and Landon, despite all the positive thoughts he's had about Ian today, shakes his head vehemently.

"No way. I'm not going out into that mob."

"You'll be fine. I'll call some security. All you have to do is stand there and let them take some pictures. Maybe some video. Let them see you. Talk about going to the studio."

"Aren't I going to the studio? What about Julian?"

"I texted Julian yesterday. You're not going anywhere."

"What? So I'll take an Uber around the block?" Landon scoffs at this. He hates, *hates*, the fabrications that he participates in, even though the ones he agrees to now are less over the top and far less harmful than the ones he used to be forced into. The only blessing is that so far Ian has kept Quentin out of them. He can only imagine how Quentin would react to this farce.

"Landon," Ian says patiently. "I know, I know, I need to be seen. For the articles." It's hard, but Landon barely holds back a sneer. PR will never be his favorite part of this business.

"Yesterday was fantastic. Better than I ever could have hoped for. But it's not a trend. It's a single day. We need to keep this going."

"Right. Into the premiere, then into the finale, if we make it, and then into album promo and then album release." Landon pauses, glances over at Ian, who is wearing that proud expression again. Landon is annoyed. "Did I get it right?"

"You know you got it right, you asshole," Ian says with a fond chuckle. "But you're still going outside. No matter how many circles you run around me."

"Fine," Landon grumbles. "Do I have to change?"

Ian looks at his threadbare sweatpants and stained t-shirt. He sighs. "Yes."

⁕ ⁕ ⁕

"I certainly hope your day was better than mine, Quen. I got papped by a mob, drove around the block in an Uber, and then spent the day going stir crazy at home and wishing I could be at the studio with Julian." Landon sighs as they rearrange themselves back on the couch. Tonight it's Chinese, not pizza, and so far there's been no re-heating. They've silenced their phones and are actually ambitious enough to attempt the quiet night in they didn't get yesterday.

Quentin sighs too. "It was good. It was productive, anyway. I liked the people I met with. They're smart and clever and know how to sell things."

"But?" Landon asks.

"But it feels like giving in, to just accept their money and let them own a piece of the business," Quentin admits. "It feels weak. It feels like I never even gave it a real shot."

Landon is quiet for a moment as he opens his carton of fried rice. "I don't like accepting help either," he finally admits.

"But?" Quentin parrots back with a smile.

"But some things, they're better if you're not on your own." Landon swallows and wonders if now is the *right* time he's been subconsciously waiting for to share the rest of his story. Maybe now is better than later. Maybe Quentin can learn from it.

"I've made some really dumb decisions career-wise," Landon continues. "Like 'against all good advice from people who knew better than me' decisions. When I came out? I was told it was better to wait. Like there were better times to do it, better ways, but I thought with my heart and not my head." He pauses. "I think what I've learned the most from four years in the entertainment business is balance. Life and career. What I want versus what I need."

"That's amazing advice. It helps, it really does," Quentin says softly, then hesitates. "Can I ask you a weird question?"

Landon stares into his fried rice. He doesn't know what's coming, but it can't be good. He nods anyway, because he's weak and he can't say no to Quentin.

"How come you never bring up Steve when you talk about coming out?"

The answer is so easy. Landon doesn't mention Steve because Landon hates talking about Steve. Not because he still harbors some misplaced devotion for the man, but because Landon had never been so humiliated in his entire life. Even the thought of Steve makes him want to hide in a dark room and never come out, never to be seen again.

Landon has never wanted to be ignored in his entire life, except for those months after Steve, and that deep, potentially fathomless pit of despair and pain terrifies him so much, even now. He won't think about it. Won't talk about it. Even with Quentin, even if he deserves to hear the truth.

Landon picks at his food. He can't look up at Quentin. "Steve was . . . Steve is . . . I don't talk about Steve."

He feels the soft brush of Quentin's hand on his shoulder. It should reassure him, but instead it makes him want to blow up and throw his food against a wall. He destroyed five cell phones during the Steve aftermath. Landon takes an unsteady breath and tries to get himself under control.

"You don't have to," Quentin says. He almost sounds like he really means it. "I didn't mean to push you."

Of course he didn't. He's a fucking saint. Some deep part of Landon wishes Quen would push him harder, make him face it and talk about it. But that's ridiculous because that's just not who Quentin is. He's *nice*.

Instead of responding, Landon just buries his face into the crook of Quentin's neck.

"Wanna watch a movie?" Quentin asks tenderly. "Netflix and chill, maybe?"

Landon lifts his head and shoots Quentin what he hopes is his good smile. As far away from the monster Steve created as possible. "My favorite kind of evening. No clothing changes required."

Sex is a good distraction. They could both use a distraction.

Quentin's smirk is back, and Landon can breathe a sigh of relief.

"No clothes required *period*."

Chapter Twelve

"We're going to be late," Quentin says as they climb into the Uber that's idling next to the curb. His voice is edgier than Landon has ever heard it. Maybe he woke up on the wrong side of the bed. Maybe he slept badly alone, even though he was the one who insisted he go back to his apartment and make sure his flower box herb garden hadn't died. Maybe it's that Landon took too long getting ready, then insisted they get coffee before catching a ride over to meet the realtor that Ian has hooked Quentin up with to help him find a space for his bakery.

Or maybe it's the truth, which is that Quentin is taking a huge step today, shouldering an enormous responsibility to invest in a business and hire employees and set himself up as the one person it all depends on. It's more adult than Landon has ever been, and maybe that's part of it.

Maybe it scares Landon more than it even scares Quentin.

"Five minutes. Not a big deal." Landon hopes his own unconcern will rub off on Quentin.

"It's a big deal to me," Quentin says, words harsher than his mild tone of voice. "I try never to be late."

Landon glances over at him and shrugs apologetically. "I hate to tell you, but you're gonna have to get used to it. I'm notorious for being late."

He watches as Quentin overcomes a brief struggle to put the annoyance behind him and then shoots Landon a reassuring smile. It's a shadow of what it might normally be, but Landon knows how big this is. He's willing to excuse Quen this morning. It would be weird if he wasn't nervous.

Unfortunately, things do not improve when they exit the Uber to find their realtor waiting on the corner.

"Hi, I'm Caleb," he says, reaching out a hand to shake Quentin's. He's medium height, slender. Hair styled perfectly, clothes equally impeccable. He's subtle about it, but he checks Quentin out top to bottom, then glances over at Landon.

It would be a lie to say that Landon is used to being recognized. It happens on a fairly regular basis, but it's always a rush, that brilliant burst of confidence that he craves, even when he doesn't need it. He still loves it every time it happens.

"Oh my god," Caleb squeaks, Quentin completely forgotten, "you're Landon Patton!"

"Guilty as charged." Landon smiles, but unlike other times he keeps it less friendly and more professional. It's a little weird to have a stranger gush over him right in front of Quentin. It never was before, not ever in front of Steve, but it feels weird now. He didn't think they were in a bad place, but maybe they are, if someone gushing over him in front of Quen makes him feel weird.

"You were so great on *The Voice*, you should've won your season," Caleb continues to gush.

The first time they met, Quen said the same thing. Landon believes he meant it. He isn't sure Caleb does. Maybe he's just one of those people who obsesses over celebrities. There's lots of those in LA, and Landon tries his best to avoid them.

"And you're here with, Quentin, is it?" Caleb says, finally remembering the job for which he was hired. Landon refrains from rolling his eyes.

"Landon's my boyfriend," Quentin says, and that edge is back in his voice. He's clearly not pleased that his real estate agent is such a big fan of Landon's.

Landon doesn't think Quentin could really get jealous; he's so easy going it's hard to imagine it. But the *boyfriend* comment is impossible to ignore.

"Aren't you two lucky?" Caleb says, and Landon doesn't even think he *tries* to be genuinely happy for them.

"The luckiest." Quentin wraps an arm around Landon, tight. It would make sense except that Landon has no intention of escaping.

Caleb gestures to the building behind them. "Ian said you wanted to see places with existing kitchens, near neighborhoods. I think this is one of your best bets. Do you want to see inside?"

Quentin takes his sweet time responding. Landon wiggles out of his grasp, finishes his coffee and wishes he could take out his phone while Quentin looks up and down the block, carefully reads every neighboring business sign, then gives a short nod. "Decent location," is all he says.

Quen will never be as loquacious as Landon is, but this is bad, even for him.

Caleb unlocks the door, and they walk in. The space to rent was a café in a former life. There are a few dusty tables and chairs, dead plants in the corners, a huge empty blackboard for a menu above the cash register.

It's small like Quentin wants, but there's no light. No space. It feels cramped, and it's basically empty already.

Quentin prowls around, though, despite that Landon can tell in the first five seconds that it's not what he's looking for.

Landon's scrolling aimlessly through email on his phone. He doesn't realize Caleb has practically invaded his space until he's *right* there. He glances up, catches Caleb in the act of trying to get a glimpse of his screen. Shoots him a patented Landon death glare.

Lesser men quail from the Landon death glare, but Caleb is dumb enough he's apparently immune. "I meant what I said. I totally thought you should have won your season," he says.

Landon could just shut him down right now, but the part of him that can't forget the way he felt the day his label dumped him still craves the validation. Craves the attention. So he doesn't. "It was a tough season, I was lucky to end up in third," he says with as much graciousness as he can dig up. Actually, in reality, he's aping Quentin and the nonchalant way he accepts compliments.

"*And*," Caleb continues, "I loved your second album. I know it didn't do as well, commercially, but it's one of my all-time favorites."

This is *not* something Landon hears very often. Or ever, actually. "Really?" he asks, the most genuine he's been since exiting the cab fifteen minutes ago. "Nobody ever tells me that."

"I thought it was really raw, really honest. Maybe too honest, before that became popular," Caleb admits. "Now it's all the trend, right? Troye Sivan and Halsey, singing about how painful it is to be queer. But you did it first."

"Maybe not the first," Landon admits graciously, but he can't believe he nearly had Caleb pegged as a fake admirer, when in reality he's one of the few who tried to understand his second album.

Unfortunately when Quentin reappears from overturning every empty box in the storeroom, or whatever it was he was doing, he finds Landon and Caleb in the middle of a chummy conversation about Landon's music.

Quentin does not look happy. In fact, Landon doesn't think he's ever seen him even slightly annoyed before, and now all at once, he looks *pissed*. Landon doesn't know what to do with it, so he shuts up. Caleb is not that smart, and doesn't know when to quit.

". . . I just really love the way you used the swimming metaphor through the whole album. The imagery, it was beautiful. . ." Caleb rambles on.

It takes him a few seconds to realize Landon isn't paying attention anymore and he looks up at Quentin.

"All finished?" he asks.

Quentin gives a sharp nod. "Though it would have been helpful," he drawls, "to have you giving me some advice and information instead of hitting on my boyfriend."

Caleb splutters. Landon nearly opens his mouth to defend the other man, then realizes that Quentin is 100% right. Caleb *should* have been helping Quentin. That is Caleb's *job*. Instead of being a loyal boyfriend by bluntly ushering Caleb to this conclusion, Landon has been standing here stroking his own ego.

"Landon, can I speak to you alone for a moment?" Quentin switches his attention to the man next to him, and his glare is *cutting*. Landon didn't even know he could look like that. "And while we talk, you can do your job and find some decent buildings that aren't full of dust and broken-down equipment."

Caleb nods mutely while Quen leads Landon outside to the still-deserted street corner. No foot traffic here. No wonder the café didn't last.

"I'm sorry," Landon gets out before Quentin can express all the ways that Landon is a fuck-up. He knows they're coming. They've been coming his whole damn life, and just this once, with this one man, Landon hoped this conversation wasn't an inevitability, but it turns out he can't avoid it.

Quentin ignores his apology. Still looks pissed. "Do you even know how important this is to me?" he finally asks. "Do you have any idea?"

That's the problem; Landon *knows*. Landon knows and he still fucked it up. He nods slowly.

"And you monopolized his time anyway? I mean, I know he was probably a persistent asshole. You seemed to realize it when we were outside. But as soon as he started feeding your ego, it was like you couldn't resist. I barely even recognized you in there."

Quentin seems less angry as he keeps talking, but more confused. Landon wants to cry. Hurting Quentin's feelings is bad enough; making him wonder if the Landon he cares about doesn't exist is another.

"I'm sorry," is all Landon can repeat. "I'm . . . weak. I need attention and too much validation. That's the truth. Maybe it's better you find that out now."

The crease between Quentin's brows deepens. "There's nothing wrong with attention and validation. We all need them. But I needed them more than you did right then."

Landon knows Quen is right. He *did* need them more, right then. And Landon stole Caleb's attention and his expertise and made Quentin feel like a nuisance and a third wheel when this whole trip is supposed to be about him. All Landon can do is apologize again.

Quentin's expression softens. "It's okay, I get it. I do. He said all the right stuff. Everything you wanted to hear. It's hard to turn that away."

"I don't want to fuck this up," Landon admits into Quen's shoulder as he pulls him in, close. "I'm so afraid I'm going to."

"You won't," Quentin promises. "We're just . . . sometimes it's a little rough figuring out a new relationship. We'll get there. It's not your fault."

It is, but Quentin is too nice to say so.

Landon pulls away with a long sniff. He knows his eyes are red and wet. He's not sure he can go back in and face Caleb. Is pretty sure he *shouldn't*. "I think I'm going to head to the studio early. Julian won't be there, but I can get some work in."

"Landon, I want you here. This is so big and I'm terrified," Quen finally admits. "I'm scared out of my damn mind."

"You're fantastic," Landon vows. "I think you'll be better on your own, really. I'm just . . . a distraction."

Quentin glances into the dirty window of the building where Caleb is waiting. "Do you think I should give him another chance?"

"You're giving me another chance," Landon counters. Frankly he doesn't know why he's defending Caleb. He shouldn't be. But then, he's never talked to *anyone* who has ever admitted to loving his second album before. Maybe Caleb has unexplored depths.

"Yeah," Quentin teases. "But you're *Landon Patton*. Caleb is just some guy who over-styles his hair."

Landon laughs and feels the tight panic in his chest begin to unwind. They're going to be okay. He didn't screw up the best thing to ever happen to him. "Don't you forget it," he teases right back.

Quentin leans in for a brief kiss, and there's a heart-stopping moment before Landon realizes that nothing *has* changed. They're still crazy about each other. Quen still looks at him like he doesn't want him to go and Landon still gets those butterflies in his stomach every time he does.

"I'll see you tonight?" Quentin says hopefully. "Dinner?"

"It's a date," Landon promises.

When he gets to the studio, he takes a quick trip to the bathroom. When he's washing up his hands in the sink, he glances up at the mirror. His eyes are red-rimmed, and there's still traces of fear in them. His stomach still feels unsettled.

He wants to be the best version of himself for Quentin. Wants to be a grownup he can count on, but deep down, Landon doesn't know if he's capable of it. It's pure selfishness that keeps him close to Quentin, loving him when he really deserves better.

❦

"What do you think our theme will be this week?" Landon asks Quentin as they head down from their green room to the main *Kitchen Wars* soundstage.

He does genuinely want to know Quentin's thoughts, but he's also trying to distract himself from remembering their fight this last week. He guesses it was a fight anyway. By the time Landon and Quentin met up for dinner later that night, Quen hadn't brought it up, and Landon had been too afraid to. They'd let it go, but Landon is afraid that instead of moving past it, it's still simmering on the back burner, ready to burn them when they get too comfortable.

Quentin starts rambling about possibilities and it turns out that the distraction isn't quite enough because Landon is still unsettled as they head to their kitchen.

Quentin must realize because at some point, he just stops and glances down at Landon, a smile quirking up the corner of his lips. "Are you okay?" he asks. "You seem distracted."

There are only four teams left. Landon can't afford to be distracted. As much as he might want to panic, he can't. Not now.

There are three more weeks of competition. He's got to focus for *three* more weeks. Surely even he can do that.

"I'm good," Landon reassures Quentin, reaching down to squeeze his hand. Offer that little bit of extra certainty. If he's reassuring himself as well as Quentin, nobody needs to know.

Filming starts, and when Zach walks out in a red lobster costume, goofy smile plastered in place, Landon can't help the giggle that escapes him. Alexis smiles, looking a little more human, and nudges one of Zach's "claws." Landon has heard a rumor that Alexis is dating Zach and has been for awhile. Landon likes to see the way her face relaxes when she glances over at him in the ridiculous outfit. It reminds him of how his own sharper edges soften when he's with Quentin.

"Yes, seafood is your theme of the week. But before you can shop and prepare a delicious dish for our judges, a little pre-shop auction, perhaps?"

Landon shifts nervously from foot to foot. He doesn't like the sound of this at all. He glances up at Quentin, who is still staring in awe at Zach. Admittedly, it must take a big set of balls to don a lobster costume on national television. Even more impressively, Zach carries it with panache.

Alexis whips a white cloth off one of their regular shopping baskets. "Let's start the bidding for this item at five hundred dollars. What for? Well, for the privilege of relieving one of your opponents of the opportunity to *use* one when they go shopping."

Ugh, this is going to suck. But Landon does not feel even the slightest need to bid on this. He's pretty sure they're going to get it regardless, because after their triumphant win last week and the interview and he and Quentin's sudden meme-worthy status, he would absolutely do the same if their roles were reversed.

But then Landon looks down at Quentin's big hands, remembers how capable they are, and figures that he can absolutely handle it.

The bidding is quick and Landon isn't surprised in the slightest when Rory and Kimber spend only two thousand dollars to confiscate their shopping basket. Honestly, Landon would have thought less of Rory if he hadn't spent the money to take it away.

Quentin just gives Landon a lopsided, painfully adorable shrug when the basket disappears. They talked about this, knew they would almost certainly be sabotaged this week. They'll be lucky if they don't get the second sabotage too.

He doesn't have to, but Landon gives Quentin a last reassuring squeeze before Quentin rushes off to the pantry to load up his hands with as much food as he can.

Landon usually doesn't pay much attention to the shopping because it's so short and usually hectic. But this time, he strains to watch Quentin through the glass doors of the pantry. When Quentin comes out, his arms loaded with ingredients and a calm smile on his face, Landon is so proud.

They rock. They can't even be sabotaged. Landon shoots a quick triumphant look to Rory who just rolls his eyes as Quentin deposits their load onto their prep station.

"Our second auction," Alexis announces, brandishing what looks like a weapon. "My favorite of the day, actually. This is a box cutter. Whoever wins this challenge can remove all the sharp implements from the team of their choice and force them to use this instead."

Quentin makes a face to indicate just how he feels about losing his knives. Suddenly Landon really hopes that this doesn't go to them.

The bidding quickly gets started, with Reed and Diego opening with $2,000. They clearly want to win this. They get into an intense bidding war with Rory, with Landon popping in a bid every once in awhile, just to drive the price up. If Quentin is going to be stuck with this "knife" then he sure as hell wants whoever buys it to pay way too much for it.

Rory drops out at $6,500. Nora, who's been quiet until now, raises Diego and Reed to $6,700. They counter with seven and it's all over.

Seven thousand dollars. Landon can't believe they just spent so much money. That's the most expensive sabotage that anyone has bought yet. Landon just prays that Reed and Diego have short-term memories and don't remember that Landon once forced them to make all their cooking utensils and cooking vessels from aluminum foil.

Diego pauses dramatically, knife cutter in hand, in front of Landon and Quentin. He's got a twinkle in his eye though, and Landon lets out a rather large sigh of relief as he changes course at the last moment and hands it to Oliver and Nora instead.

Thank god.

"Normally," Alexis says next, and god, Landon wishes she would *just stop talking,* "you'd start cooking now. But I've got one more little surprise."

"We're going to have a little trivia contest," Alexis continues, as pencils are distributed to the chefs, but not the celebrities, "to prove how well you've gotten to know your celebrity. Whoever answers the most questions correctly will not only receive a large stock pot, exclusive for their use, but also a fresh Maine lobster. Succulent and delicious, I assure you."

Quentin perks up at this and Landon can't help but giggle under his breath. Is there any person on earth that doesn't think they have this in the bag?

Rory clearly does because he calls out, "This is totally unfair, I'll have you know."

Alexis just laughs maniacally. "There is no fair!" she pronounces. "There is only the war!"

Landon hears Rory continue to grumble as the celebrities are ushered out of the room. He isn't happy that he won't get to watch Quentin answer questions about him *or* see him own everyone's asses. But he's very, *very* confident that the latter is going to happen. They're actually *together*, and while according to Quentin, Rory has been continually trying to get into Kimber's bikini bottoms, he has yet to be successful.

Landon glances over to where Kimber's standing. She's clearly fretting over the unexpected challenge, and he suddenly feels like maybe it wouldn't hurt to pretend they're not competitors.

"It'll be fine," Landon promises as he sits down next to her. "Rory's smart."

Kimber gives him a rueful look. "I don't think it's going to matter how smart he is," she retorts.

That *is* true.

Landon tries again, because you never know when you might need an Olympic athlete on your side. "You know, I hear a lot of things about you and Rory," Landon offers with an eyebrow waggle.

She laughs, and he can see some of the tension melt from her face, and he takes that as a solid win. Rory should be grateful because he definitely doesn't deserve Landon comforting his partner after that whole lazy Susan prep table fiasco.

"Certainly not as much as I hear about you and Quentin," Kimber retorts.

Landon blushes. "He's wonderful."

Kimber has the nerve to look very smug. "I figured as much."

"Everybody knows, don't they?" Landon asks, not even the tiniest bit upset by this.

"Everybody knows," she says seriously with a little nod of confirmation.

He makes a face and she laughs again.

Rory really owes Landon now, but it's still nice to chat with Kimber for the next few minutes. She's funny and kind and Landon decides that if Rory is a lucky man, maybe he'll be successful in winning her over.

When they walk back onto the soundstage, Quentin's triumphant smile tells Landon everything he needs to know. He won (big surprise) and he won big.

Alexis starts the cooking time with a flourish and off they go again. Except this time, Landon feels relaxed and prepared. Like they've got this and nothing can shake their confidence.

"What happened?" he asks Quentin as he gets the large pot on to boil.

"The questions were so easy," Quentin says softly, like he's afraid Alexis will hear them and suddenly decide to make their lives harder for the next hour.

"What did they ask about?" Landon wonders as he paws through the groceries Quentin carried back to their station. He's got shrimp and lots of garlic, pasta, herbs, cherry tomatoes, lemon, and some parmesan cheese. "Scampi?"

Quentin nods. "The lobster will really bump up the flavor I think. I stuck with simple in the pantry because I had to carry it all, but the lobster takes this to the next level."

"Glad you won it then," Landon says earnestly.

"The questions were honestly all things I even knew back from *The Voice*," Quentin confesses. "So maybe that crush on you came in handy after all."

Landon shoots him an affronted look. "I think it more than came in handy."

Quentin's smile is easy and free as he picks through the shrimp. "Can you chop some herbs for me? The basil and the parsley."

They've been cooking at home together enough that Landon knows them both by sight and smell and surprises even himself at how calm he is, chopping them up as requested. He remembers a few weeks ago when he was afraid to even touch one of Quentin's knives.

Speaking of knives, Landon glances over to where Oliver and Nora are working at the next station. They got saddled with the horrible box cutter, and Landon is really hopeful that it is going to make their time much more difficult.

He seems to be right, as Oliver is bent over the cutting board, cursing fluidly and in great detail over how terrible the box cutter is at slicing up his vegetables.

Quentin comes over to look. "Should've changed his game plan," he whispers. "Came up with something that required less knife work. His cuts look *horrible*."

"Does it really matter that much?" Landon asks, even though he already knows the answer. He knows the answer because Quentin didn't force him to chop carrots for hours just because he liked the way his hands looked on the knife and how his eyes narrowed in concentration. Of course, maybe Quentin *did* like those things, but knife work is *also* important.

As predicted, Quentin just rolls his eyes. He puts the lobster in the boiling water, after tossing in some of the lemons he's already juiced and zested. "For flavor," he adds. "It's subtle but I think it'll add something."

"Are you afraid our dish is too simple?" Landon asks as Quentin slices up a baguette.

"If it's perfectly executed it shouldn't matter," Quentin says confidently, but that isn't really an answer and Landon knows it. He knows Quentin well enough at this point to know all the things he leaves unsaid. They twist the tension in his stomach tighter, and Landon is suddenly glad he didn't eat before filming.

Thirty minutes passes by quickly but not so quickly that they don't have the time to take the right amount of care with their dish. It's as perfect as they can make it.

Quentin is precise in a way that Landon hasn't ever witnessed before. He's focused and there's much less time for flirting or small talk, though they do discuss the dish and what Landon can do to help. He grates parmesan cheese, finds the right serving vessel, brushes the baguette slices with olive oil and is then put on broiler duty as they toast.

"Just until they're golden brown," Quentin warns for the fiftieth time.

"I know, I know," Landon complains as he carefully slides them out of the oven. They look flawless, and he begins to get more excited. Is it possible they might win a second week in a row?

He glances down the line. Nora and Rory are making a hearty seafood chowder. Rory is grilling oysters, bending over the flames as he watches them diligently. Reed and Diego have embarked on cooking an entire fish, stuffed with fennel and citrus.

Will their simple pasta be enough to carry the day? Landon hopes, but he can't help but be nervous as Quentin sprinkles parsley over their plated dish. Alexis counts down and suddenly Zach is back with the other judges, *sans* costume.

Landon feels his heart beat a bit faster as the trio of judges start with Rory and Kimber's oysters, which he describes as a modern take on Oysters Rockefeller.

"These are delicious," Simone observes. "*Really* delicious, in fact."

"They *are* good," Jasper agrees, his brow wrinkling. "But with only a few more weeks in the competition left, I'd expect something a little more elaborate."

Landon's heart sinks a bit more. Elaborate? When Rory has roasted vegetables as a side as well as a parsnip puree? How will the judges take their own simple pasta dish?

When the judges move on to Diego and Reed, Zach speaks up for the first time and he effuses over their branzino. "Beautiful and ambitious," he says. "Very tender fish, perfectly cooked and seasoned."

When the judges move on from Diego and Reed, they give each other a high five and Landon can't help but wonder if they're really the pair to beat.

Oliver and Nora are next up and they present the steaming bowls of broth and seafood as a cross between cioppino and a traditional seafood stew.

However, it becomes clear very quickly that something has gone wrong. "These vegetables," Jasper says with a wrinkle of annoyance, "they're very unevenly cut. Almost a bit too rustic for my tastes."

"Definitely too rustic for me. And unevenly cooked as a result," Zach adds. "I just got a bite of raw onion."

"I'd also like to see a bit more flavor developed," Simone points out. "Though for only a thirty-minute cooking time, it's amazing what you *did* get into the broth. It's pretty good."

Finally, it's Landon and Quentin's turn to be judged. Landon feels like they have a very strong chance of at least moving on to next week and a good shot at potentially second place or maybe even first.

The judges dig into their bowls of pasta with gusto, Zach immediately digging for the chunks of lobster that Quentin tucked into the strands of spaghetti.

"Delicious," Zach pronounces and Quentin's smile is so bright it could light the soundstage. Landon is unbearably proud. His boy is so damn good at what he does.

"Really beautifully cooked. Great flavor. Love the herbs and the lemon. It's a simple dish but it's a damn good one. I can't find a flaw."

"I'd say texture," Jasper objects. "It's all a little one note to me. But the garlic rubbed crostini does help a bit."

"Gives it a good crunch when you need one," Simone agrees.

The result is that when judging happens, Landon is feeling more relaxed than he ever has, facing Alexis.

"Overall great food this week," she says. "You should all be proud of what you've accomplished, making it to the final four. But I can only take three teams to the semi-final. And unfortunately, the team going home will be . . . Oliver Glines and Nora Hsu."

Oliver looks chagrined but not surprised. Landon isn't either. The box cutter was truly their downfall—though as Quentin said, maybe if they had adjusted their strategy, it might not have been enough to send them home.

"Our third-place team, with a place in the semi-final, is Rory and Kimber."

Everyone claps politely and Rory looks less than pleased, for the first time in Landon's memory. He was probably hoping he would get a better placement and therefore more money to use in the semi-final and final rounds.

Landon reaches out for Quentin's hand as Alexis announces the second-place team. "And in second, Diego and Reed with a beautifully executed branzino. Really impressive in the time you had," Alexis says.

Landon doesn't get it for a moment then it hits them. Alexis didn't say their name. That means . . . that means . . . they *won*. *Again*.

Quentin's throwing his arms around Landon as Alexis repeats their names, a bit of a smug edge to her voice. Landon doesn't like to think these things are pre-determined, that maybe they'd have had a shot even *without* the interview and suddenly becoming a food world sensation, but he's certain that it doesn't hurt.

"We did it," Quentin whispers into Landon's ear. "We're almost there."

Landon hugs him back just as tightly. He no longer wonders if these shots will make the final edits. *He knows.* But it's okay. He's made his peace with how this has turned out. As long as Quentin gets his bakery, he's good.

Better than good, really.

CHAPTER THIRTEEN

Quentin is in the kitchen, doing more recipe testing, when Landon comes bursting in, excited about the idea that just popped into his head.

"We should be matchmaking!" Landon announces as he plops down on one of Quentin's bar stools. Quentin hums and wanders over, hands floury. He brushes a quick hello kiss across Landon's lips, keeping it short and sweet to avoid dusting Landon with any more flour than is absolutely necessary.

Quentin raises an eyebrow as Landon's words sink in. "We should be matchmaking?" he asks dubiously.

"Rory!" Landon exclaims. "And Kimber!"

Quentin's dubious expression grows. "So you're saying we should give one of our only advantages to one of the two groups of competitors that are left?"

Landon frowns. He didn't think of that. He's just been sitting in the studio all day, unsuccessfully trying to develop a hook for one of the new tracks he and Julian are working on, and all he could think of was how sweet Kimber was in the green room and how much Rory clearly likes her.

And if *Landon* has managed to get everything he wants, then surely some other people should be able to benefit too. It's only fair.

"What about this?" Quentin asks, leaning against the counter. "There was a space I liked so much today that Caleb thinks I should borrow it for an afternoon and see how I like it. It's got a kitchen in it already. Why don't we have ourselves a little double date?"

"You found something you liked today?" Landon asks excitedly.

"It's definitely a front-runner. Great big space, beautiful light, a courtyard and a garden, but with a homey feel. The kitchen needs revamping but there's something to start with, instead of having to build from scratch . . ."

Landon feels a smile bloom on his face, and there's no way he could even dream of holding it back, not when Quentin is so lost in his plans and the world of his new bakery, excitement ripe in his voice. It's the way Landon feels every time he and Julian submerge themselves into a new song.

"I can't wait to see it," Landon says and he reaches over, pulling Quentin to him, never mind the flour. This is a big occasion. Quentin might've found his bakery today. And Landon, who's been giving him plenty of space on this, didn't mess it up.

Quentin's eyes are shining. "I can't wait for you to see it. The more I've thought about it this afternoon, the more I want it to be *the* location." His brow furrows. "I hope it works out."

Landon smooths a reassuring hand down Quentin's back. He, usually a neat baker, has managed to get flour not just on his front, but all over his back too. Landon is hopelessly endeared. He wants Quentin to smudge him with flour forever.

And well.

That's a thought.

Landon's brain stumbles at first then keeps going. It does make sense. He's in love with Quentin. Why wouldn't he want to spend the rest of his life with him? He doesn't have to take the steps *now* to make that happen, but there's nothing wrong with thinking it every once in a while.

"It'll work out," Landon promises. "If it's right, it's gonna work out."

Quentin leans his head on Landon's shoulder. "It's a lot to take in," he finally admits quietly.

"Then maybe we should do what you suggested, make a night of it, hone our matchmaking skills a bit. I know mine are rusty."

Quentin raises his head and shoots him an incredulous look. "You tried to matchmake the mailman and your neighbor across the way just last week!"

"That was amateur hour," Landon sniffs. "Rory and Kimber deserve my finest work." He pauses. "And *your* finest work too."

"Does that mean we're on?" Quentin asks. "Should I call Caleb and make some arrangements?"

"Tell Rory he's responsible for at least *asking* her himself." Landon sniffs again. "No shirking."

"So if the point is to test out the kitchen, we should really make our own dinner."

Landon makes a face, but it's not a bad idea. Sadly, he's reluctantly come around to the idea of cooking lately, but it's never going to be his first choice. And why would it be, if he has such a brilliant cook for a husband?

Landon freezes, even though he didn't even say the word out loud.

Husband.

The word reverberates inside his head like bass in an underground club. In an instant, he can see it: Quentin in their kitchen with their kids, baking sugar cookies, and decorating them with a mess of pink and purple icing. There's glitter in his hair, but he's laughing like he can't stop. And Landon is there, and there's an impromptu singalong, everyone grooving in their stocking feet to Landon's latest album.

And the only word Landon can come up with to describe it is right.

It feels *right.*

It's magical and staggering, to realize your life is laid out in front of you and you suddenly know exactly what you hope it'll look like. And who you hope to share it with.

"Landon?"

Landon comes back to reality with Quentin repeating the name with amusement as he returns back to his mixing bowl.

"What are you making?" Landon asks stupidly, even as he thinks *sugar cookies. With pink and purple icing. And you've got glitter in your hair.*

Quentin smiles back at him. "Apricot tarts with an almond *macaron* shell," he says, and Landon lets out the breath he didn't know he was holding.

"Sounds fancy."

He's both relieved and disappointed they're nothing like the big clunky sugar cutouts that he was envisioning in his dream. It's wonderful to *know* what he wants, but that doesn't mean he's ready. He hasn't even managed to tell Quentin he's in love with him yet. An important first step that he still needs to take. *At some point.*

They're good together, but the fight last week proves they aren't perfect.

"It *is*, but it isn't, if you get my drift," Quentin explains as he carefully dusts almond flour into the bowl. "The hearty filling of the apricots, and the gentle, delicate shell, traditional and French. A beautiful juxtaposition."

Landon laughs and leans back against the counter. He loves to watch Quentin in the kitchen, his arm muscles straining against the sleeve of his t-shirt as he whips the egg whites by hand, moving terrifyingly fast and with such confidence it takes Landon's breath away. He's never been that confident a day in his life. He has to let the songs he and Julian write grow on him, needs to talk himself into knowing they're good. But Quentin always *knows*. If he adds sugar and butter to flour, he knows what he'll get, every single time, and it never fails to be delicious.

There's a beautiful certainty to Quentin that Landon loves. And really, Landon could rant and rave about that all day, but he'd sound like a lunatic. So he keeps it simple instead. "Juxtaposition?" he teases. "And here I thought you were a simple purveyor of baked goods."

"Food is most extraordinary at the intersection of opposites," Quentin tutors. "Sweet and sour. Hot and cold. Bitter and sweet."

"Like dark chocolate," Landon says.

"Or like those sour peach gummies rolled in sugar that I know you hide and eat by the bagful," Quentin teases back.

Landon blushes. "Like those."

"You always want different flavors, different textures. People don't want to be bored when they eat. They want to be surprised, even when they claim they don't."

Over the last week, Quentin has been imparting these tidbits of food philosophy to Landon, as if he has some inkling of what is to befall them in the next two weeks of *Kitchen Wars* filming. And Quentin's probably not wrong. At some point, Landon will have to stand on his own, without Quentin holding him up.

He's not sure he's ever really going to be ready for that, but Quentin's going to make sure he's properly armed when it's just him and the stove.

"Did you finally figure out the savory pastries?" Landon asks. "This is the first sweet you've made in a while."

"Put the finishing touches on the chicken and tarragon puff this afternoon," Quentin says as he carefully pipes out tartlet shells onto the parchment paper-covered baking tray. "And it felt like the right time to start something sweet."

Landon bats his eyelashes and Quentin giggles, bubbles escaping from his pastry bag. He makes a face at the ruined shape and scoops the batter back into the bag, one quick movement after another, so he can start over. "Yes, you're definitely sweet enough."

"What's for dinner then?" Landon asks.

Quentin's piping out the almond tart shells now, his concentration locked in and so Landon wanders over to the takeout drawer and starts debating between curry and kung pao.

Quentin doesn't emerge from his zone until he carefully slides the tartlet shells into the oven. He rises, stretching his back. "Sorry," he says, "didn't want the egg whites to fall."

"It's okay." Landon waves a hand absently. "I was just trying to decide on dinner."

"I could whip something up," Quentin says, because *of course he can*. But he sounds tired, there's the edge of it in his voice. He's been cooking for most of the day. He could probably use a break.

"Nah." Landon smiles over at him. "Let's get takeout. Maybe watch a movie."

"Maybe pizza?" Quentin wonders as he wanders over to examine the menus over Landon's shoulder.

Quentin's arms wrap around Landon's body, coasting down his chest, and resting perilously close to the zip of his jeans. Landon feels himself go a bit breathless. He keeps expecting this to start feeling normal or routine, but it never does. His blood still, *always*, heats like it's the very first time Quentin put his hands on him. He's beginning to think maybe this feeling is endless.

"So what do you think?" Quentin asks, as they walk into the cavernous space, loaded with grocery bags.

Landon is still trying to get his bearings. The outside of the space is not much to look at—it's rather narrow and dark and unassuming, actually—but once you step inside, the entry widens into this great hall of a room, with soaring ceilings and *god*, the light coming from the enormous skylights. It's like they're filtering in the best of the California sun into this room. There's a counter installed along the side, long and topped with a slab of incredible natural wood, buffed to a high gloss finish. The glass cases look like they've been removed along with all the tables and chairs in the room. There's just that incredible counter and a huge expanse of hardwood floor.

"It's so empty, I know," Quentin continues, before Landon can even get his breath back to answer. "The previous renters took most everything with them, anything they could really, though *thank god* they couldn't seem to move the counter. And of course, most of the kitchen equipment. I'll have to go through what's left and see if any is even worth salvaging."

Landon knows how bright his smile is when he turns to Quentin. "It's perfect though. Empty or full, really."

Quentin sets his bags down gently on the counter and gazes around. "It is. The light is spectacular. And," he continues, clearly enthusiastic about the possibilities, "there's enough room that if I wanted to expand to a full breakfast or lunch menu, it's got the space."

Landon would be daunted by the logistics and work required to put this kind of operation together from scratch, but Quentin isn't even the tiniest bit. He's buoyant with happy enthusiasm, his nerves from earlier seemingly gone.

"You want to see the kitchen?" Quentin asks.

"I'm the worst possible judge of a kitchen," Landon laughs. "You know I never used mine before I met you."

"A regular Carrie Bradshaw you were, darling," Quentin says with an indulgent smile and a squeeze of Landon's bicep as they walk behind the counter and through the doorway to the kitchen. "Practically kept your sweaters in the oven."

It's all stainless steel, gleaming and spotless. Quentin said Caleb had sent a cleaning crew in preparation for tonight, and they did a great job because Landon thinks the floor looks cleaner than any of the surfaces in his apartment.

There's a lot of big equipment, some of it more worn than others, and Quentin goes around pointing out the huge ovens and the mixers and the stoves.

"Well," Landon says when Quentin finishes. "It certainly looks big enough."

There's a flash of uncertainty in Quentin's eyes. An uncertainty that Landon hoped he'd moved past, but it's understandable that Quentin hasn't because this is a *big* undertaking, even with the kind of financial and business support that Ian's connections are bringing to the table.

"Any smaller though," Landon continues, "and it wouldn't be big enough."

"I mean," Quentin says and the uncertain tone is in his voice now, and Landon can't take it. Quentin is so full of life and promise and possibility that the idea of him sounding nervous is difficult to hear.

So Landon just interrupts him. "It's perfect. It's absolutely fuck-ing perfect, Quen. Stop worrying." He pauses. "*Please.*"

Quentin reaches over and wraps his arms around Landon, tug-ging him tight against his body. "Thank you," he murmurs into Landon's shoulder.

A knock coming from the back of the kitchen interrupts their moment. "That must be the rental company," Quentin explains. "Tables and chairs."

"I thought this was just the four of us," Landon wonders.

"It is, but we still needed a place to sit down," Quentin says, moving towards what must be the stockrooms and the back door, Landon trailing behind him.

After Quentin's signed for the table, chairs, the simple place settings and linens the rental company delivered, Quentin makes an impatient gesture to Landon. "You can go, you know. I know you have a meeting. I'll be fine here. I've got prep to do and dessert to bake."

"You'll be fine here?" Landon asks, even though he already knows the answer. Quentin is insanely self-sufficient and besides, the last thing he probably needs is Landon's assistance, which is inconsistent at best and a hindrance at worst.

"Seriously," Quentin says, digging out his portable speaker from one of the bags and his wooden box of knives. "I'll be perfectly fine here."

Landon leans over and gives him a quick kiss that is in the middle of turning into a much longer, much hotter, full-on make-out session, when his phone buzzes in his pocket and reminds him that he has an important meeting to get to.

Quentin knows it too, and gently, but firmly, pushes him out the door.

As Landon slides into his cab, he thinks that Quentin is maybe beginning to understand him a bit too well.

"We love the way the album is coming along."

The woman on the other side of the conference table is a clone of the producer at the first *Kitchen Wars* meeting, down to the navy-blue Max Mara suit she's wearing.

"Good." Landon squirms in his chair and wishes he'd asked Ian to come to this marketing meeting. He thought it would be silly stuff, like picking the font for his album title, and talking about the cover photoshoot. But only having one marketing executive meet with him for that doesn't make sense and a bad feeling is growing in the base of his stomach.

"I wanted to talk to you specifically about Quentin Maxwell, and what sort of promotion you'd be willing to do with him to support it."

"To support the album?" Landon should have known this conversation was coming. It was inevitable. They're big news right now, and with *Kitchen Wars* starting to air in a few weeks, their exposure will only increase. It makes sense to ask the person the album is *about* to participate in some of the promotional appearances.

"Yes, to support the album," the woman confirms a little testily.

"It's *my* album. It doesn't have anything to do with Quentin." Landon can only imagine how Quentin would like this conversation. He doesn't love the spotlight like Landon does, and the idea of being paraded around as the love interest subject of an entire album would probably be hellish for him. Landon can't help but remember all those interviews he'd watched on YouTube, when

Quen had turned away every ounce of personal attention and cred-it.

The sick feeling in Landon's stomach grows.

The marketing executive taps a pen impatiently on the glass tabletop. "Nothing to do with it? I didn't realize you were planning on hiding your relationship."

"We're not. We're . . . not." That's as far as they've gotten. They haven't decided how to confirm it yet, but at the very least, they know they're not trying to hide.

"You don't think people will naturally assume it's about him?"

They would have to be deaf, dumb and stupid. Landon does not say this, and wishes Ian was here so he could get some brownie points for holding back.

"Of course they will," Landon retorts. "But I'm not going to shove it down people's throats."

Landon watches warily as she regroups.

"I would think Quentin would be proud to be part of this. He must be so proud of you."

It's so fucking presumptuous of her to assume how Quentin would feel. She's never even *met* him before. It pisses Landon off even more that she's pegged it *perfectly*. Quentin would do this even if he didn't want to. He'd volunteer himself into an entire press junket that he'd hate.

"Can we at least talk about it? Get back to you?" Landon says, gritting his teeth. He was so looking forward to tonight, but all he can feel is a faint dread at the thought of having to discuss this with Quentin.

The problem with this whole conversation is that she hasn't been wrong once. It would be *great* promo to include Quentin. Landon can completely understand why Epic wouldn't want *Kitchen Wars* to monopolize how adorable of a couple they are.

"Of course," she says with a bright smile. Like she already knows what he's going to come back with.

She knows he wants to be a big star. The best, easiest way to that is to utilize his love for Quentin. The problem is that Landon knows this is the very last thing Quentin is going to want.

Chapter Fourteen

When Landon returns to the bakery a few hours later, it's like he's walked into a totally different space.

The lights are dimmed, and there are candles scattered everywhere, their glass jars glowing bright green and yellow. There are flowers grouped across a long trestle table, daffodils and white hydrangea, and in the niches throughout the room. It's fresh and bright and fragrant and it makes Landon wonder what Quentin's capable of with more than a few hours and some temporary staging. His apartment is lovely and elegant but simple, and Landon *knew* he had good taste, but seeing it executed like this, like the beginning of Quentin's internal vision, is breathtaking.

There's bottles of wine chilling in a rustic stainless ice bucket next to the counter and four wine glasses sitting on top of it, along with a large wooden cheeseboard, scattered with cheese and dried fruits and nuts.

It's inviting and homey, and Landon didn't think that was even possible to achieve in such an empty, blank space.

Quentin walks out of the kitchen and lights up, his lips curving into a bright smile. "I thought I heard someone come in," he says, reaching for Landon and hugging him tight. "What do you think?"

I think I'm in love with you and *I think I want you to create a home for me and our future kids. I think I want to keep you forever.*

Landon's throat clogs a bit and he can only hug Quentin tighter. "It's perfect," he mumbles into Quentin's neck. His hair is tied up in one of his buns, a few loose tendrils tickling Landon's nose. "*You're* perfect." He's too perfect. Too kind. Too giving. Until the moment that he realizes he's lost himself and he leaves just the way Steve did.

Landon pushes the thought away. This is an important night for Quentin and he refuses to ruin it. He'll think about the marketing angle of the album tomorrow.

Quentin pulls back a little and the look on his face is as wondrous as Landon knows his own must be. They're like two infatuated fools, gazing at each other like they've discovered the secret of the universe. Landon is wondering if he can maybe convince Quentin to have that make-out session they didn't get earlier, but of course, before he can suggest it, the front door opens and closes again, and they both reluctantly part as Rory and Kimber walk in.

"You two are the worst," Rory exclaims. He glances over at Kimber, his eyes twinkling. "Can't leave 'em alone for a moment."

Landon gathers himself, remembering a bit belatedly that while this night can't help but be a *tiny* bit about him and Quentin, considering where they're at, it's *mostly* about Rory and Kimber.

When Quentin had suggested the plan initially to Rory over speakerphone, so Landon could, *naturally*, listen in, Rory had explained that Kimber *seemed* interested enough, but had seemed nervous and shy about accepting any of his rather broad hints at invitations. Not wanting to face certain rejection, he'd avoided saying anything more pointed. But Landon knows how Kimber looks at Rory when he's not watching. Kimber might be concerned, but she's definitely interested.

Which is what Landon had told Rory in order to convince him to actually bite the bullet and ask her.

Rory had texted back ten minutes after hanging up that she'd said yes, *and* seemed quite excited about the proposition.

It seems to Landon that there isn't much more work to be done. Unless Rory screws it up, he and Kimber are on their way to figuring everything out. At least their intertwined hands seem to indicate strong movement in the right direction.

Landon's gaze drops to them and then back up to Rory's face for a long, pointed moment. He has the nerve to flush.

"What's for dinner?" Rory asks. Landon isn't sure if he's thinking with his stomach or he's trying to change the subject.

Quentin gestures them behind the counter, which Rory admires profusely, through the door to the kitchen, like the Pied Piper leading his children.

"Welcome to my new kitchen!" Quentin exclaims.

Rory drops Kimber's hand and throws his arms around Quentin, catching him by surprise, and they embrace, hopping around the kitchen like two enthusiastic puppies who've just been given a brand-new bone.

Kimber leans over. "They're pretty cute, aren't they?"

Landon observes the two of them for a moment. They're holding each other still, Quentin excitedly and in extreme detail describing all sorts of foodie things that Landon can't understand. He just *really* loves this man.

"Tolerable, I'd say," Landon says with a quirk of his lips. He's afraid if he says more, it's all gonna come tumbling out, unbidden. Kimber is a nice person. She doesn't need to know about that little panting gasp Quentin makes when he gets really turned on and Landon is nosing at his pants-covered cock. Or the way Quentin curls around Landon in bed when he's had a bad day, even though Landon will loudly and vociferously claim he is *always* the big spoon. The way Quentin's hair gets stuck in his mouth and Landon not only doesn't mind, he *likes* it.

"Are you two finished over there or are you going to keep gossiping while we slave over the stove?" Landon looks up to see Quentin's eyes twinkling. "So?" he asks again impudently.

"Let's cook," Landon says with a lopsided smile. "And yes, for the record, I actually said that."

Landon is painstakingly chopping vegetables for a salad, which isn't really all that interesting when he can see Rory and Kimber giggling over the grill top, cooking beef tenderloin medallions wrapped in bacon. He doesn't know how he *ever* thought Rory needed assistance with Kimber. The two of them aren't quite as wrapped up in each other as he and Quentin are, but it's closer than Landon realized.

Quentin comes up behind him. "How's it going?" he asks, snagging a piece of tomato.

Landon gives an exaggerated sigh. "I don't know why I ever thought they needed help."

Quentin's expression is innocence personified, though Landon thinks he maybe knows better. "Trying to make me feel necessary was nice," Landon continues. "A great touch."

Quentin shrugs. "Rory would've asked her out at some point. You just speeded along the process. That was important."

It isn't really. Quentin's being nice. But Landon always likes it when Quentin is nice, so he lets it go.

"They're cute," he pronounces as he tosses the rest of the veggies in the wooden salad bowl, "but not as cute as us."

Quentin smacks an exaggerated kiss onto Landon's cheek. "Not even close," he says, as he turns around to check on the potatoes in the oven.

"You know who's *really* cute," Rory says, wandering over, followed closely by Kimber, who's holding the tray of steaks. "Reed and his boyfriend."

Landon does a double take. He had no idea Reed had a boyfriend. Or that Reed liked boys at all.

Kimber swipes a cucumber slice from the salad bowl. "I take it from your astonished expressions you don't know about Reed and Jordan."

"Jordan who?" Quentin asks as he dishes up his potatoes onto a platter, handing Landon a bowl of yogurt whipped with feta for the potatoes.

"Jordan Christensen," Rory explains patiently as they all load up their arms with food and move out of the kitchen towards the dinner table.

"The name sounds familiar," Quentin confesses as they sit down.

"He's a football player," Kimber supplies.

"He plays for a team that just relocated to LA. That's why Reed's doing a lot more work in California, lately, and why he agreed to do *Kitchen Wars*," Rory explains. "He owns a restaurant in Chicago right now, but he wants to open one in LA."

"I thought being out wasn't okay for football players," Landon says, even though as soon as he says it, he feels like a complete dumbass. It wasn't okay for pop singers either, and Landon did it anyway. And not even for as good a reason as Jordan.

"Wait," Landon continues before anyone could comment. "I said that without thinking. It doesn't matter if he's out or not. Or if he's a football player. He should do what's best for him."

Quentin looks over at him pensively. "It's a legitimate question," he says softly. "When Colin O'Connor came out as bisexual last year, he faced a lot of backlash."

"The pressure in that world is unrelenting," Kimber offers. Landon realizes she would know, not only being an Olympic swimmer, but going through the very public war with her mother. "Everyone wants something out of you, but all they want are the same things; variations on the same themes. They want to be able to package you and sell you easily, and that only works with what they're familiar with. So they force you into the pattern and hope you don't fuck it up by saying or doing the wrong thing."

It's the most Kimber has said this whole evening, and it's by far the most profound. Midway through cutting his first bite of steak, Landon freezes and lifts his eyes to her. There's heat in her words, and a fierce intelligence. She won't be forced into *anything*, that much is clear. And he likes her more for it.

She blushes. "Sorry that was so serious. Here we were, having a good time, and I had to go bring down the meal."

Quentin is the quickest to speak up. He reaches over and covers her hand with his own, squeezes. "On the contrary, all you've done is elevated the conversation."

She flushes brighter when Rory casually wraps an arm around her waist. "Really, what Quentin's saying is that you're a hell of a lot smarter *and* stronger than the rest of us. Two chefs and a singer. You're slumming it tonight, babe."

Kimber's very shy, sweet glance in Rory's direction, like he's everything she's wanted but afraid she couldn't have, is the last bit of reassurance that Landon needs that he did the right thing in planning this double date. He might not be completely responsible for this bit of matchmaking, but he will certainly take credit for speeding up the inevitable.

After finishing off the bitter chocolate crème brûlée with the salted caramel hazelnut whipped cream, Quentin and Landon are in the kitchen, doing a last cleanup. They'd sent Kimber and Rory off to go get drinks (or to go back to his place for a drink, as Quentin had whispered with the cutest giggle in Landon's ear). Kimber had half-heartedly protested, but Quentin and Landon had been unyielding, and so off they'd gone, with stars in their eyes.

"They're good for each other," Landon pronounces as he jumps up on the stainless steel counter, letting his legs swing carelessly.

"Agreed," Quentin says, as he finishes packing up their last bag of supplies to take back to his apartment. He turns, and lets out a groan. "What have I told you about sitting on counters?"

Landon smirks. "That it's a very naughty thing to do?"

Quentin's laughing as he sets down his bag and walks over to where Landon is sitting, resting one hand on each of his knees, situating himself in-between Landon's legs. Right where he should *always* be, if Landon has any say in the matter.

"I told you," Quentin says, very seriously, but he's smiling so wide it feels like his mouth takes up half his face, "not ever to do it."

Landon shrugs. That's never really stopped him before. Besides, he likes riling Quentin up. And he certainly looks riled up right now.

Quentin just sighs, tilting his head and looking unbearably fond. "That's what I love about you."

It's very stupid, because it's not like Quentin actually *says* it—then again, he kind of *does* say it—but it doesn't matter because Landon freezes anyway, like Quentin has, in fact, said those three magic words.

Quentin doesn't even realize it, doesn't even notice that Landon has frozen, his eyes big and wide, just keeps babbling on about Landon's stupid jokes and teasing and all these other things that are usually important but right now just feel quite silly in the face of what Quentin has just said.

"Did you mean that?" Landon interrupts him breathlessly. Finally. This is the end of the line; the end of all those endless rounds of mental interrogations he has with himself.

Quentin looks perplexed. "Did I mean what?"

Landon isn't amused. This is not the time to be joking around.

"Did you mean that you loved that about me? Or that you loved me?" The words are frankly out of his mouth before he can even dream of taking them back. It's been too long, and he's been holding them back for enough time that they just tumble out now, gracelessly.

"Because I love you," Landon continues in a jumble as Quentin just stands there, a bit shocked. A good kind of shocked Landon interprets, and fervently hopes that he's not wrong.

And suddenly, Quentin's confusion smooths into the brightest smile, his eyes gleaming like jewels in the dimly lit kitchen. It feels appropriate, Landon decides a bit hysterically, that this is coming to a head in a kitchen.

"Of course I love you," Quentin finally says. "I love you so much. I thought that . . . I thought that was obvious? That I'm absolutely crazy about you? We're practically living together. I don't even like being in a different room from you. All of my pastries are suddenly inspired by you. I'm completely crazy about you."

It hits Landon like a wave, and he's drowning in love for a moment, but when he reaches the surface and can breathe again, it's the best gulp of air he's ever had. "Ditto," he giggles, hooking his legs behind Quentin's back and tugging him close until he can lean down and kiss him.

The kiss only stays sweet and soft for a moment, but Landon's heels dig hard into Quentin's back, pulling him impossibly closer. It gets deep and dirty, tongues sliding together wetly and Landon is gasping into Quentin's mouth as his hands creep up Landon's thighs, thumbs digging into his muscles.

"Love you," Landon whispers against Quentin's lips, *"love you."*

Quentin murmurs it back, not just twice, but a litany against Landon's skin, over and over. Until he feels branded with it and he's never been happier in his entire life.

"Let's go home," Landon suggests with a dirty eyebrow waggle that only a man in love might appreciate.

"This is going to change everything," Landon admits in the cab as they head back to Quentin's place.

"Or nothing," Quentin corrects softly. "I feel like I've loved you for so long, I'm not sure of any other way to be. Like, I knew so much about you from *The Voice* and when you walked in that day and couldn't even cut a carrot properly, that was all it took."

The cab stops in front of Quentin's apartment building and they lug the bags up the stairs. Landon has never seen Quentin treat kitchen equipment or groceries roughly once so it comes as quite a surprise when he drops the bags he's carrying right in the tiny entryway and crowds Landon up against the door.

"You were so beautiful and cute and *clueless*," Quentin repeats and he's smiling so brightly that Landon can't look away.

"Clueless, huh?" Landon can't help a smirk.

Quentin just giggles though.

"I . . . I loved you the moment you joked about getting the mixer attachment in the hole," Landon confesses. It's so outside of his realm of experience to have someone who actually *wants* to talk about these things, who revels in the joy of falling fast and hard. With Quentin, there's no shame, no hiding his feelings so he doesn't feel stupid and cliché. There's only love, holding them together in this perfect bubble.

"You finally going to let me listen to your music now?" Quentin asks.

This is the moment Landon should say yes. His whole body is thrilling with the love Quentin feels for him. The right thing to do would be to pull out the thumb drive he has with the latest version of the album on it, but he doesn't, and he can't help but think of the marketing meeting he had today. "Yeah, but *later*," Landon says, reaching to kiss him again. He won't let himself think that he's distracting Quentin, but he definitely knows he's distracting Quentin.

It feels like a complete no-brainer to kiss again. A lot. Against the door. Until Landon's knees feel just about ready to give up the ghost and melt into jelly. It's the way Quentin kisses, probably—like Landon is the only person he wants to kiss, ever. Landon doesn't know how he wasn't more certain before this that Quentin loves him. It's in every angle that Quentin bends himself to, so he can surround Landon completely. It's in every delicate lick of his tongue against Landon's. It's the way his thumbs caress his cheekbones and then drift to his collarbones.

It's also in the way that the moment Landon feels like he's gonna just slide to the floor, Quentin scoops him up and carries him to their bed.

"Our bed," Landon says dazedly, realizing for the first time that whatever bed they're in, Quentin's or Landon's, it's still always going to be *theirs*. That's a heady realization that sends the rest of his blood straight to his already hardening cock.

"Wanna make love to you," Quentin says, and Landon can only nod helplessly. He *really* wants that too. He's so turned on his blood seems to boil with it.

The first slide of skin on skin feels like a revelation, a ghost even of when they did this the first time, when Quentin went out of his way to make it romantic and sweet. It feels so much more now, so much *bigger*, that Landon nearly cries when Quentin slides the first finger inside him. But it's Quentin who moans brokenly.

Landon thinks he's been in love before, but it's never felt like this with another man before. Every movement, every touch, every frisson of pleasure is *more* somehow, and being in love hasn't changed anything; it *still* feels like more. As Quentin slides inside of him, he knows he wants him this close for the rest of his god damn life. He's never letting this man go.

"Perfect," Quentin groans into Landon's neck, his teeth catching on the tendon, roughing him up the tiniest bit as his strokes are so long and slow and even that they're driving Landon out of his fucking mind. Quentin knows how to make it hot and good, but that isn't even why Landon loves him.

But it certainly doesn't hurt.

"Quen," Landon gasps out as Quentin refuses to speed up, despite Landon's intense efforts to persuade him that leave him panting in more ways than one, "*please.*"

"Need a hand, baby?" Quentin asks with a smirk, and then, in such an infuriatingly Quentin way, suddenly starts fucking him into the mattress. It turns out that Landon *doesn't* need a hand; he just needs Quentin to stop teasing.

"That was good," Landon says later, when they're clean and dry, tucked back into the cocoon of Quentin's bed. "But it really wasn't all that much different. I thought it might be, but no."

Quentin laughs softly into Landon's shoulder. "We've loved each other for a while. Besides, while being slightly more attuned to each other's desires, and maybe a trifle more selfless, how is having sex while we're in love any different really than having sex if we merely like each other?"

Landon is perplexed for a moment. He's never thought about this before. "I mean, it *wasn't* all that different. It felt like more of the same, like *better* more, sure, but still just more."

"I'm still going to want to ride you, I'm still going to want to fuck you into the mattress. I'm still gonna want to bend you over Rory's desk and eat you out until you cry and beg for it. That's part of loving you too."

"Even if I wanted it rough?" Landon asks, because he's beginning to discover that he does. And so does Quentin. They're a good, if rather incendiary, combo.

"Especially if you wanted it rough. Or I wanted it rough, actually," Quentin laughs with a bit of a self-deprecating edge. "It's all about trust, baby."

❧ ☙

Landon thought he might, faced with Reed and Diego, think of them slightly differently now that he knows why Reed is doing this show in the first place. That Reed wanting to be closer to his boyfriend might somehow trump Landon's insatiable desire to win. After all, Quentin's going to get his bakery now regardless. He's signed the papers. The building is his. They don't *need* to win.

But Landon wants to win anyway. He's just not that good of a person.

"You better be ready to lose," Rory calls out as they assemble in the kitchens for filming. "I brought my A game today." Next to him, Kimber blushes, and Landon debates whether his whole match-making idea was smart. Rory looks ready to take on the world today.

Landon glances over at Quentin. They sure should be too, after exchanging exceedingly sappy I love yous upstairs in the green room before coming downstairs to compete in this semi-final round. He raises his chin a bit. He'll take Rory's just-been-fucked glow and raise it one my-boyfriend-told-me-he-loves-me, thank you very much. He would be completely, one hundred percent transcendently happy if he could just forget that he keeps putting off Quentin's polite, never invasive questions about the album.

Landon doesn't think Quen will run when he hears how serious Landon is about him. That's a given at this point in their relationship. The problem is when Quentin falls asleep next to him, Landon stays up and thinks too much. Thinks about how Quentin doesn't really enjoy the spotlight, not like Landon does. That when this album comes out, a few months after *Kitchen Wars* ends, everyone who listens to it will know exactly who it's about, and Landon, who went into this very much feet first, brain scattered and no thought whatsoever, realizes that might not be something Quentin wants. The marketing department at Epic is already pushing for Quentin to participate in the release.

But Quen might not want to read tabloid articles about his private life when he's standing in line at the grocery store. He will definitely not want to get papped with Landon—that much Landon already *knows*. Quentin won't want to be asked questions about his relationship in interviews, when he wants to talk about his bakery and his creations instead.

The conclusion Landon always comes to, in the grey of the morning, is that there's no conclusion at all. He doesn't know how to fix things that aren't changeable. He can't make Quentin like the spotlight more. He can't make himself like it less. He can't write a different album. This is *the* album.

Landon knows he's only postponing an inevitable conversation he doesn't want to have, so he puts it off, and every time, Quentin gets that confused little wrinkle between his brows. It hurts each time, but it doesn't hurt enough to make Landon risk the peaceful happiness they've found together.

"Welcome to our semi-final round," Alexis says as filming starts. Landon tries to shake off his melancholy and look involved. *Alive.* "Where things start getting . . . good." She cackles for a moment. "Or progressively more evil," she continues, "depending on how you think of it. Let's get started, shall we?"

"As our dear judge Zach's restaurants are most famous for their Italian roots, I thought it would be appropriate if we celebrate the art of pasta today," Alexis concludes. Landon nods. Pasta. Okay, he loves pasta. He also really loves it when Quentin cooks him pasta.

The sixty second shopping time comes and goes, and Quentin comes back with a satisfyingly full basket of ingredients. Landon thinks he spies tomatoes and cheese and of course, the ingredients to make fresh pasta.

"Now for the first auction item," Alexis says with an extra dramatic flourish. "This is an oldie but a goodie, I think. A real classic."

Someone wheels out a kitchen that looks like the one Landon's younger sisters played with a few years ago. *When they were toddlers.*

Everything is tiny, including the stove and the oven, which is so small that it can't actually be a functioning piece of equipment. He looks over at Quentin, and sees his eyes grow wide.

They'd already discussed potentially bidding for and buying one of the sabotages today. Landon knows there are two, so it's a risk to bid for the first one, but he can't possibly imagine anything worse than this. He doesn't know how you'd actually *cook* anything on that stove and since cooking is a required element, this is going to have to go to Rory or Reed.

"Let's open the bidding at five hundred dollars," Alexis says.

"One thousand dollars," Landon shoots right back.

"Fifteen hundred dollars," Rory chimes in. Landon is sweating a little; the one person he didn't really want to bid against was Rory. Rory's proven to be both relentless and completely unconcerned about the amount of cash he has available to him. Not a great combination.

"Three thousand dollars," Landon responds, hoping to scare him away with how high the number is already. He does seem to have scared off Diego and Reed, if they were ever even considering bidding in the first place.

"Four," Rory yells happily.

He and Quentin have never spent this much on an auction item before, but then again, they've won two weeks in a row now. They've got the extra funds. He might as well use them.

"Five," he calls back again. Alexis' eyebrows shoot up and Landon stares her down, trying to pretend he isn't flushed and flustered. He doesn't like the auctions, but he has to do *something*. He can't ask Quentin to do ninety percent of the cooking and bid as well.

"Fifty-four hundred dollars," is what almost instantly comes from Rory. Landon gnashes his teeth in frustration. Why won't he just *stop* bidding?

"Fifty-five hundred dollars," Landon grits out and Rory finally throws up his hands in mock surrender, grinning the entire damn time. Which immediately makes Landon think all he was doing was driving up the price.

Landon is not amused, even after he gives the tiny kitchen to Reed and Diego, who have the nerve to not even look slightly panicked. He can only hope this isn't a repeat of the foil pan and utensils sabotage which didn't phase them at all.

Landon continues to be not amused as the next auction item is revealed. It's a spoon. They all stare at it, mystified. Landon wonders if they're going to use it to scrape out each other's eyeballs, a little bit at a time.

"I know you're wondering, what could this possibly mean?" Alexis asks. She's got an absolutely conniving expression on her face and Landon knows that means *nothing* good is about to happen. *Nothing.*

"We're going to auction off . . . the ability to taste your own food."

Landon fully expects Quentin to groan out loud next to him. He's always telling him, over and over again, how important tasting the food at every stage of cooking is. But when Landon looks over, he's perfectly calm and relaxed. *Serene.*

It's not like Landon could have bid for this sabotage even if he'd wanted to, though, so he gets to sit back and watch Rory and Diego fight for it, all while knowing that it is almost certainly going to be given to him and Quentin.

The spoon is, for the affordable price of $3,800, delivered to their station by a very smug Rory Dargan.

Landon regrets ever wanting to help him win Kimber.

"Oh"—Alexis smirks—"*and* your challenge this week." She whips her arm around and she's holding a rope. "You'll be *tied* together for the entirety of the thirty-minute time period."

There is a large chorus of groans. Everyone except him and Quentin that is. Landon just smirks at Quentin, who smirks back. He wonders if Alexis's been listening in on some of their conversations. They've been discussing introducing some light bondage into the bedroom, and Landon thinks this is a great start.

They get tied up, and Landon rolls his eyes when the knot is tied purposefully loose, with all kinds of give, and it's only one hand.

This is a joke. Alexis could have made this so much harder. Sure, he and Quentin will have to work together on any task that requires more than one hand, but they're so in-sync anyway, Landon doesn't see that being an issue.

"Aren't you worried about not being able to taste anything?" Landon asks Quentin as they unload their ingredients from the basket. There are tomatoes and a big hard brick of cheese. Landon sniffs at it and is surprised at how pleasantly nutty it smells. There's herbs and sausage too.

"Nah," Quentin whispers conspiratorially, "I can make Bolognese in my sleep. The ingredients are so standard, it shouldn't be too much of an issue. Besides, I think we're going to be a lot better off than those two." He nudges Landon's hip in the direction of Diego and Reed in the tiny kitchen. He can already hear frustration in their voices as they try to navigate the minuscule space, all while tied together.

"What's Bolognese?" Landon asks.

Quentin rolls his eyes but still looks endeared. "Basically, tomato sauce with meat."

"Oh, *that* pasta," Landon exclaims. "That's delicious. Of course it's delicious when you make it for dinner, but my favorite is probably when it's late at night and I'm hungry from, *you know*, and I sneak back into the kitchen and eat it out of the Tupperware cold."

"Is it sneaking if I know you're doing it?" Quentin asks fondly.

"Yes," Landon insists, ignoring the way his stomach twists painfully. If Quentin knows he's not falling asleep after sex, why hasn't he asked him what's wrong? Landon doesn't know if he could be honest about his feelings, but maybe it's worse that Quen doesn't seem concerned.

Together, they start a big sauté pan with the sausage and onion and garlic. Landon has to hold the onion while Quentin chops. It takes them a bit longer and some trust, but they get it done. Quentin eschews chopping the garlic, decided to use the knife to smash it to a paste instead. The smells from what they're already cooking are delicious. Landon feels rather unbearably smug, as he glances over to where Rory and Kimber are clearly bickering, and then to where Diego and Reed are struggling with an oven that seems to be heated with a lightbulb.

"Stop gloating and come help me get the pasta machine," Quentin laughs.

They cart the machine over to their station and Quentin mixes together the pasta dough with his one hand. "Are we being too ambitious?" he wonders quietly as they begin to feed the dough through the machine.

"It's the semi-final. I don't think there's such a thing as too ambitious," Landon pronounces."Besides," he adds with a tiny brush of his lips to Quentin's cheek, "your fresh pasta is delicious."

Quentin blushes. "Maybe it's even worth the annoyance of chopping the herbs with one hand."

The pasta dough takes forever to get rolled thin enough and then they have to carefully feed it through the cutter that divides it into long, wide strips. They take breaks periodically to check the sauce, to add tomatoes, to add spices and herbs, to add salt and pepper with a look of intense concentration on Quentin's face. Landon gets it. If he can't taste it before he presents it to the judges, Quentin has to be deliberate about everything he adds to the sauce.

With five minutes to go, and the distinct sounds of swearing coming from the tiny kitchen, they pop the pasta quickly in a pot of boiling water and then Quentin, with lots of Landon's assistance, combines it with the sauce, and then carefully positions it into a beautiful swirl in the center of their bowl. Landon holds the parmesan cheese steady as Quentin swipes a grater over the surface, dusting the pasta with cheese. A sprinkle of herbs and they're done.

Quentin wipes his brow when they sit back and Alexis re-enters to count down the final seconds. Landon feels as apprehensive as he looks. Rory has a beautiful dish of what looks to be scampi, and even Diego and Reed have put together something that at least *looks* good. It might not be cooked, but their presentation is gorgeous.

This time, the judges start with Quentin and Landon.

"Pasta Bolognese with herb fettuccine and some parmesan cheese," Quentin explains politely as he nervously eyes Zach Emory. He *is* the Italian here.

"Pasta is perhaps a trifle soft," Zach pronounces, "but the herbs are delicious, and the flavor of the sauce stands up well against them. A great job."

"I'm going to eat this whole bowl," Jasper jokes, which sends Landon's heart into an unsteady rhythm. Jasper doesn't tend to joke. He's unreasonably serious most of the time. And he is probably the pickiest person that Landon has ever met in his entire life. He could find fault with *anything*.

"An excellent dish of pasta, boys," Simone adds. "Could have used a tiny bit more salt, though."

Quentin raises his eyes skyward and Landon *knows* he is thinking about how he was literally *not allowed* to taste the food before it was put in front of the judges. Frankly if a bit of salt is all they're missing, it's a miracle.

Still, Landon feels confident about them heading to the final. They didn't have a single major flaw.

Of course, Rory and Kimber don't really either.

"This is really good," Zach claims, as he wraps the pasta around his fork. "Though I get that bit of woodiness that I usually do from dry pasta. I'm assuming this isn't fresh."

Landon doesn't think he imagines the quick, dirty look that Rory shoots Quentin.

"No, it's not fresh," Rory admits.

"Fresh pasta and a sauce in thirty minutes isn't easy," Zach says understandingly. Landon doesn't want him to be understanding, but then he keeps going. "But your competitors did it and did a credible job."

"Still, this is delicious," Simone says.

"I think my shrimp might be overcooked," Jasper adds, and there is the picky judge that Landon knows—and doesn't love at all. "Just a tad. How are yours?" he asks the others.

"Mine are a bit on the rubbery side too," Simone admits.

Landon thinks they're barely inching out Rory and Kimber when the trio of judges hits the wild card of the day, Diego and Reed. They could have done something spectacular with that tiny kitchen, but Landon is betting (hoping) that they didn't.

"A spicy raw tomato sauce," Reed explains politely. Maybe Landon should feel bad that he condemned them to serving raw sauce, especially now that he knows about Reed and his boyfriend, but Landon isn't that selfless.

It takes a long time after that first bite before Zach says anything. Landon feels like his breath is clawing out of his lungs and there's a hush that's fallen on the entire set as everyone waits for what he thinks of this "raw" sauce.

Zach, of course, figures it out. "This doesn't strike me as a particularly 'raw' sauce," he finally says. "Not the purpose of raw anyway. It more strikes me as a sauce that just isn't cooked."

The oven and stove with their lightbulb heating elements have done their job. Landon wants to give himself a high five. He settles for giving Quentin a low five under the cover of their station.

Jasper and Simone make similar comments, and even though everyone protests that the taste is good, Landon knows it's not going to be enough to save them.

It isn't. Landon doesn't feel a single ounce of remorse when fifteen minutes later, Diego and Reed are sent packing.

Landon and Quentin have made it to the final.

Chapter Fifteen

You promised me **I could listen**, is the text message Landon gets from Quentin three days later. **Tonight. Please?**

Shit. Landon's palm is sweaty as he slides his phone into his pocket, message unanswered.

This is the fifth time Quentin has asked, and the most direct he's ever been. Landon's run out of excuses that aren't the truth, and the thought of admitting what he worries about in the middle of the night makes his palms even more damp.

He's kept hoping that the longer he puzzles out this problem of their fundamental differences, the greater chance he might stumble onto a solution. Landon can't believe that he spent so many rapturous hours in the beginning of their relationship obsessed over how alike they are.

The similarities haven't changed; Landon's just become more and more aware of their differences. If he was still going to his therapist, he has a feeling she'd be tossing around phrases like "honeymoon period" and "adjusting to the reality of a serious relationship."

Landon is not ready to face the possibility that someday Quentin will get fed up with the attention Landon craves and *leave*. Steve leaving was devastating, but Landon isn't sure how he'd make it through Quentin leaving. The stray thought is enough to send him into a cold sweat.

His phone vibrates in his pocket again. He pulls it out, and this time it's not a text. This time it's Quentin calling. Probably because he knows Landon read the text and ignored it.

Quentin calls three more times over the next hour, and by the end of it, Landon is a mess. Julian has to call his name multiple times, at increasing volume, to even get his attention. Finally, he throws his hands up and tells Landon they'll meet back up tomorrow. "Go home," Julian says, "and get your head on straight."

Landon wishes that would be enough to do it.

He putters around the studio for another twenty minutes after Julian leaves, but he can't put it off any longer. Feels sick at the possibility of dragging this out any longer.

Maybe it's a good thing Quentin is forcing the issue. Landon can finally stop worrying about what happens when the subject inevitably arises.

Quentin's got something delicious-smelling simmering on his stove, some sort of soup, and he's hunched over his laptop on the counter, typing something that's made the crease between his brows grow even more pronounced.

"Something going on with the bakery?" Landon asks. He's deliberately avoiding the real issue, and as Quentin glances up, it's clear he knows it too.

"You have your phone on silent today?" Quentin asks casually, but it's not a casual question. Landon never has his phone on silent.

The lie sticks in Landon's throat. Finally, he shakes his head, *no*.

Quentin sighs and Landon hates the long-suffering edge it has. "Are you gonna tell me what's up with you? Why suddenly you're not responding to my texts? Dodging my calls? Making a bunch of shitty excuses that a five-year-old could see through?"

This whole time Landon has kind of wanted Quentin to call him on his bullshit, but now that's happened, all he wants to do is run away. There's no more excuses Landon can make. He's *done* all the things Quen is accusing him of. Quentin has the patience of a saint and has miraculously withheld judgment, but there's no way that'll continue.

"You sick of me? Done playing house? Is that it, Landon? You want me to give up on you?" Quentin's voice is creeping upwards in volume.

"That's the last thing I want." It's the only truth Landon can give.

Quentin jerks to his feet and shoves a hand through his unruly hair. He starts pacing in the living room, frustration ripe in every jerky movement of his body. "Then *what the fuck*, Landon," he finally says. Stops. Turns towards Landon. His gaze is burning blue, intense and angry. It's ironic that this reaction was the very one Landon was trying to avoid, yet here they are all the same.

"I've been trying to avoid this." Another single nugget of truth.

"Well, you're doing a terrible job," Quentin snaps.

"I know," Landon says, miserable and sick. "Maybe I should just go . . ." It's a terrible thought; Landon has a feeling that once he walks out that door, he won't be coming back anytime soon.

"No." Quentin practically yells it. "I want you to tell me what the fuck is wrong with you. Why you're not sleeping. Why you'll let everyone else hear your music except me. Is the album about Steve? Is that it? You're not over him?"

Landon wraps his arms around himself. In a different scenario, he might be amused how Quen could get so close, yet be so far.

"I'm over him; I'm not over what he did to me," Landon admits. So far it's the closest to a dangerous truth that he's gotten.

"He left you," Quentin states, and his voice is a little calmer. "I'm not going to leave you, unless you god damn force me. And you're forcing me right now, by pulling this."

Landon knows it. He's been caught between this rock and a harder place for weeks. Maybe he should just spit it all out and let the cards fall where they will. Maybe it means he'll lose Quentin, but maybe losing Quentin would be better than driving him away like this.

Landon reaches into his pocket and pulls out the thumb drive with all the songs. "You want to listen? Fine. Listen."

Quentin grabs the drive like his life depends on it and wastes no time shoving it into his laptop. If Landon thought he was going to share this experience and it was going to be beautiful and glorious, that moment has long passed. He feels a hairline fracture in his heart as he realizes that the first time Quen will ever listen to all the songs about him, he'll be angry. Angry at Landon.

Quentin pulls his headphones on, and spends the next forty-ish minutes listening in silence, his face completely blank. Landon knows because he stares at him for the entire time, barely blinking, halfway to tears, desperately wondering what Quentin is thinking as he listens.

It must finally end because Quentin braces his arms on the countertop, and bows his head. He seems overcome by some sort of emotion. Landon hopes it isn't pure rage. He doesn't think that an album full of love songs could diminish Quen's feelings, but Landon's tested them both these last few weeks.

He pulls the headphones off and turns towards Landon. His voice is rusty, gruff. "This is about me, about *us*. Why would you hide it from me?"

"If I come out with these songs, everyone is going to know it's about you."

Quentin still looks confused, so Landon is forced to continue, forced to utter every single damning word. He wants to cry.

"You don't like the attention. You don't *want* the attention. Not like I do. I want to yell about how much I love you in front of thousands of people. You're more comfortable in front of a few. I thought we were perfect for each other . . . but I think I was wrong."

"Is this because of the thing with Caleb?" Quentin asks, still confused.

"Yes. No. Sort of." Landon doesn't know how the thought originally germinated, but it's been growing and that particular morning fed it. The meeting with the Epic marketing executive cultivated it. The way Quentin has constantly and consistently turned every bit of personal attention away is what gives it life.

"You're wrong," Quentin says, and the certainty in his voice punches the breath out of Landon's lungs. "You're so fucking wrong." He reaches for Landon, for the first time since he walked in, and Landon feels his knees sag a little with relief as Quentin holds him close, tucking him under his chin. "I can't believe you wouldn't talk to me about this."

"When Steve left," Landon confesses, voice wobbly, because he *hates* talking about the way Steve made him feel like a stranger in his own body, "it wasn't only humiliating. It wasn't only rejection. It was *everything*. All of it. I can't do that again. Not with you."

Quentin cradles him like he's precious. And despite his fucking stupid behavior, maybe he really is, to Quen.

"Not going anywhere," Quentin vows. "Not today. Not tomorrow. Not in a year when you pull another stupid-ass stunt. I *know* you. I know you blossom under attention, that you crave it. I don't care. You could put me on some stupid reality TV show, make me a Kardashian, I don't give a shit, as long as it's with you. *Fuck*, I already put myself on a reality TV show. How could you think that would make any difference? I *love* you. Not sometimes. Not only if you do stuff I like. *All the time,* Landon."

Landon stands there for a long moment, feeling the rapid heartbeat under his cheek, and knows that Quentin's telling the truth. It doesn't make sense, but it's the truth.

"You really mean that." Landon still can't quite believe it.

"I really mean that." Quen pauses. "Also, you're a genius. I love the album, I'm sorry I didn't tell you right away, I should've. I was just … blown away that it was about me, when I'd sorta convinced myself that you wouldn't let me listen because it was about Steve and how much you still cared about him."

This actually makes a sick sort of sense. Landon wouldn't talk about Steve, and avoided playing Quentin his songs. He can't blame Quentin for wondering that. Besides, if anyone here needs to apologize, it's Landon.

"I'm sorrier," Landon says. "I was a total shit."

"A real brat," Quentin says, but his voice is affectionate. Like he knows it, and accepts it, and it doesn't bother him.

"You're going to get sick of it, I promise you," Landon says. *Warns.* He is still a little bit afraid, and will be afraid for a long while longer. Only time can give Landon the reassurances he really needs.

"Doubtful." Quentin slips a hand under Landon's chin and lifts his head gently, so he can press their lips together. "I told you I love you."

Landon deepens their kiss. He's said everything he can; maybe it's time to show Quentin how he really feels. His hand trails down Quentin's arm and intertwines their fingers. He gives Quentin a little tug. "Maybe I should show you how much I love you," he says and when Quen giggles, Landon lets out the breath he didn't know he was holding.

❧ ❧

Landon settles his knees further into the comforter and arches his back, pushing the curve of his butt deeper into Quentin's face. "Like that, Quen?" Landon croons as he wiggles just the tiniest bit, giving Quentin a taste of his own medicine.

If he had the available brain cells to truly consider it, Landon might think that he enjoyed this other side of their relationship too—when they flip the power and he gets Quentin literally on his knees, then on his back—but he doesn't. He just doesn't. Because Quentin's slipped his tongue down his crack, and is now teasingly circling his hole and the pleasure is hot and thick in his veins.

"We should do this after every fight," Landon breathes out unsteadily, his voice high and breathy.

Landon can feel Quentin's chuckle, and it's way hotter than it should be.

That's another thing he loves so much about Quentin; the bedroom isn't always serious. They can laugh and joke and tease and still make each other moan all in the space of five minutes. It's brilliant.

Landon leans forward, careful to not move from where Quentin is finally applying himself to his work, and lets just his breath ghost over Quentin's hard cock. It's hard and bright red at the tip, pre-come bubbling out of his slit. There's a wordless whine from the general direction of where Quentin's upper half is buried under Landon's body. Landon just laughs.

"Yeah, you want it," Landon croons to Quentin's dick as he leans a bit further down, close enough that he can swipe just his tongue across the head, gathering the taste of Quentin there.

Quentin's hips stutter upwards, chasing Landon's mouth, but Landon places his hands on his thighs and presses hard. Hard enough to leave blooming red marks across the pale skin. He trusts that Quentin will do something if he hurts him, but all Quentin seems to want to do is flick his tongue against Landon's hole harder and more insistently. Which Landon is pretty okay with.

"Don't move," Landon insists. "And if you want more, you'd better give me something."

Quentin's reaction is almost instantaneous. Landon gets a spit-slick finger sliding next to Quentin's tongue almost before he can imagine what it is that Quentin will do. A tiny whine escapes from Landon's throat and he can't help but want to arch his back even more insistently into Quentin's face.

But Quentin's so good, Landon wants to reward him. So he leans forward again and this time his mouth sinks down onto Quentin's cock, his fingers still holding on to Quentin's thighs to keep him in place.

It gets hot so fast, Quentin's cock practically down his throat, and Quentin's tongue and fingers practically wrenching Landon's orgasm from him.

It doesn't take Quentin much longer, his entire body tensing as he shoots into Landon's mouth.

Landon reaches for a spare sock next to the bed and wipes down his tummy as Quentin lies back against the pillows, curls frizzing around his face, a smile on his face.

"Liked that, didn't you?" Landon teases.

Quentin just shrugs, radiating calm from every pore. Landon throws the sock to the floor, damn Quentin's inevitable scream of betrayal when he goes to put it on the next morning, and snuggles up next to him.

"Do you want to talk about it?" Quentin asks. "I feel like maybe we should talk about it."

Landon would rather walk over burning hot coals than talk about his sexual kinks, newly discovered or otherwise, but he and Quentin are in an adult relationship and they love each other. He was stupid before, keeping it all inside. He can't do that anymore, as much as he wants to. Quentin deserves better, and the love pulsing through Landon makes him *want* to be that better man.

But he sure as hell isn't going to look Quentin in the eye while they talk about it. He buries further into the pillow and ignores Quentin's quiet chuckle. "I like it," Landon finally says. "Don't you like it?"

"I do like it. I like that it's something we share. That we can both take control. And that we don't always have to do it." Quentin's voice is soft and though he doesn't say a word about Landon's hiding his face, Landon still feels like he's being coaxed out of his hiding place.

He finally glances up when he feels like his flush is finally fading. "It's fucking hot," Landon admits.

Quentin chuckles louder now. His eyes are soft and hot and knowing all at the same time. Landon loves him more in this moment than he has ever before. "Maybe if we go further, we should talk about what we like and what we don't."

Landon squirms. He absolutely doesn't want to do that. Besides, he isn't even sure what the answer to that question is. Before Quentin, he sure as hell never trusted a partner enough to even want to explore this side of him.

"Or we could address it as things come up," Quentin offers, like he knows without being told that Landon would rather hide under the blankets forever than discuss it. "How about we just agree on a word we can both use when it becomes too much?"

That's easy enough. Landon can do that. "Pancake," he says decisively and Quentin makes a soft sound of agreement.

They're quiet for a few moments longer before Quentin finally murmurs into Landon's skin, "We're so good together. Better every day, even. The Dream Team."

Landon falls asleep and stays that way, until 6 a.m. when he wakes up to Quentin's screech of annoyance and frustration when he discovers his sock is full of Landon's come.

Landon can't help but smile into his pillow; they really are the Dream Team.

Chapter Sixteen

"Are you sure you're ready?" Ian asks for about the millionth time in the last hour.

Landon, who's cuddled up next to Quentin on their couch in the green room, looks up and sighs in exasperation. "Are you trying to make us nervous?" he demands of their manager.

Quentin laughs next to him.

"No," Ian counters defensively.

"I know," Landon says, "that you're not used to not being needed at a time like this. You've probably never had two clients in something together before. Isn't there some sort of press release you can go write or something?"

Except Landon knows there are a few press releases that have already been written, waiting for when the shows start to air. One of them talks about them winning. One of them is them being gracious losers. And a third, which is still the source of some conflict, is publicly confirming Landon and Quentin's relationship.

Not that the world really believes otherwise. Everybody knows. Every interview they give now feels like an unspoken confirmation, though every host tries to unobtrusively ask for one. Ian has threatened both Landon and Quentin with every bad thing he can think of to keep it under wraps until what he calls, "the right time."

Landon was worried at first that "the right time" was going to be never, but Ian set him straight quickly, outlining how a lot of their post-*Kitchen Wars* promotion is better with them publicly together. But Landon is still antsy during interviews. The past never really leaves you; it just becomes easier to deal with.

Ian is always endearingly annoyed afterwards, but it's worth it for the way Quentin laughs at some of Landon's snarkier responses.

"Fine," Ian grumbles. "I'll go wait somewhere else."

They're finally alone. "Are you ready?" Quentin asks, even though he's asked a version of this question about half a dozen times in the last two days.

"I'm fine," Landon says, and to his own surprise, it's true. He really wants to win, but also he knows it's not strictly necessary. And that fact has added considerably to his rather calm attitude.

"You know, you're probably going to have to cook," Quentin says gently.

He's been working up to this one too, like Landon isn't perfectly aware that part of the show's point was to teach him how to cook. If he and Quentin weren't practically living together and Landon hadn't absorbed some of his newfound knowledge by osmosis, no doubt he wouldn't have learned a thing. But he has, and though he's not sure how to use all of it, surely some of it will come in handy today.

"I know," Landon says.

"Keep it simple," Quentin suggests. "Don't worry about fancy. Whatever you have to make, we'll keep it as simple as we can."

If Landon felt even a hair more confident in his cooking skills, he'd be offended, but the truth is, simple is probably all he's capable of.

Ten minutes later, after a final hair and makeup check, they head to the filming kitchen.

As filming begins and Alexis walks in, Landon is totally fine. Not nervous at all. If he has to reach out for Quentin's hand as Alexis introduces the theme of the week, then that's completely understandable.

"For today's challenge," Alexis continues, "we have a culmination of everything you've learned on the last weeks of *Kitchen Wars*. Landon and Kimber will be doing *all* the cooking. Quentin and Rory are allowed to talk them through their dish, to *help* and to *assist*, only. No touching of any food or equipment in this kitchen during the next thirty minutes."

Landon knew it was coming but it still feels like a blow. He glances over at Kimber and to his relief, she looks a little pale as well. At least he's not absolutely terrified alone. Quentin grips his hand a little harder, a quick squeeze that says everything he can't say out loud—"you're fine," "you're good," "you're going to be brilliant," and, "I'm going to be right here with you the whole way."

"Your theme this week is *personal inspiration*. Anything goes. You'd better be able to tie it back to your life, *somehow*. Before your sixty second shopping time, I believe it's only fair to allow you a minute to consult with your chef," Alexis says, pretending like she's generous when in reality it's still only *sixty seconds*.

Landon turns to Quentin. "Grilled cheese," Quentin says before Landon even asks him. "With a roasted tomato soup. Get bread, cheese, butter, tomatoes, onion, garlic, cream, basil. Very simple, but with strong, memorable flavors."

Normally, Landon trusts Quentin completely when it comes to cooking. After all, that's what Quentin *does*. But this dish sounds so simple, when he's sure that Rory and Kimber will attempt something more complex. Landon opens his mouth to argue, but Quentin presses his finger to Landon's lips before he can even start to argue. "Yes," Quentin continues, "Rory and Kimber will try something harder. But your execution will set you apart."

It should be weird. Landon hadn't even voiced his concern, and here Quentin is, answering it like Landon said it out loud. But maybe that's what else sets them apart—they are absolutely on the same wavelength.

Even if they had more to discuss, they don't have the time. Alexis announces it's time to shop and this time it's Landon who grabs the basket and races off to the pantry. He still remembers where a good portion of the ingredients he needs are kept—that too makes it lucky, that one of the two times he was in here, he was making a very similar dish. Maybe Quentin *has* thought this through.

Landon moves through the pantry like a whirlwind, desperately trying to remember every ingredient that Quentin rattled off, and picking up additional besides, because it can't hurt to have more options, especially with the auction coming up.

He scoots past the glass pantry doors with a half a second to spare and a full basket which he plops down on their station. Quentin glances through it, a thoughtful expression on his face.

"Now for our final two auction items. First," Alexis says, "a true challenge for our celebrity—whoever wins this auction can doom their opponent by removing all knives and utensils from their station and forcing them to make do with this!" Alexis whips a Leatherman tool from behind her back. She spends the next thirty seconds, going through some of the available items besides the tiny knife, but Landon has already made up his mind. Kimber is going to have to deal with this. They have a lot of money—quite a bit more than Rory and Kimber, in fact—and there is no reason to save it. This is it. So he bids fast and high, Rory and Kimber sending them glares of pure annoyance as Landon jacks the price up.

He finally wins the auction at $11,000. It's ridiculous, but Landon wants to win more than they need the money.

"Next item up for auction," Alexis continues, "is the power to remove a single item from your competitor's basket. I would definitely take your time choosing the best thing to remove, should you win this, because that could easily be enough to sink them."

Landon's heart is what sinks. If Rory and Kimber win this, and they likely will, as they currently have more money than Landon and Quentin, they could take their bread. Or their cheese. Either vital ingredient is gone and Landon and Quentin will have to design a new plan from scratch.

The bidding on this item goes even higher.

Once they reach ten thousand dollars and a determinedly stubborn look settles onto Kimber's face, Landon decides he can't avoid it but he also won't let her have it easy either.

She wins it at $13,600.

Kimber and Rory hold a brief, smug consultation, and Kimber saunters over to confiscate their bread. Landon makes a face and doesn't even care if the camera catches it. They're going to have to rethink their entire dish now. He almost wishes he'd gotten stuck with the utility tool.

Alexis kicks off their thirty-minute cooking window and Landon's heart clenches as he begins to unload their basket. Can they even make something from what he grabbed absently from the shelves? Quentin has a serious look on his face as Landon places the items onto their prep station.

"Well," Quentin muses, "it's not ideal."

That's an understatement, Landon thinks, and his heart sinks even further.

"I think we still make a soup," Quentin suggests after another long minute contemplating the lineup of remaining ingredients. "Some sort of Italian minestrone, maybe, with a parmesan *frico* to add texture. You've got vegetables and herbs, and you even grabbed this pasta. We won't have beans, which are pretty integral, but we can have good flavor."

It sounds so much like settling that Landon wants to throw something, but he's a professional. This is all designed as a game, but it's so much more. Landon *knows* it doesn't really matter if they win or lose, as long as they continue to look good doing it.

It's still hard to face the possibility they've lost before they even start cooking.

"If I'd known they could take a major ingredient, I wouldn't have suggested a dish that relied so heavily on one item," Quentin says mournfully as Landon carefully chops up an onion and some cloves of garlic.

"How could you possibly know?" Landon asks. "You don't have Alexis' sadistic imagination."

"I heard that!" Alexis calls out from her position up front, but she's smiling. Sadistically, maybe, but she *is* smiling.

"Speaking of sadistic," Quentin says, his voice dropping down until Landon can barely hear it. "I know we're frustrated, but they're not much better off." He shoots a pointed glance over at Rory and Kimber's station, where she is clearly struggling with the limitations of the utility knife.

"Everything is so damn tiny," Rory exclaims in frustration, as Kimber tries and fails to cut through a potato.

Following Quentin's basic instructions, Landon gets the pot on the stove, heats olive oil and some butter—"We have it," Quentin says with a shrug, "we might as well use it!"—and starts to sauté the onions and garlic. He's also turned on the oven, and they're still going to roast the tomatoes to try to extract the most flavor they can from them. He slides the sheet pan in the oven, and then they go through their available ingredients again. Landon can tell that Quentin's trying not to mourn what they don't have, but it's hard. There are so many gaps, because this dish wasn't what he'd shopped for.

"I'm just afraid it's going to be lacking sophistication," Quentin says as Landon chops herbs for the broth.

"Don't you always tell me simple food with great flavor is better than complex food with subpar flavor?" Landon points out.

"True," Quentin admits.

"Then let's make great flavor," Landon says, digging deep to find some optimism. He could glance over to Rory and Kimber's station, but it doesn't much matter. Landon has begun to feel this is almost a personal crusade, completely separate from whatever Rory and Kimber are doing. If he can make a delicious soup out of these random ingredients, then he can at least hold his head high during the judging.

Quentin helps Landon build the soup one flavor at a time, adding chopped carrots and celery to the onions and garlic, covering it with chicken broth, and letting it simmer and steep with the fresh herbs they add next. Landon grates a mound of parmesan, and then sticks the rind into the stock, hoping to add what Quentin calls a "lovely, nutty flavor."

Landon bakes the grated parmesan in lovely, mounded piles, until it turns melted and pliant, and Landon risks burned fingers to mold it into fun shapes at Quentin's insistence.

When the tomatoes are done, Landon puts them through a food mill, bitching the whole way about how difficult it is. But the lovely mound of tomato pulp left is worth it, he thinks. And also the camera, which just caught them in a very cute and very snarky conversation over Landon's new least favorite kitchen appliance.

The tomatoes go into the pot along with the ditalini pasta. Quentin suggests Landon add cream, more fresh herbs and some finely minced spinach leaves. Then all there is to do is check the seasoning, scoop into a beautiful shallow white bowl, and top it with a final chiffonade of basil and the most acrobatic of the parmesan *fricos*.

It's a beautiful dish, actually, steaming and fragrant, and Landon feels confident for a single moment. Then he glances over to where Rory and Kimber are standing behind their dish, and she's prepared a whole *steak* with an equally ambitious acrobatic mound of thin fried potatoes. It looks like a whole meal, whereas their soup looks like a measly lunch. They don't even have any meat.

The judges' encouraging smiles when they walk into the kitchen with Alexis can't sweeten Landon's spirits. He feels like he's let Quentin down, even when Quentin reaches over and intertwines their fingers together, giving him three brief, reassuring squeezes.

Landon knows what they mean: *I love you.*

And they do help, they *do*—but Landon wanted to win this so badly.

The judges approach Kimber and Rory's station first. Landon's heart is in his throat as they cut into their steaks, examining the doneness and tenderness, and deconstructing the elaborate cloud of fried potatoes. Landon can't help but wish that he'd sunk them with the second sabotage—not the first, because the first seems to have not affected Kimber at all in the end, and they truly would have been done if they'd lost their beautiful cuts of meat.

"First off, congratulations on making it this far," Zach says, with a smile on his face. "Second, I feel like I speak for all the judges when I say your flavors on your steak are spot on, *but* I wish the peppercorn crust had been a little more evenly ground up. I have some big chunks on mine, and it is a bit disconcerting. Some big bites of pepper."

"The fries are well-seasoned, but the cuts aren't that great when you look closer," Jasper points out. "All in all, a good dish, with some small flaws when examined more closely."

"And I would've liked a sauce," Simone adds. "It's all a little . . . dry, honestly. But Zach is right, decent execution."

If Landon's heart was in his throat listening to Rory and Kimber's critique, it's nothing compared to how he feels when the judges approach and it's *his* dish they're tasting.

"Delicious," Zach declares, and a little bit of the breath that Landon was holding so close loosens. "Simple, but delicious. There are so many layers of flavor here that it's hard to say it's *just* a soup."

"But it *is* just a soup," Simone says. Landon can barely hold back the glare. Quentin's fingers are on his again and they're holding tight and fast. "Albeit a tasty one."

"I do like that you attempted to add some texture with the *frico*," Jasper says. "Unfortunately, no matter how tasty, it is just still only soup."

The judges retire to the green room to debate. Rory and Kimber turn their direction, and it nearly kills Landon but they all exchange friendly handshakes. Rory and Quentin even share a brief hug. He can tell Quentin is trying to brush it off as not mattering, but Landon can see the tension in his shoulders as the judges return to the kitchen.

Of course Alexis makes a big dramatic speech. All three judges speak again, giving similar critiques. But it doesn't matter because he knows what's going to happen. He should have seen it coming, but he was too crazy in love to notice. The producers haven't been prepping Quentin and him for the winner's edit. They've been prepping them for second place.

"And our runners up today, in a very respectable second place, beating out many quality pairs for the second spot in our final, are Quentin Maxwell and Landon Patton."

Landon halfway expected it, even strongly suspected as they cooked today and stood silent through the judges' comments. It still hits him like a brick, the knowledge that they couldn't pull it off. Quentin's arms are around him in an instant, and they're gripping each other so tightly. He can hear, in some far-off distant part of reality, Rory and Kimber celebrating and the judges congratulating them. He doesn't care. He just wants to hold on to Quentin forever and never let him go.

But he can't. He has to be a professional. He finally lets go as Alexis expresses her condolences for their loss. She does honestly look disappointed, but frankly this episode is no longer about them. After all they didn't win. So they're escorted perfunctorily back to their green room.

Landon shuts the door behind them and tries to dredge up something he can say to comfort Quentin. To *apologize*, for letting Kimber win the second sabotage, when she couldn't have handled it herself, for not cooking better today, even though all the judges said that the dishes' disparities only came in their level of complexity.

"Landon," Quentin says softly. The kind, sweet edge to his tone isn't deserved, Landon knows that. He knows Quentin is almost certainly secretly angry that they lost. That he must blame him. Them. Anyone. Landon should have made sure this didn't happen.

He still can't turn around and face him.

"Landon," Quentin repeats again, and he's a touch firmer this time. "It's really okay. I have the bakery. You have your album. We're going to be fine."

Landon finally turns. "I hate losing," he says and his voice is trembling. He hates how much this reminds him of Steve and the aftermath of his second album. That stinging regret of failure.

Quentin enfolds him into his embrace almost instantly. "I know, I know," he murmurs against the cotton of Landon's shirt, his breath warming the skin beneath as they hold each other. "But we didn't really lose."

Landon, who is halfway to tears, pulls back abruptly at this statement. "We lost," he grinds out. "I was there, we most definitely lost."

"No, we didn't," Quentin corrects again, softly but surely. Like he knows something that Landon doesn't.

"I found you," Quentin says and holds his hand up to stop Landon from speaking. "I know, it's horribly sappy, but I don't feel like I lost today."

This is a whole different take on the situation. When Landon came in third on *The Voice*, he definitely lost. But he also won, because the winner's contract was total shit. Third place got him only a marginally less shitty contract, but even the tiny difference was worth celebrating.

Today? Today he has a lot more to celebrate. A partner and a life and a *future*. None of which would have been possible if he hadn't gotten his head out of his own ass and made peace with the fiendish appliance otherwise known as the oven.

"No," Landon says, a smile dawning across his face, "we didn't lose."

Epilogue

"I thought this would be easier," Landon says as they lean up against their faux-kitchen counter and wait while the camera crew adjusts for what feels like their fiftieth shot of the day.

Landon refuses to check which take it actually is. Quen has no such compunction and glances over at the clapboard. "It's only been six takes, Landon," he says, still easy-going even though it's a thousand degrees in this hellhole masquerading as their house.

Landon would never keep their house at ninety fucking billion degrees.

"Also," Quentin continues, "you're the one with all the television experience. I thought you knew what this would be like."

"*Reality TV*," Landon hisses at Quentin. "I've never filmed a cooking show before. And don't say *Kitchen Wars* was a cooking show. We both know it wasn't. Not like this."

When Ian approached them with a proposal for filming a cute fifteen=minute cooking show for *Five Points*, a sports and pop culture blog looking to diversify more into the latter spectrum, Landon had laughed. "They *really* don't want me to teach people how to cook," Landon claimed, while Quentin had lovingly rolled his eyes at Landon's dramatics. "Quen, now, he's a genius and could teach a rock."

"They want both of you," Ian had insisted. "They're considering calling it *Dream Team.*"

"Well, that's a ridiculous title," Landon scoffed. "It's perfect."

Landon knew he'd been seduced by the adorable title, the prospect of more, cute on-air bantering with Quentin, and also the surprisingly good compensation package *Five Points* had put together.

During all of that, he'd never once considered what filming a strictly cooking show might be like.

What it's like is the most boring twelve hours of Landon's life. The only saving grace is that Quentin is here with him, and he's been entertaining himself by balancing a dozen pieces of fruit around Quentin's cute little top knot. The "bun" is just about as silly as *Dream Team's* name, which means that Landon loves it.

"I'm gonna call you Carmen from now on," Landon proclaims, as he gets a particularly large bunch of grapes to drape artistically down the side of Quen's head. Unsurprisingly, the person who makes a face isn't Quentin, but the director, who, after an entire day of wrangling a bored Landon, has completely run out of patience.

Quentin, obviously a saint in a former life, just grins.

"Landon," the director snaps. "Let's focus. We just need one more shot of you and Quentin taking the casserole out of the oven."

"You mean the casserole *someone else* cooked?" Landon asks archly. Maybe he didn't start the day trying to be difficult, but he's run out of patience himself. He never expected that compared to *Kitchen Wars*, this show would feel like only smoke and mirrors. They barely chop anything. They don't prepare anything themselves. They barely cook. They play act with food that other people prepared. Landon doesn't even have to taste this casserole to know that even though it's an exact replica of Quentin's, it won't taste right because Quentin didn't make it.

In the last year, Landon has become a food snob—as in he doesn't like to eat anyone's cooking except for Quentin's.

"Landon, let's just get it over with." It's the most straightforward Quentin has been all day, and Landon's been making a concentrated effort over the last year to listen more when he gets that edge to his voice. Trusts, like he implicitly trusts Quentin, that he wouldn't use it if he didn't need to.

"Okay, let's go."

Quentin pulls the grapes down just in time, and they start the take.

"Quen, I'm starving, is it done yet?" Landon barely refrains from rolling his eyes at this horrible canned dialogue that doesn't sound like anything he'd say. He'd wanted to ad lib all his lines, but then he'd gone off in so many different directions, many of them too explicit for the channel, that they'd written him an actual script.

Landon rolling his eyes ruined the last three takes of this scene, but this time he makes it through. A few months ago when Landon had suggested to Ian he should start shopping him for the requisite power musician-actor crossover, Ian had flatly refused, claiming the only person Landon was good at being was Landon.

Like everything else, Ian isn't wrong about Landon's acting abilities either.

"It's finally done," Quentin says, actually making the line sound authentic. If he wasn't completely committed to his bakery, maybe he could make a go of the acting thing. Of course, it's a great distraction that his job is to pull out the barely warmed, pre-prepared casserole out of the cold oven. Landon's only task is to react.

"Looks delicious!" Landon exclaims, which is only half a lie.

"You want to make sure it's a really nice golden brown. Don't undercook it," Quentin counsels seriously, as Landon jostles him, trying to slip a fork in to grab a quick bite. Quentin gives him a quick elbow jab, and they jostle back and forth, before Quentin deigns to feed Landon a forkful.

It's one of the few scripted moments that actually feels authentic.

"For this recipe, and others, make sure you check out *Five Points'* website," Landon says through a big bite of cold casserole. Luckily for him, the casserole isn't just out of the oven and he didn't just fry his tongue.

It's finally, *blissfully*, over, at least for two weeks, when their busy schedules have jived enough to be able to get together for another full day of filming. Landon is not looking forward to it.

When they return to their green room, Landon is so tired he doesn't even try to seduce Quentin.

"I can't believe we have to come back and do this again," Quentin says, and *that's* the most brutal thing he's said all day. Maybe in his entire life. Landon smiles. Quentin finally getting fed up is enough to boost his own mood.

"They need to find a better person to write the scripts," Landon says. He doesn't even bother to argue they don't need scripts. He lost that fight during the screen test when he accidentally brought up blowjobs three separate times.

"You sound like a caricature of Landon," Quentin agrees, eyes drooping as he lies back on the couch. "Like a weirdly peppy cheerleader."

"Also less cooking and more dressing you up as Carmen Miranda," Landon adds, though the chances of them being allowed to do that are slim to none.

There's a knock on the door, and Landon groans loudly. He isn't in the mood to meet and greet Duncan Snyder, the CEO of *Five Points*, who was apparently going to stop by after filming finished for the day.

Quentin shoots Landon a dark look and struggles to his feet. Yeah, whoever's at the door probably heard that. Landon doesn't feel the tiniest bit guilty.

But when Quentin opens the door, Duncan Snyder isn't standing there. Instead, it's a young-ish-looking man, *really* tall and slender, with a buzzcut and a pair of startling green eyes.

Landon might be otherworldly happy with Quentin, but he can't help but give the man a second glance. He's in love, not dead.

It's been a hellish, exhausting day, but curiosity propels Landon off the couch to catch what the man is saying to Quentin.

"... a fan," Landon catches. "Had a chance to see you on set today, and thought I'd stop by and say hi."

"Hi, I'm Landon," he says, grabbing the door out of Quen's hand. "Wanna come in?"

"Jordan Christensen," the man says as he nods and walks in, Landon closing the door behind him. For a split second, Landon can't place the name, even though it sounds *very* familiar, and then it hits him all at once. This is why Quentin's been so weirdly quiet since he opened the door. This is Reed's ... well, Landon heard they broke up. So this is Reed Ryan's *ex*-boyfriend.

Logically he knows he and Quentin aren't responsible for their breakup. Maybe even if Reed had won *Kitchen Wars*, it still would have ended. But even a vague possibility they're responsible for what happened is enough to make Landon tense as hell.

"I have to tell you how sorry we are," is of course what Quentin says when he decides to open his mouth.

Jordan chuckles, and if Landon wasn't listening for it, he might have missed the tiny edge of bitterness. "You really don't have to apologize." He shrugs. "Reed knew it was an outside chance that he'd win. But I'm not here to talk about *Kitchen Wars*, I'm here to talk about your new show."

Landon makes a face.

"Yeah," Jordan says, lips quirking up in a quick smile, "I caught some of the filming today. Why did you let someone script you?"

"We . . . well, *I*, am incredibly easy to distract," Landon admits. "I was rambling all over the place. They said the show would need to be twice as long if I didn't stay focused."

"I mean, you can tell me to go to hell," Jordan says, "but I watched *Kitchen Wars*. I know why they wanted to make *Dream Team*, and it's not because you can stay focused or because you can credibly cook something in fifteen minutes. They wanted you because you're *great* together."

"And we're losing all that," Quentin observes morosely. Landon wants to hug him. He sounds exactly how Landon feels. This *Dream Team* thing was supposed to be a lot different.

"You've lost it completely," Jordan states. "But I think you could get it back, if you could find someone to script you who got your dynamic."

"Who could do that?" Landon asks, refraining from the over-dramatic addition that *nobody* gets them as well as they do, and he and Quen are definitely not going to write their own scripts. They're busy enough, thank you very much.

"Me." Jordan sounds deadly serious.

"You?" Landon squawks. "But *why*?"

Jordan has really nice eyes; such a deep, rich green, and Landon is almost certain he recognizes that deep sadness buried in them because he's felt it too. It makes him want to both apologize and to *help*, but Landon isn't dumb enough to think either of those things might make a difference to Jordan.

Jordan hesitates. "Because I work here now and I think I'd do a good job—at least a *better* job than what you have now—writing you some lines."

"They're not going to want to reshoot," Quentin warns.

"Leave that to me," Jordan says. "I know some people. I'll talk to them, let them review the footage. They're not going to waste your chemistry together, and right now, that's what they're doing."

Landon looks over at Quen. They've developed an unspoken language over the last six months. Sometimes Landon even knows what Quen is thinking from the way he breathes on the phone when Landon's away, promoting his new album. He knows that Quen wants to reshoot, and that's because Quentin is a perfectionist who won't let anything less than flawless ever cross his bakery counters. Not only would Quentin not want to see his brand diminished, no doubt he's worried over what a *Dream Team* failure might do to the future success of the bakery.

"We're on board," Landon speaks up for both of them. "Anything you need, you got it."

They discuss details for a few more minutes, and then Jordan leaves, claiming he has some arms to twist.

"So I guess he left the NFL," Landon says as he pulls on a jacket. "And now he wants to be a writer."

"He *is* a writer," Quentin corrects. "And I feel responsible for that. I don't think I should, but I do."

Landon shoots his boyfriend a sympathetic smile. Normally he might insist Quentin is too nice, but he's too tired and Quentin's right. "I do too."

"Makes me wish I'd gotten to know Reed a little better."

"All I remember about Reed is *muscles*, those serious eyes, and how well he made those foil pans when I sabotaged him," Landon says.

"I think that was his partner, but yeah, me too. He kept to himself a lot," Quentin says, jamming his hands in his pockets as they walk out towards the parking garage where his car is parked.

"It's still really nice of Jordan to offer to help. I wonder who he knows." Landon's curiosity is insatiable at the best of times. Right now, his interest is undeniably piqued, but he and Quen know almost nobody at *Five Points* yet.

It's another very early morning when Quentin lets them into the back door of the bakery. Landon hates the early mornings, will probably never stop hating them, but is slowly becoming resigned to them because often it's the only time he can get a moment alone with his boyfriend.

The downside of being both the cutest couple on the planet, and *also* individually brilliant, is that Landon longs for the days when their *Kitchen Wars* schedule felt hectic. They live in the same house now, which Quentin had to move them into while Landon was doing the publicity tour for his very successful album, but quiet evenings cuddling on the couch are hard to come by. Quentin is still needed at the bakery every day—wouldn't have it any other way, in fact—and gets up painfully early the six days a week they're open. Landon is in demand everywhere and finds himself even turning down appearances occasionally because sometimes the thought of dragging himself on *another* plane for *another* week away from Quentin is cringeworthy.

Landon both loves and hates these early morning trips with Quentin to the bakery. He loves Quentin and loves watching him be his most amazing self. He does not love getting out of his warm, cozy bed with the man he would just about kill to have morning sex with.

"Coffee," Landon slurs, propping himself up against one of the big stainless steel counters where Quentin and his small staff create the pastries and goodies for which they're quickly becoming renowned.

"Already heating the machine up," Quentin echoes from the other side of the cavernous kitchen. After almost a year together, he knows Landon isn't really coherent until his second cup of strong coffee.

Landon boosts himself up on the counter, ignoring his boyfriend's half-hearted glare. He still likes being taller, and Quentin still loves to lecture him about breaking the rules. Landon hopes nothing will ever change.

Except maybe the being so busy they can barely breathe thing.

"I talked to Ian yesterday," Landon tells Quen when he brings him a steaming cup of cappuccino, dark espresso swirled with lighter foam, lightly sweetened, just the way Landon likes it.

"You talk to Ian every day," Quentin says absently as he heads over to the walk-in cooler, and begins loading a beat-up hotel pan with pounds and pounds of butter.

"Not about getting out of a contract," Landon retorts.

Quentin glances up in surprise. Landon makes a face. "Here's the thing," he says. "Between this crazy schedule you have at the bakery, and my own crazy schedule touring the world, we barely have time together. But we said we'd do *Dream Team* anyway, because it sounded awesome."

"Except it wasn't awesome." Quentin finishes Landon's sentence before he can. Landon loves it when he does that. It's a visceral reminder that from the first moment they met, they've always been on the same wavelength. Even when Landon is being an asshole.

"It wasn't awesome," Landon agrees.

"I like Nick. I like *Five Points*. I still like the promotional package they were talking about. Lots of bakery tie-in promo."

Landon knows Quentin still worries about the bakery making it. Margins are so slim. He likes buying the highest quality ingredients and charging just as much as he has to for his products. He's only taking a small salary, a minuscule amount compared to the time and energy he puts in. Landon, on the other hand, has never been more comfortable financially. He's got lots of money in the bank, and Ian is making rumbling noises about hiring some fancy financial planner. But Quentin wants to pull his own weight between them, and though it's never come up, Landon *knows* he refuses to ever depend on Landon's money.

The generous compensation package *Five Points* as well as the boosted promotion for the bakery are two of the biggest reasons Quentin wanted to do the show. Even if he was already halfway working himself to death.

"Ian is having the lawyer look at the contract," Landon says casually.

Quentin, elbow deep in croissant dough, jerks his head up. "I didn't realize you were that serious about getting out of it. You didn't tell me."

Yeah, because Landon is positive that his reaction would be similar to the one he's getting now. Extreme reluctance.

"Because you're determined to work yourself to death." Landon tries to say it without the hurt edge to his voice, but it's hard to hold it back. There's a reason he's up at four in the morning, sucking down caffeine like it's going out of style—he *loves* Quentin and he's determined not to lose their relationship to a lack of quality time.

Quentin opens his mouth to say something, but Landon jumps down off the counter, and plants a warm, coffee-flavored kiss onto his lips. When he pulls back, the fight has gone out of Quentin's eyes. "If it was awesome and going to work out, you know I'd be the first in line. I loved the idea of doing something with you. We do too much apart these days."

There's guilt hovering in Quen's tired blue eyes. Landon wishes he would listen to it a little more.

"What about the adjustments Jordan wanted to make?"

Landon shrugs. "We'll look at them before we make a decision. But I'm not losing more time with you over something miserable we don't enjoy and that probably isn't going to be a success. End of story."

Quentin brushes flour off his hands and leans back against the counter, gaze suddenly appraising as it sweeps from the top of Landon's bedhead to the sneakers he shoved his feet into before they staggered out the door this morning.

"Who are you and what have you done with my boyfriend?" Quentin asks, the side of his mouth tilting up into a grin.

"Are you saying I was careless and thoughtless before?" Landon exclaims in mock outrage. "How dare you."

Quentin shrugs, amusement replacing the haunted look in his eyes from earlier.

"Well," Landon pronounces. "Better not let that happen. Nobody will be here for another forty minutes. Better be spontaneous now." Before Quentin can even begin to wonder what Landon has in mind, he slides to his knees and runs a hand up Quen's jean-clad leg, resting it on his fly and on the thickening bulge behind it.

If Landon gets flour in his hair, then nobody is there to see but the two of them—and it's not like it hasn't happened a thousand times before.

❦ ❦

Landon hates being wrong.

"These changes are fantastic," he tells Jordan, and if he sounds a little incredulous, *sue him*. Jordan Christensen, before he came to work at *Five Points* and decided he could rewrite Landon and Quentin's *Dream Team* script, was a professional football player.

How was Landon supposed to know that he could write so well? Or fucking *nail* their dynamic as a couple?

"I might have watched *Kitchen Wars* a few dozen times," Jordan admits quietly, tucking a pen behind his ear and looking surprisingly studious and incredibly unlike an ex-football player as they stand on-set, ready to re-film the three episodes they'd done last week. "And the editors loved you two. But then, you already knew that."

"Oh." Landon doesn't know what to say. He wishes there was something he could say or do to assuage Jordan's broken heart. But from his own experience with Steve, Landon knows there's nothing anyone can do. The only thing that helps is time and perspective.

Jordan glances over at him, and probably sees the resigned panic on Landon's face as he tries to figure out how to dig them out of this conversational black hole.

"It's fine, really," Jordan says, and there's a glimmer of a smile on his handsome face. "Glad it came in handy for something."

"Why'd you leave football?" The question slips out before Landon can grab it back. At least it's one of the milder ones, with nothing to do with Reed.

Jordan shrugs, his attention turning back to the script pages he's reviewing before they go into the teleprompter. "Felt like the right time. Always wanted to be a writer. This job came open and it was a no-brainer. Besides, I was never going to be a huge star. I'm good, but not great."

"I have no idea," Landon admits. "I mostly watch for the tight pants. Quen keeps trying to teach me the rules."

"You watch football together?" Landon wishes he couldn't hear the wistful note buried in Jordan's voice.

"Sometimes, yeah. My mild-mannered, sweet-as-pastry boyfriend is a Raiders fan," Landon tells Jordan. "You should come over sometime and watch with us."

Maybe Landon can't fix what broke Reed and Jordan; he doesn't even know what it was, and he isn't cruel enough to ask Jordan about it. But maybe Landon can be a friend.

"You don't gotta do that," Jordan says. "You don't owe me anything."

"I know," Landon says calmly. "But I like you. You laugh at my terrible jokes. And two people teaching me the rules is probably better than one."

"I'll think about it," Jordan says gruffly, and Landon is almost certain there's a note of apology in his voice. "Now, let's get this show on the road. You boys ready?"

Landon shoots Jordan a triumphant look. "I was *born* ready."

Quentin emerges from their green room onto the sound stage, and he's balancing an entire fresh fruit Carmen Miranda headdress on his curly blond hair. He looks fabulous.

When the cameras start rolling, Landon reaches over and plucks a grape from Quentin's head and eats it. "Tasty," he observes, his most innocent smile plastered on his face.

Quentin glances over, affection overflowing out of his gaze. "Hungry, babe?"

"Starving," Landon says. "Let's cook."

Read the bonus scene for a fun and sexy snapshot of Landon and Quen discovering their own fanfiction.

To read Jordan and Reed's book, click here.

347

INTERESTED IN READING MORE OF
BETH'S BOOKS?

CHECK OUT A FULL LIST OF TILES
BY SCANNING THE QR CODE
OR VISITING HER WEBSITE

WWW.BETHBOLDEN.COM/BOOKLIST

WANT TO FOLLOW BETH?

MAKE SURE YOU NEVER
MISS A RELEASE?

SCAN THE QR CODE BELOW
OR VISIT HER WEBSITE
FOR A SOCIAL MEDIA LIST,
NEWSLETTER SIGNUP,
AND SO MUCH MORE!

WWW.BETHBOLDEN.COM/ABOUT

9 781964 691015